THE LAST
SHOGUN

THE LAST
SHOGUN

The Life of Tokugawa Yoshinobu

RYOTARO SHIBA

TRANSLATED BY
Juliet Winters Carpenter

K

KODANSHA INTERNATIONAL
New York • Tokyo • London

This book was published in collaboration with the Japan Foundation.

The publisher gratefully acknowledges the contribution of the Association for 100 Japanese Books toward the cost of translation.

The translator wishes to thank Doshisha Women's College for generously granting her a yearlong leave of absence in which to work on the translation, and the College of William and Mary for accepting her as a visiting scholar during that time.

Kodansha America, Inc.
114 Fifth Avenue, New York, New York 10011, U.S.A.

Kodansha International Ltd.
17-14 Otowa 1-chome, Bunkyo-ku, Tokyo 112-8652, Japan

Published in 1998 by Kodansha America, Inc.

Library of Congress Cataloging-in-Publication Data
Shiba, Ryōtarō, 1923–1996
  [Saigo no shogun. English]
  The last shogun : the life of Tokugawa Yoshinobu / Ryōtarō Shiba : translated from the Japanese by Juliet Winters Carpenter = [Saigo no shōgun / Shiba Ryōtarō chō].
      p. cm.
  ISBN 1-56836-246-3
  1. Tokugawa, Yoshinobu, 1837-1913. I. Carpenter, Juliet Winters. II. Title
  895.6'35—dc21   97–38774

Book design by Jessica Shatan

Manufactured in the United States of America on acid-free paper

98 99 00 01   10 9 8 7 6 5 4 3 2 1

Contents

CONTENTS

Introduction

BY FRANK GIBNEY

When Commodore Matthew Perry brought his squadron of "black ships" into Tokyo Bay, this was widely regarded as the "opening" of Japan. After two and a half centuries of determined self-isolation from the rest of the world, the island nation was forced to open its ports to foreign trade. With this, inevitably, the process of modernization had begun. There is no doubt of Perry's importance. Although the Japanese had had brushes with foreigners in the past, the military threat posed by modern steam-driven warships was both formidable and immediate. Japanese leaders, awed and furious at the display of the West's superior technology, did not wish to repeat the earlier failure of the Chinese emperor's troops to drive out the Western imperialists with force.

In fact, Perry was more of a catalyst than a prime mover. His ships arrived off the coast of Japan at a time when the Japanese people and their governments were already in a state of ferment. As the country moved toward modernization, the next fifteen years became a confused struggle among xenophobic patriots, militant clan leaders, and eager students of Western technology. It came to a climax with the fall of the Tokugawa shogunate in 1868, an event that forms the centerpiece of this book. Its central figure, Tokugawa Yoshinobu, was the last of his line to hold power.

The Tokugawa shoguns had ruled Japan like a dynasty since the early seventeenth century. By the mid-1800s, they were already weakened by a shattered economy, popular discontent, and military pressure from their unruly vassals in the feudal clans. The Meiji Restoration of 1868—as history calls it—toppled the shogunate, and brought a seventeen-year-old boy emperor back from the secluded imperial palace in Kyoto to preside over what amounted to a political and cultural revolution. With this, Japan's extraordinary self-modernization began in earnest.

The shogunate did not dissolve instantly. The final victory of the reformers came only after several years of battles, intrigues, and forced compromises. The ostensible winners were the rulers of Satsuma and Choshu, two leading anti-Tokugawa clans in southwest Japan. But it was really a group of young samurai-bureaucrats from these and other clans who set up the new government at the shogun's castle of Edo, now renamed Tokyo, and began the forcible modernization of their country. The fact that they succeeded so quickly was due in great part to the conduct of Tokugawa

Yoshinobu. Yoshinobu reigned for barely one year. A modernizer himself, he sympathized with the wider goals of the reformers. It was his surrender of authority at a crucial point that made the transfer of sovereignty relatively peaceful.

To understand the drama of Yoshinobu's brief rule as well as the circumstances that defined it, we must go back to his ancestor, Tokugawa Ieyasu, and examine the peculiar political and social structure he had put together. Like the British Isles in Europe, Japan's islands lay off the coast of Asia, providing its inhabitants with a kind of insular seclusion. Unlike Britain, however, Japan was never successfully invaded, at least until World War II. The Japanese drew their higher civilization from nearby China and Korea, much as the British had gotten theirs from Rome and France. But they were by and large peaceful borrowers and adapters. Only once did they attempt to attack the mainland—in Korea in 1598—and that unsuccessfully.

For centuries emperors reigned in the old capitals of Nara and Kyoto, but over the years they gradually lost their political power. Yet they remained, well garnished by myth and tradition, as spiritual pontiffs. The real power was assumed by a military class, and the feudal society that evolved resembled those of Britain and France in the European Middle Ages. The leaders of these military clansmen came to bear the title of *sei-i-tai* shogun, literally "barbarian-subduing generalissimo." Like the French "mayors of the palace" in Carolingian times, these Shoguns developed their own family dynasties and all too frequently fought it out for primacy in the realm.

The fall of the Ashikaga shoguns in the early fifteenth century was followed by almost one hundred and fifty years of brutal warfare in which rival military leaders vied for supremacy. This was literally the age of the storied *bushi*, or samurai, whose greatest virtue was loyalty to his superior, and whose leaders cultivated a kind of Spartan simplicity that owed much to Confucianism as well as the more austere sects of Buddhism.

By the beginning of the seventeenth century, one of these chieftains, Tokugawa Ieyasu, managed to set himself up as first among equals. At the famous battle of Sekigahara, comparable in some respects to Britain's earlier Battle of Hastings, Tokugawa established himself as the supreme ruler and took on the title of shogun in earnest.

Ieyasu was far more than a mere military leader, however. A shrewd politician, he institutionalized the feudal order of clans at the time of his victory, changing their shape and status only insofar as his allies were rewarded and his enemies banished to remote regions of the Japanese islands. Borrowing heavily from China's Song Dynasty's neo-Confucianism, Ieyasu established four classes—the samurai warriors, farmers, artisans, and tradesmen—the so-called *shi-no-ko-sho*, which defined the social status of the realm.

At the time Tokugawa took power, traders and missionaries, mostly from Portugal and Spain, had established a presence in Japan. They had gained, to his way of thinking, a dangerous hold over thousands of Christian converts. Although the Japanese had prized the sixteenth-century Western technology they received—firearms principal among them—Tokugawa feared that trade and proselytizing would be followed by military invasion from European powers. To protect his domain, he and his immediate descendants enforced rigid rules of seclusion against further contacts with foreigners.

Tokugawa's principal contribution to his country, however, was the universal peace that his arms enforced. His writ was observed throughout the Japanese islands. Although clan leaders (called daimyo) held supremacy each in his own territory, they were bound by various forms of fealty to the shogunate, whose rule was also enforced by a nationwide network of spies and bureaucrats. The samurai themselves, with no more fighting to do, developed into a huge bureaucracy that administered the various feudal domains. For a century and a half, Japan prospered under the shogunate. Trade and arts and crafts developed to a high degree—to the point where the lowly *shonin*, the merchants, originally the low men on the Confucian totem pole, were becoming richer and more powerful than the samurai, many of whom led a hand-to-mouth existence, derived almost solely from the rice subsidies they received.

By the early nineteenth century, the clan domains (*han*) were quite restless. The shoguns were never quite able to deal with the money economy that was growing up to supersede the feudal economy of rice subsidies that Shogun Ieyasu had created. The outside clans (*tozama*), that is, those leaders who had lost at the battle of Sekigahara, became in turn powerful and continued to cherish hopes of revenge on the shogun's dynasty. Meanwhile, scholars and political theorists had become increasingly vocal in asserting the right of the emperor, not the shogun, to rule the country.

At the same time, a thin trickle of "Western learning" seeped into Japan through books and other materials first imported via the Dutch trading post at Nagasaki, the one place in the empire where foreigners were allowed limited access. Two crosscurrents were in conflict. On the one hand, there was great interest in borrowing Western technology. But proponents of a revived emperor cult were eager to use the emperor's age-old legitimacy as a weapon to crush any "barbarians" who might attempt to invade Japan again. It was into this tangled web that Commodore Perry steered his ships at mid- century.

In fact, the demands of Perry to open Japan to foreign trade and coaling stations, seconded by visiting British and Russian squadrons, put the shogunate in a difficult position. If the shogunate were to yield to foreign pressure, it would be denounced as betraying Japan's sacred interest and accused of disloyalty to the secluded emperor in Kyoto. If the Tokugawa forces resisted the foreigners, they ran the risk of defeat in a full-scale war. Already scattered brushes between visiting warships and shore batteries quite convincingly underscored the European and American superiority.

Tokugawa Yoshinobu, who was born in Edo in 1837, was the son of Tokugawa Nariaki, the leader of the anti-foreign school. At this time there were three main branches of the Tokugawa family, of which his father's was one. Foreign incursions, intensified after Perry's visit, prompted the daimyo to import their own guns and instructors from the West. By the 1860s Tokugawa power had been seriously weakened by internal dissension in the capital. While several weak shoguns were installed, advisers desperately tried to import enough

European instructors and materials to produce something like a modern army. It was too late. By 1867 troops from the feudal domains had poured into Kyoto, allegedly to guard the emperor, led by a remarkable group of young samurai-bureaucrats who had studied Western technology and hoped to modernize the country. Conflicting calls came, variously, for a union of the shogunate and the clans, or direct imperial rule.

Enter Tokugawa Yoshinobu. Young, vigorous, and progressive, he was pressed by the shogunate's council first to take over the regency of the realm, and then, after the feeble shogun Iemochi died, to serve as shogun himself. This was hardly an attractive prospect. By the 1860s the authoritarian polity Ieyasu had constructed was in pieces. Throughout Japan, people were restless and looking for a change. Various clan leaders, particularly those from Satsuma and Choshu, were bent on destroying the shogunate altogether and bringing the emperor back to direct rule. Tokugawa himself was of two minds. While he wished to maintain the family dynasty, he was at heart a modernizer. He did not have any particular quarrel with restoring the emperor.

The policy of his brief reign reflected this indecision. At first he attempted to subdue the rival clans by force. This expedient failed. In fact, by 1868 the Satsuma and Choshu forces had gained control of the imperial city of Kyoto. They soon marched on Edo. In two small battles the shogun's armies were totally defeated.

Yoshinobu was nothing if not a realist. Fearing that further fighting would lead to warfare and destroy the country, he sent one of his most trusted retainers, Katsu Kaishu, to negotiate with the now-imperial forces. In the summer of 1868, Yoshinobu left Edo and retired to the Tokugawa ancestral holdings in what is now Shizuoka Prefecture.

It is tempting to play "what might have been" historical games with the likes of the last Tokugawa, who had to abdicate at the age of thirty. What if he had succeeded to the shogunate five years before? Could he have then mobilized all the gathering forces of modernization behind the shogunate castle in Edo rather than the imperial palace in Kyoto? The pattern of his life before his accession showed a man of considerable competence, who was capable of making fast and often difficult decisions. It is the same question one asks of other people who stood at the cusp of history and failed to fulfill their promise—Kerensky in the Russian revolution, for example, or Lafayette in the French. For Yoshinobu, unlike many of the shogunate's retainers, had a pretty clear idea that to survive as an independent nation, Japan must modernize—and do so very swiftly.

Yet at that point in history we must conclude that he had succeeded to an impossible job. In the passage of two centuries, the firm governance that his Tokugawa ancestor brought to an exhausted Japan had long since played out. What started as law-and-order decision-making had ended up in bureaucratic indolence. So long solitary in its power, the shogunate grew into a nest of protocol-happy courtiers, with so many prejudices to be counted, so many interests to be satisfied. It was next to impossible to govern decisively. The one man who had tried it, Ii Naosuke, the great chief retainer of the Tokugawa, had tried to mobilize Japan against the foreigners while modernizing. He was assassinated for his pains in 1862. Yoshinobu could make decisions and did, but he no longer had the machinery for executing them.

Against him he had arrayed the fifty-odd young samurai-bureaucrats who remodeled Japan in what history must record as one of the first great modern cultural revolutions. The Meiji Restoration was created by young and extraordinarily far-seeing planners like Okubo Toshimichi and Saigo Takamori from Satsuma, Ito Hirobumi and Kido Koin in Choshu. They set out with speed and deliberation to turn Japan into a modern state. Although they had grown up indoctrinated with all the anti-foreign rhetoric of their time—"*sonno joi*" or "respect the emperor and destroy the barbarians" was the watchword of the fifties—they had the vision to see that they could best move Japan into the present century by mobilizing the ancient slogans of the past in the interest of detente with the Western powers. Given relative autonomy by the daimyo of their respective realms, who were rather afraid of them, the young Meiji reformers set out to construct a modern nation state. To do so, they had to destroy the whole creaky edifice of codified feudalism that the Tokugawa regime had left Japan.

In his afterword to this book, Ryotaro Shiba comments on how Tokugawa must have envied Okubo, a man of almost the same age, with probably the same objectives, who succeeded so triumphantly where Tokugawa failed. If Tokugawa Yoshinobu was no hero, still he had one achievement that should not be underestimated. In 1868, the year of total change and turnover, he had the wit to realize that the shogunate could no longer be restored. Ordering his generals to sign a truce, he left the palace peacefully. His loyal followers, disgusted with his retreat, held out for some months afterward. The Aizu clan in northern Japan, loyal to the last, was only subdued by the new Meiji army after months of heavy fighting. Aizu, however, was the exception. By bowing to the inevitable, Tokugawa made peace an immediate possibility. He and his immediate retainers were not only pardoned by the new emperor, many of them were welcomed into the Meiji administration. Tokugawa himself lived peacefully in retirement. Ennobled a prince in the new European-style nobility of the Meiji era, he lived on until 1913, when he died peacefully on his estate. In a worldly sense, therefore, he was a lot luckier than his leading opponent, Okubo, who was tragically assassinated in Tokyo at the height of his power in 1877.

The facts Shiba provides us in this account of Tokugawa Yoshinobu are unquestionably true. Yet *The Last Shogun*, when published in Japan, was, like the rest of Shiba's multivolume historical narratives, published as a novel. If Shiba lived in the United States, his book would be regarded as straight history, in an era when Americans seem to have lost the distinction between fact and fiction. The Japanese are more meticulous in these matters. To their mind *The Last Shogun* remains a novel, because Shiba has used a few of the novelist's narrative devices. In its accuracy, however, it is a faithful depiction of events of that now-far-off time, and can safely be called history for all practical purposes.

In conclusion let me say a few words about the author. Shiba Ryotaro (the Japanese surname is first), who died just two years ago at the age of 72, was justly acclaimed as Japan's national writer. He was the author of some 40 books. In his work, he combined the curiosity of a good journalist with the reflection and ability of a true scholar. Most of what he wrote was intimately bound up with the Japanese experience. Whether in a long series like *Saka no Ue no Kumo* (Clouds Above a Hill) or more general essays like *Meiji to Iu Kokka* (A Nation Called Meiji), he could weave together the warp and woof of one nation's history. He remains immensely popular. In Japan, his name on a book virtually guarantees a wide readership.

As a novelist he made history live far better than most academic practitioners of the historian's trade. Yet he was also an internationalist—*Kokusaijin*, to use that much-abused Japanese phrase. His acquaintance with world cultures was a wide one. His knowledge was informed by a curiosity that was benign but insatiable. He saw his own country more clearly through the prism of a wider knowledge about the world outside it.

Shiba was particularly fascinated by the events of the Meiji Restoration, this turning point in Japan's modern history, and the stormy last years of the Shogunate that preceded it. No one could recall so well the drama of Japan's great cultural revolution. Significantly, he wrote almost nothing about the militarists' era of the 1930s and 1940s. Although mobilized for war service—he was a probationary Navy officer trainee when the war ended—he regarded Japan's "Greater East Asia" war as a cruel and tragic mistake.

I was privileged to know Shiba rather well. I never ceased to wonder at his far-ranging curiosity about the history and manners of different countries and cultures.

Yet this extraordinary man, one of the world's great "public intellectuals," was almost unknown outside his own country. He never attained the international visibility of novelists like Kawabata, Mishima, or Oe, largely because his work was rarely translated. Perhaps his focus was too narrowly fixed in Japanese history and culture. Shiba wrote, also, in the discursive manner so common to Japanese, but too singularly hard to render, concisely, into non-Japanese languages. Happily, in the *The Last Shogun*, Juliet Carpenter has done a really excellent job of translation, nicely conveying both the style and substance of Shiba's prose.

In Japan, far more than in the United States (where nonacademic "public intellectual" writers are being crowded out by journalists on one hand and professors on the other), authors like Shiba are still respected as the "wise men" of the national society. Such indeed Shiba was.

Translator's Note

Ryotaro Shiba, one of Japan's most highly acclaimed writers, is that country's narrative historian *par excellence*. Of American writer-historians he perhaps most closely resembles novelist Shelby Foote, author of a monumental narrative of the American Civil War. Foote closes his third and final volume of that narrative with a note stating that "nowhere along the line have I had a 'thesis' to argue or maintain—partly no doubt because I never saw one that could not be 'proved,' at least to the satisfaction of the writer who advanced it." It is a sentiment that Shiba Ryotaro—similarly driven to write millions of words about a series of roughly contemporaneous, equally cataclysmic events in Japan—would no doubt have found to his liking. Moreover, Foote's avowed purpose of "re-creating [the Civil War] and making it live again in the world around us," a purpose to which he devoted twenty years of his life, also seems to find an echo in Shiba's lively and detailed retelling, in book after book, of events before, during, and after the Meiji Restoration.

Certainly the story is told in *The Last Shogun* with a wealth of detail that bears testimony to Shiba's voracious reading habits. As Shiba notes in his afterword to the Japanese original, "The political turmoil of Yoshinobu's time is . . . a vital part of an era just beginning to gel into history." Shiba was determined to examine that era closely, to seek to understand the motives and forces that came into play during it, and above all to tell the story of the men who shaped it. Yoshinobu (born 160 years ago this year) he saw as "one of history's victims," and yet as much more: it was his realization that "the shadow cast by Yoshinobu on history was clearcut and intense," he tells us, that moved him to write this narrative. He brings out the essential irony in Yoshinobu's life: that he was a man of enormous ability who took power at a time when his country desperately needed leadership, but whose greatest contribution had to lie not in the exercise of power, but in the relinquishing of it.

The story is told for Japanese readers, who of course bring considerable background knowledge to the story; here and there I have slipped in a bit of explanation, or done a bit of trimming as seemed necessary. Names follow the traditional Japanese order, family name first.

JULIET WINTERS CARPENTER
Ikoma, Japan,
November 21, 1997

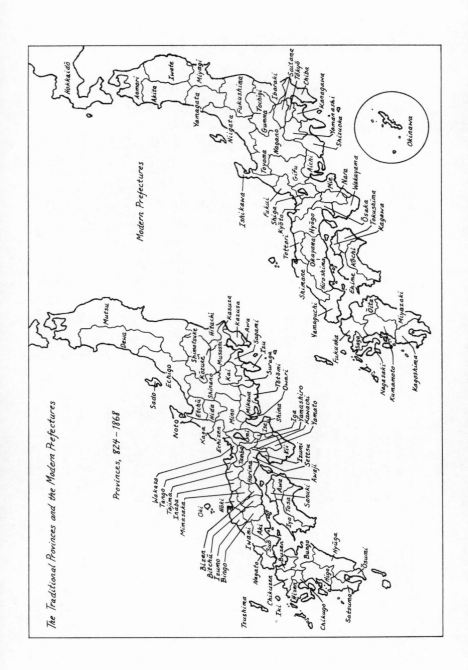

The Traditional Provinces and the Modern Prefectures

Provinces, 824–1868

Modern Prefectures

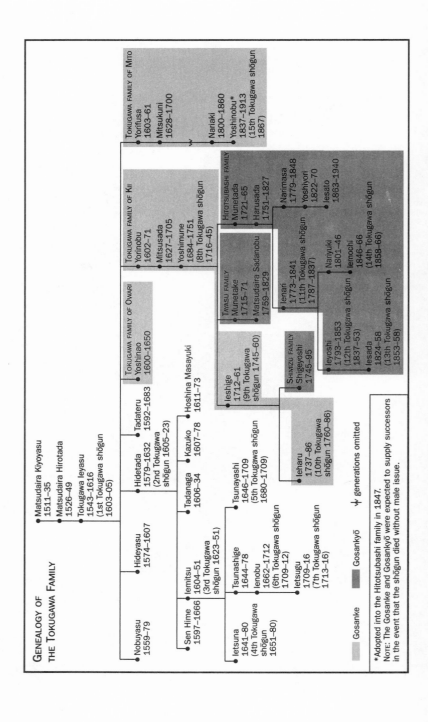

List of Characters

ABE MASAHIRO (1819–57)
Daimyo of the Fukuyama domain (now part of Hiroshima Prefecture) and chief senior councillor of the Tokugawa shogunate from 1843 to 1857; architect of the shogunate's policy of opening Japan to diplomatic and trade relations with Western nations.

ANEGAKOJI KINTOMO (1889–63)
Antiforeign, antishogunate noble who assisted Choshu loyalists by issuing false edicts in the name of the emperor. Assassinated in Kyoto after heading a mission to Edo.

ARISUGAWA, PRINCE (1835–95)

Member of the imperial family; adopted son of Emperor Ninko (1800–46) and kin to TOKUGAWA YOSHINOBU through his mother. Active in the movement to overthrow the shogunate, he led imperial army troops against the shogunate in the civil war of 1868 to 1869.

DATE MUNENARI (1818–92)

Daimyo of the Uwajima domain in Iyo Province (now Ehime Prefecture). One of the reform-minded "wise men" who supported HITOTSUBASHI KEIKI.

ENOMOTO TAKEAKI (1836–1908)

Captain of the *Kaiyo-maru*, which carried TOKUGAWA YOSHI-NOBU from Osaka to Edo in 1868. Refusing to surrender to the new government, he escaped to Ezo (now Hokkaido) and held out until 1869.

FUJITA TOKO (1806–55)

Leading Confucian scholar of the Mito school; main adviser to TOKUGAWA NARIAKI and an exponent of nationalist views. Masterminded the early campaign to promote the candidacy of HITOTSUBASHI KEIKI for shogun.

GOTO SHOJIRO (1838–97)

Samurai of the Tosa domain (now Kochi Prefecture) and proimperial activist who urged TOKUGAWA YOSHINOBU to return rule peaceably to the emperor.

HARA ICHINOSHIN (1830–67)

One of HITOTSUBASHI KEIKI's strategists, succeeding HI-RAOKA ENSHIRO as his main adviser and confidant. Beheaded by Mito fanatics at his home in 1867.

HIRAOKA ENSHIRO (1822–64)

Faithful retainer and right-hand man of HITOTSUBASHI KEIKI. Assassinated at Horikawa Bridge in 1864, in the wake of the Ikedaya Incident.

HITOTSUBASHI KEIKI (see also TOKUGAWA YOSHINOBU)

Born a Mito in Edo (now Tokyo), Keiki was adopted into the Hitotsubashi family at an early age. After the failure of his first candidacy for shogun, he became shogunal guardian for the fourteenth shogun, IEMOCHI. Later, under the name TOKUGAWA YOSHINOBU, he became the fifteenth and last Tokugawa shogun.

II NAOSUKE (1815–60)

Daimyo of the Hikone domain (now part of Shiga Prefecture) who as tairo (great elder) of the Tokugawa shogunate was virtual dictator of Japan from 1858 to 1860. His signing of trade treaties with Western powers triggered a backlash, causing him to clamp down with the Ansei Purge. Assassinated March 24, 1860, outside Edo Castle.

ITAKURA KATSUKIYO (1823–89)

Daimyo of the Matsuyama domain (now part of Okayama Prefecture); chief senior councillor and a close adviser of TOKUGAWA YOSHINOBU, whom he persuaded to become the fifteenth shogun. A Tokugawa diehard, he fled to Hokkaido rather than submit to the new government.

IWAKURA TOMOMI (1825–83)

Court noble and chamberlain to EMPEROR KOMEI. With OKUBO ICHIZO and SAIGO TAKAMORI, he engineered the takeover of the imperial palace that initiated the Restoration.

KATSU KAISHU (1823–99)

Rose from relatively humble origins to prominence, becoming commissioner of warships in 1862. When the shogunate collapsed, he argued for surrender and followed TOKU-GAWA YOSHINOBU into retirement, though he later returned to service as naval minister.

KOMATSU TATEWAKI (1835–70)

Senior elder of the Satsuma domain (now Kagoshima Prefecture) and coordinator of various anti-Tokugawa factions.

KOMEI, EMPEROR (1831-67)

Reigned from 1846 to 1867; favored the two-hundred-year-old policy of seclusion and opposed the overthrow of the shogunate. Died of smallpox shortly after TOKUGAWA YOSHINOBU took power.

KUSAKA GENZUI (1840–64)

Samurai of the Choshu domain (now Yamaguchi Prefecture) and a leader of the ultraradical proimperial, antishogunate, antiforeigner campaign.

MATSUDAIRA KATAMORI (1835–93)

Daimyo of the Aizu domain (now part of Fukushima Prefecture) and Protector of Kyoto. Organized the Shinsengumi, ronin troops of the bakufu used to quell anti-Tokugawa extremists in Kyoto. In 1863 he succeeded in driving extremists from Kyoto altogether, and repelled them again the following year. Along with his brother Sadaaki, he resisted the imperial takeover to the bitter end.

MATSUDAIRA SHUNGAKU (1828–90)

Also known as Matsudaira Yoshinaga. Reform-minded daimyo of the Fukui or Echizen domain (now part of Fukui Prefecture) and adviser to the shogunate. As political director, he attempted to reform and modernize the shogunate with HITOTSUBASHI KEIKI, who became shogunal regent.

NAGAI NAOMUNE (1816–91)

Inspector general who became TOKUGAWA YOSHINOBU's private secretary in Kyoto.

NAKAGAWA, PRINCE (1824–91)

Activist court noble siding now with Satsuma, now with HITOTSUBASHI KEIKI.

NAKANE CHOJURO

First retainer of HITOTSUBASHI KEIKI and immediate superior of HIRAOKA ENSHIRO, whose indiscretion led to his assassination in 1864 outside Kijibashi Gate by Edo Castle.

OKUBO ICHIZO (1830–78)

Also known as Okubo Toshimichi. A Satsuma domain official who participated actively in the proimperial movement. With SAIGO TAKAMORI and others he negotiated a secret Satsuma-Choshu alliance against the shogunate and subsequently helped lay the groundwork for the new Japanese state. He was assassinated in 1878 by six conspirators from Satsuma.

SAIGO TAKAMORI (1827–77)

A Satsuma-born leader in the overthrow of the shogunate and the establishment of the Meiji government. He helped pave the way for a Satsuma-Choshu alliance, and as commander of Satsuma troops in Kyoto he defeated the shogunal forces at Toba and Fushimi in late 1867. Ten years later he led Satsuma rebels in an ill-fated rebellion, and committed suicide.

SAKAMOTO RYOMA (1836–67)

Proimperial activist from the Tosa domain (now Kochi Prefecture) who was virulently opposed to opening Japan to trade with foreigners. A key figure in formulating proposals leading to TOKUGAWA YOSHINOBU's resignation, he was killed in December 1867 by a shogunate patrol squad in Kyoto.

SANJO SANETOMI (1837–91)

Court noble and political leader who supported the anti-Western, antishogunate campaign along with ANEGAKOJI KINTOMO.

SHIBUSAWA EIJIRO (1840–1931)

Also known as Shibusawa Eiichi. An ex-farmer who was enlisted as a retainer for the Hitotsubashi family in 1864. After the Restoration, as an entrepreneur and business leader he played a central role in the establishment of modern industry and banking in Japan.

SHIMAZU HISAMITSU (1817–87)

Regent daimyo of Satsuma domain (now Kagoshima Prefecture). Supported *kobu-gattai*, union of the court and the shogunate. Had TOKUGAWA YOSHINOBU appointed shogunal regent in 1862.

SHIMAZU NARIAKIRA (1809–58)

A progressive daimyo of the Satsuma domain (now Kagoshima Prefecture) and strong advocate of westernization. He was one of HITOTSUBASHI KEIKI's main backers as successor to IESADA, whose third wife was his adopted daughter. He died just as the Ansei Purge was getting under way, thus escaping punishment.

LIST OF CHARACTERS

SHINMON TATSUGORO (1800–75)

Edo firefighter and aide of TOKUGAWA YOSHINOBU; his daughter Suka was sent to TOKUGAWA YOSHINOBU in Kyoto, and stayed with him thereafter, a favorite.

TAKEDA KOUNSAI (1803–65)

Samurai activist of the Mito domain (now part of Ibaraki Prefecture), a strong supporter of TOKUGAWA NARIAKI's reforms and a leader of antiforeign insurgents. He was executed for his role in the Mito civil war.

THE TOKUGAWA FAMILY

IEMOCHI (1846–66)

The fourteenth shogun, reigned 1858 to 1866. Born Tokugawa Yoshitomi, he became shogun at age twelve with the backing of II NAOSUKE. Later married Princess Kazu, sister to EMPEROR KOMEI.

IESADA (1824–58)

The thirteenth shogun, reigned 1853 to 1858. Feebleminded and sickly, he died childless.

IEYASU (1543–1616)

The first Tokugawa shogun (reigned 1603 to 1605), he founded the Tokugawa shogunate after his decisive victory in the Battle of Sekigahara (1600). Credited with bringing peace, unity, and stability to Japan.

IEYOSHI (1793–1853)

The twelfth shogun, reigned 1837 to 1853. Uncle by marriage to TOKUGAWA YOSHINOBU; his wife, the former Princess Sachi, was sister to Yoshinobu's mother. His failure to name an heir touched off a succession dispute.

MITSUKUNI (1628–1700)

Popularly known as Mito Komon. The second Mito daimyo, he was the driving force behind the compilation of a scholarly history of Japan that formed the basis for the nationalistic Mito School of Learning, a source of friction between the Mito and the bakufu.

NARIAKI (1800–60)

Mito daimyo and father of TOKUGAWA YOSHINOBU. Championed both Western learning and the proimperial, antiforeigner cause. Idolized by loyalists.

YAMANOUCHI YODO (1827–72)

Also known as Yamanouchi Toyoshige. Reformist daimyo of the Tosa domain (now Kochi Prefecture), he became adviser to IEMOCHI and was one of TOKUGAWA YOSHINOBU's main supporters.

YOSHINOBU (1837–1913)

Also known as Tokugawa Keiki. Fifteenth head of the house of Tokugawa, and fifteenth of the Tokugawa shoguns, reigned 1867. See HITOTSUBASHI KEIKI.

YOSHITOMI *see* IEMOCHI

High Hopes

SOMETIMES A MAN'S LIFE RESEMBLES A NARRATIVE. IT HAS A distinct theme.

Tokugawa Yoshinobu, the fifteenth and last Tokugawa shogun of Japan, embodied the nation's fears and aspirations during the first half of his life as few have ever done. That circumstance forms the dominant theme of his life.

He was not born into a shogunal family. He was born into the Mito, a branch of the ruling house of Tokugawa. It was one of three senior collateral families, the others being the Kii of Wakayama and the Owari, with headquarters in present-day Aichi Prefecture. Of the three great houses, the Mito (in present-day Ibaraki Prefecture) had the smallest stipend and the lowest prestige. The others could each boast a chief councillor of state, but the Mito had produced nothing higher than a middle councillor. Kii and Owari sons were eligible to succeed to the shogunate should the main Tokugawa family fail to produce an heir, but sons of Mito were not. To that degree, they suffered discrimination.

Yet there was one way in which Mito received preferential treatment. All daimyo, or domainal lords, were required by law to maintain households in the administrative capital of Edo (modern Tokyo), but only the lord of Mito was free to remain there permanently, unburdened by the standard obligation to spend alternate years in Edo and his home fief. The system of alternate attendance (*sankin-kotai*) required all the other daimyo to reside in the shogun's capital in alternate years, leaving their heirs and wives behind as hostages in the interim. As he alone was always present in Edo with the shogun, the head of the Mito domain became known informally as "vice shogun of the realm." From the time of the famous Mito Komon (as national historian Tokugawa Mitsukuni, grandson of founder Ieyasu, is commonly known), Edoites bestowed this title of respect on the lord of Mito. Officially, no such post existed, but that was a detail that the bakufu graciously overlooked in view of the Mito family's privileged status.

That was the family into which Yoshinobu—or Keiki, as he was known until his accession, and as we shall call him for now—was born.

Keiki's father, Tokugawa Nariaki, the Mito daimyo, was the hero of all loyalists—political activists professing supreme loyalty to the emperor, and hostility to the shogunate for what they saw as unlawful usurpation of power. The "Mito patriarch," as they reverentially called him, was an ardent advocate of reform measures aimed at keeping foreigners out of Japan and increasing the power of the emperor and the great daimyo. As long as he was around, they believed, the hated incursions of the foreign barbarians would end, and Japan would be saved. Foreign intercourse was banned in the Tokugawa regime, a time of prolonged national seclusion when Japan withdrew into itself, eschewing all but a minimum of contact with the outside world. Gradually, however, international pressure was mounting for Japan to open its ports and engage in foreign trade, with foreign warships turning up increasingly in Japanese waters. Outraged at this threat to Japan's sanctity, fearful of the superior military power of the West, yet determined to deny the foreigners right of entry to their country at any cost, loyalist patriots all but fell and worshipped at Nariaki's feet. Their extreme veneration was, however, the product of an illusion born of the desperation of the times.

Tokugawa Nariaki was a man of modest ability but bold spirit, with a staff of extraordinarily able advisers headed by the great Confucian scholar Fujita Toko. The Mito family was also the source of Mitogaku, a nationalist school of historical studies founded in the late seventeenth century that formed the philosophical underpinnings of the impassioned *sonno joi* ("Revere the emperor, expel the barbarian") campaign in the closing years of the Tokugawa era. Nariaki himself, highly conscious of being "vice shogun," bore himself around Edo Castle with dignity and pride. Small wonder indeed if in the patriots' eyes he loomed a hero.

Nariaki was in fact a pathological philanderer. He even went so far as to penetrate into the Ooku ("great interior"), domestic quarters of Edo Castle occupied entirely by ladies in the shogun's service, and attempted to force himself on the residents there. As a result, the ladies in the powerful Ooku hierarchy despised him. His lack of supporters among them was to cost him dearly in his political life. And yet philandering has its uses: Nariaki sired twenty-one sons, of whom twelve survived to adulthood, along with six girls. His numerous progeny were a boon to the family fortunes.

Nariaki's wife was from Kyoto. She was a woman of imperial blood, from the family of Prince Arisugawa, the adopted son of Emperor Ninko, and before her marriage was known as Princess Tominomiya Yoshiko. When the match was first proposed, Emperor Ninko happily gave his consent, commenting, "The Mito are a family of military retainers, but for generations they have served the court well. This is an ideal match."

The princess was highly regarded in the palace for her cleverness and beauty, rumor of which had come to the Mito family as well. Nariaki was devoted to her, and said, "Beauty fades, but intelligence is irreplaceable. I hope to have a fine son by her." Before long a son was duly born to them. Nariaki already had fathered a son by another woman, but naturally his son by his official wife would be next in line as head of the Mito domain. That was Tsuruchiyo, later Yoshiatsu, the tenth head of the house of Mito, a man with the mild appearance and demeanor of a Kyoto aristocrat. His personality was unprepossessing, and he lacked the military bearing that Nariaki preferred. Disappointed, Nariaki declared that the effeminate blood of the court had won out in his son.

Five more sons were born to him, one after another, but

not all by his wife. These were given names reflecting their birth order: Second Son, Third Son, Fourth Son, and so on. The second and fifth were by his wife, but of those, one died in infancy and the other, like Tsuruchiyo, had the etiolated features and character of the court nobles. Nariaki lamented the dominance of the Kyoto blood in his progeny, overwhelming his own contribution. Then in 1837 his wife gave birth to Keiki, whose infant name was Shichiroma, Seventh Son. From the time the baby was in diapers, Nariaki kept a watchful eye on him, impatient to know the answer to the all-important question: Which side of the family would he take after?

Nariaki was a man of many idiosyncrasies, one of which was a passion for education. Unlike most daimyo, he took a keen interest in how and what his sons were taught. As a boy, he himself had despised being taught by a nurse. "A man must be raised by men," he had declared to his father, persuading him to replace the hated nurse with a couple of robust retainers as private tutors.

By law, daimyo children were to be kept in Edo at all times, hostages under the *sankin-kotai* system. Even so, Nariaki had petitioned successfully to have special allowances made for his children. They would be born in the Mito quarters in Edo, but taken back during infancy to be raised at the rougher hands of samurai in the home province. Nariaki was determined that his sons not be spoiled by a life of luxury in the capital.

This pattern became the rule for the family, and Keiki was brought up in the same way—not as an Edoite, but as a genuine son of Mito. The year after his birth he was sent away from his parents to live in Mito Castle in Hitachi. When he was ten his father returned home and saw with pride what a fine youth he was growing to be. Over the years, during intermittent stays in Mito, Nariaki had noted his son's progress with increasing satisfaction, even predicting confidently to the shogunal council of elders with all the assurance of a physiognomist, "Mark my words, that boy is going to turn out different from the rest." For once, he meant, a son of his did not look like a weakling Kyoto prince.

In his heart he expected Keiki to be a reincarnation of Ieyasu, the great founder of the Tokugawa dynasty. "See that you discipline him properly," he counseled everyone involved in rearing the child, from domain elders and tutors to the women who retained separate quarters in the castle. Naturally, the Mito samurai shared his high expectations for the boy. But Nariaki believed that a daimyo had to be stronger than an ordinary samurai, and his sons were trained with according rigor. The greater his expectations for Keiki, the more rigorous Keiki's upbringing became.

That a warrior had to lie perfectly straight when asleep was part of Nariaki's creed, and he took to entering Keiki's bedchamber without warning to check on the boy's sleeping posture. Invariably, it was unsatisfactory. Finally he summoned an attendant and issued a stern order: "If he rolls around in bed like that, he'll never make a true samurai. Set a sword blade on either side of his pillow." From that night on, Keiki was forced to sleep with his wooden pillow set between two swords standing vertically like a pair of horns. Unless he turned over with extreme caution, he ran the risk of cutting himself badly about the head and face.

Nor was that all. Keiki's tutor, Inoue Kanzaburo, was constantly after him to sleep with his right arm beneath him. That way, even if as a warrior he should be surprised by the enemy while sleeping and lose one arm, he would still retain the use of his good right arm, and be able to fight back. As a result, it became Keiki's lifelong habit to sleep with his right arm beneath him.

As a boy, Keiki never questioned the value of all this training, even though, because of his father's belief that a daimyo was a chosen warrior, the regimen he followed was far stricter than that of other samurai boys. His clothing and bedding were all of coarse hemp or cotton, without a scrap of silk. His day got under way at first light of dawn. After washing up, he read aloud a portion of the four books and five classics of Confucianism, supervised by an attendant, and then had breakfast. After that he practiced calligraphy until ten o'clock. Then he went off to school together with the other boys, returning at noon. After lunch a short playtime was allowed. The remainder of the afternoon was devoted to martial arts. In the evening, after supper, he would finish whatever remained from his early-morning reading assignment. That ended his daily schedule. No deviation was permissible.

Despite the rigor of his upbringing, Keiki was not docile by nature; it was Nariaki who forced him to submit to this regimen. The boy poured himself eagerly into his martial arts lessons, but detested reading. His desperate teacher warned, "If you won't read, then I will have to burn your finger." Finally, he had the boy hold out his index finger and placed a large amount of burning moxa on it, cauterizing the skin. The pain was searing, but Keiki bore it uncomplainingly, declaring that anything was better than reading Chinese classics aloud. He was punished that way so many times that the finger festered and swelled, but he was unrepentant.

At a loss, the teacher reported the situation to Nariaki, who ordered that the boy be immediately confined. One corner of the parlor was screened off for this purpose. The screens were bound fast, and the boy left inside to languish without meals. This treatment proved too much for him, and he did become somewhat more tractable. His attitude toward his studies, however, remained halfhearted. Until his twenties Keiki demonstrated little interest in book learning. His early education is summed up in the disapproving words of the prominent bakufu official Kawaji Toshiakira: "Seven parts martial arts to three parts book learning! Until the proportion is balanced, he's no true son of Mito."

In general, as a child Keiki was rash and heedless, a tad wily, and lacking in charm. Among the ladies of the castle he was no favorite. Fifth Son, his elder brother, was a quiet child fond of setting out *hina* dolls with the maids. One day Keiki burst into the room where his brother was playing and yelled, "This is a stupid thing for you to do, Brother!" Grabbing the dolls from the tiers where they were on display, he threw them to the floor, smashing them to pieces. The maids attending his brother whispered together that this Seventh Son was an insufferable brat.

Despite these bursts of truculence, one reason Nariaki always entertained high hopes for Keiki was the vigor and boldness of his calligraphic style. A person's hand was believed indicative of its owner's nature, and on that basis alone Nariaki was convinced that the boy would go far. Secretly, he may well have harbored hopes of one day making Keiki shogun.

Once, a request came from the Kii branch of the Tokugawas for a Mito lad to adopt as heir. It was a golden opportunity to marry into the powerful Kii line. When Fujita Toko broached the matter to Nariaki, he was quickly warned off Keiki, whom Nariaki wanted to save should anything happen to Tsuruchiyo, his heir apparent. "I'll let them have Goroma, Fifth Son. He likes to plays with dolls and will never amount to anything, for good or for ill. Perfect for sending off to be another family's heir." Nariaki's unwillingness to send the young Keiki even to the Kii family, dominant among the three branch lines, was a certain tip-off that he had other plans for the boy beyond keeping him around as a "spare." (As it happened, the adoption scheme somehow fell through, and Keiki's brother ended up going, instead, to the Ikeda family of Tottori, becoming known in time as Ikeda Yoshinori, lord of Tottori.)

For Keiki, another fate lay in store. In 1847, the summer he was ten, Abe Masahiro, chief senior councillor of the Edo shogunate, summoned an administrator of the Mito family affairs named Nakayama and told him, "I have been informed in confidence that the shogun wishes Keiki to be adopted into the Hitotsubashi family." Confidential or not, the news was tantamount to an order from the twelfth Tokugawa shogun, Ieyoshi.

Nakayama's response was swift and adamant: "Why not another of the master's sons? Let it be anyone else!" He went on to explain Nariaki's high hopes for the boy and reluctance to let him go.

9

The man was a fool, thought Abe Masahiro impatiently. Could he not see what lay behind the request? Himself a man of great perspicacity, Abe enjoyed a reputation as the ablest of all the bakufu politicians of his time. He found something attractive in the dangerous man Tokugawa Nariaki of Mito, despised though he was by the bakufu and the shogunal families for his fanatical insistence on returning the country to imperial rule. Secretly, Abe planned to forge an alliance with him in order to cope with the knotty problem of Japan's maritime defense.

The "black ships" of U.S. Commodore Matthew Perry would not make their stunning entry into Japan's waters for several years yet. Still, the occasional appearance of Western warships kept the authorities in a constant dither. Abe saw nothing to do but fall back on the brains, courage, and popularity of Nariaki, who was not only antishogunate but also an ardent advocate of driving off foreigners by force. But of such things he could say nothing in public, Nariaki having been placed under house arrest here in Edo as punishment for the radical nature of his political views and conduct.

On the theory that even a poisonous plant could be put to medicinal use if one only knew how, the practical Abe was determined to curry favor with Nariaki for future benefit. That this marriage proposal from the Hitotsubashi would be all to Nariaki's liking was clear to him. He sent Nakayama home with the advice that he ought not to attempt making such a big decision on his own. "Talk it over with the boy's father," he urged.

At his domicile in Koishikawa, a section of Edo, Nariaki was told of the shogun's confidential desire. Abe Masahiro's reading of the man had been correct. He accepted the offer on the spot.

Keiki could become shogun. The analysis that led Nariaki to that conclusion was as intricate as that of a chess master seeing far ahead into the game. To begin with, the present shogun, Ieyoshi, was not in good health and could not be expected to live long. His heir, Iesada, moreover, had been frail and sickly from birth, and because Iesada's condition ruled out the possibility of sexual relations with a woman, he appeared destined to die young, without issue. The Tokugawa mantle would go to an adopted son. Candidates could come only from the other two senior collateral families, the Kii and the Owari—or from the three junior cadet families of the Hitotsubashi, the Shimizu, and the Tayasu. And Keiki was now to marry into the Hitotsubashi family. There was a chance.

In fact, it was a very good chance. Of the two senior families, the Owari family was out: Having recently been forced themselves to adopt a son from another line, they were in no position to offer up a scion as future shogun. And young Lord Narimasa of the Kii family had died less than a year before, leaving a posthumous infant son named Kikuchiyo. Under the circumstances, neither family could possibly provide a candidate for the succession. In the three cadet families, moreover, Yoshiyori, the head of the Tayasu, had only recently attained his majority and had yet to father a child, while the Shimizu family currently lacked a head, Narikatsu having left hastily the year before to fill the vacuum in the Kii. That left only the Hitotsubashi.

Here, too, tragedy had followed upon tragedy. For generations the family had had to adopt sons to carry on the line, but strangely enough, all had died young. The current heir, Masamaru, a young fellow from the Owari, lay even now on his deathbed. So Keiki would be adopted into the Hitotsu-bashi family—and then should the shogunal family find itself in need of an heir, there would be nowhere else to turn. And so the Mito family might end up producing a shogun after all.

Nothing like this set of events had ever occurred before in all 250 years of the Tokugawa shogunate (or in the preceding five centuries of other military rule, for that matter). That was what appealed to Nariaki. If such an eventuality did come about, as father to the shogun he, Nariaki, would wield great authority in Edo Castle. He could lead the shogunal cabinet and silence the powerful Ooku hierarchy. The prospect enthralled him. He was an ambitious man, misunderstood and shunned for that reason by the senior councillors on the shogunal cabinet, but his ambition arose from his deeply patriotic concern and indignation about the state of the country, which he saw to be under imminent threat of foreign domination. One way or another, he was determined to grasp the reins of Japan's government.

"That fellow Abe is no slouch," he thought admiringly of Abe Masahiro, whose secret overture had opened the door. In fact, he barely knew the brilliant twenty-nine-year-old lord of Fukuyama and leader of the senior councillors. To find Abe extending a hand to him in this subtle way came as a surprise. He gave his assent through his chief retainer.

On hearing news of Nariaki's acceptance, Abe gloated privately at the accuracy of his political instincts. Of the young Keiki he had no personal knowledge whatever. All he'd had to go on was rumor of the ludicrously high hopes that Nari-aki entertained for the boy.

And so it was that Nariaki's fatherly expectations occa-sioned rumor, and rumor carried his seventh son to a place of inconceivable destiny.

Raising a Future Shogun

TEN-YEAR-OLD KEIKI NATURALLY KNEW NOTHING OF ALL this. When he set out on the journey from Mito Castle for Edo in 1847, his father having commanded him to come quickly, it was early autumn. He traveled on horseback, attended by thirteen samurai including his tutor, Inoue Kanzaburo. It took three days for the entourage to arrive at the Mito residence in Komagome, Edo.

On the morning of the first day of the following month, Abe Masahiro and Toda Tadamasa, another senior councillor, called on Nariaki as envoys of the shogun Ieyoshi and formally conveyed His Excellency's desire to have the boy installed as Hitotsubashi heir. The family had a yearly budget of 100,000 *koku*. The Hitotsubashi were not independent like the three senior branch families of the house of Tokugawa, nor did they have a fief. Because the family was not a *han*, or feudal clan, moreover, it had no vassals of its own. Instead, the family was served by *hatamoto*, shogunal vassals who retained their status as direct retainers to the shogun, and of whom there were just enough to see to Keiki's personal needs, no more. Because the three cadet families of the Hitotsubashi, Shimizu, and Tayasu were among those who might by law supply a shogunal heir, their retainers in the three junior cadet families ranked as being in direct service to the shogun, and were considered on loan from him. The system was begun by the eighth shogun, Yoshimune, in order to pool the shogunal bloodline. The families' sole obligation to the shogunate was to carry on their line in good health; beyond this, they had no earthly role or purpose.

So Keiki joined the Hitotsubashi family. It was whispered in the shogunate that as a Mito, his blood bond to the central Tokugawa line might be a bit tenuous. This could not be helped. The Kii and Owari had close blood ties to the shogunate, and a shogun of such antecedents would have had impeccable credentials; but for a Mito to be in line for the succession was unprecedented. The Mito founder was Ieyasu's eleventh son, Yorifusa. Since his day there had been no further intermarrying with the shogunal line—so that even though the Mito was a cadet family, its only blood tie to the Tokugawa was the shared ancestor Ieyasu, a link now two hundred years old. For Keiki, the youngest scion of that branch, to fall in line for the position of shogun was nothing short of extraordinary.

The shogun Ieyoshi, however, was well pleased. His beloved

wife, the former Princess Sachi, was sister to Keiki's mother, making him the boy's uncle. This was reason enough for him to be favorably disposed toward Keiki before ever setting eyes on him. "They tell me our nephew is a bright and promising fellow," he told his wife. Abe Masahiro had alertly sniffed out this connection and its political implications.

On meeting Keiki, Ieyoshi was more and more taken with him. "*Gyobukyo*, attend to your studies," he told him with an affectionate smile, calling him by the special name for the head of the Hitotsubashi. The previous head of the family, a boy named Akimaru, had died of illness just before Keiki's adoption. To raise a child of high birth to manhood was no easy matter. In fact, Ieyoshi himself was a second son, having acceded to power after his elder brother, Takechiyo, died young. He was a genial fellow who bore no one ill will.

Now the Tokugawa hatamoto, who were retainers of the shogun, did not feel as familiar toward Nariaki, the lord of Mito, as they did toward members of the Kii and Owari families. The two others seemed family, but toward the Mito everyone felt slight hostility and a deep-rooted alienation. One reason was the tenuous nature of the blood tie between the families, as we have seen; another was the Mito family's role in promoting the imperialist school of thought advocating the overthrow of the shogunate and a return to direct imperial rule. Over the years, the Mito had spent vast sums of money on gathering opposition scholars to work on the compilation of the vast *Dai Nihon Shi* ("History of Great Japan"), which was strongly nationalistic and proimperialist in philosophy. It paid reverence to the Kyoto court, and scorned the military rulers. For example, where the latter honored the fourteenth-century military commander Ashi-kaga Takauji for his role in restoring power to the Genji, in the sight of the Mito scholars he was an outlaw for fomenting civil war and forcing Emperor Go-Daigo to flee the capital. Instead, they promoted the brilliant military tactician Kusunoki Masashige as a paragon of virtue for his determined, though doomed, opposition to military rule.

The Mito view of history constituted a scathing indictment of the Tokugawa bakufu. "Insurrection runs in that family": Such was the vague impression of the Mito among the shogun's retainers. Rumor had it that there was a secret saying in the Mito family dating back to the days of the patriarch Mitsukuni: "If there should ever be war between the Tokugawa rulers in Edo and the imperial court in Kyoto, cast aside your weapons and serve the court." (That this saying was no mere legend, but had a basis in fact, was revealed in later years by Keiki himself.)

It was in that sense a house to be shunned. Nariaki, moreover, was known as a dangerous thinker. Certainly for the shogun Ieyoshi he was a man to steer clear of. One day Ieyoshi spoke privately of Nariaki to Asahina Masatoshi, his chief of affairs, as "a man to guard against." Ordinarily, however, he spoke of him openly to his associates as a "notable man"—presumably meaning a man of special importance even for the branch families. Together, the two statements are typical of Ieyoshi's balanced approach. As head of the house of Tokugawa, he sought to view Nariaki and Keiki separately, each on his own terms. Not only that, he apparently had some thought of adopting Keiki himself, as the following anecdote suggests.

One of the most influential men in any shogun's immediate staff was his grand chamberlain, a sort of personal secretary. In Ieyoshi's case, that post was filled by a man called Hongo. Observing with regret that his friend Asahina Masatoshi had yet to receive an increase in stipend, Hongo broached the matter respectfully to Ieyoshi one day.

There was good reason why Asahina's stipend should be raised: He had been in charge of organizing the shogun's deer hunt, a time-honored event held once in the reign of every shogun. It was traditional for the coordinator of the deer hunt to receive an increase in stipend of some 500 *koku*, yet Asahina had not had word yet of any such raise. Even so, Ieyoshi rejected Hongo's intercession, telling him, "That will not be necessary. It is only a matter of time before Asahina rises to the same rank as you anyway."

It was a portentous remark, not only for Asahina but for Hitotsubashi Keiki as well. When Keiki was adopted into the Hitotsubashi family, Asahina had gone to great lengths to be of service to him. Were Keiki now to become shogun, Asahina would certainly be made grand chamberlain, in the highest level of the shogunate bureaucracy. That was Ieyoshi's implied meaning, and that was why the raise was not urgent. Clearly, Ieyoshi foresaw a brilliant future for Keiki.

Word quickly spread among castle officials that the shogun had privately expressed his endorsement of Keiki. On the castle staff was a group of men called *bozu* ("priests") who performed various odd jobs such as waiting on tables and serving tea, dressed in priestly attire. They also frequented the daimyo residences that were maintained in Edo by every feudal lord in the country, and would obligingly leak castle secrets and gossip to whoever was there. The money they were paid for this service nicely supplemented their incomes.

Because the "priests" passed on the rumor, Ieyoshi's whispered comment was soon common knowledge among all the daimyo. In the blink of an eye the name Hitotsubashi Keiki, belonging to a youth still in his teens, took on enormous weight in Edo. In such ways is a man's destiny set.

The Hitotsubashi residence was soon visited daily by a stream of daimyo, high-ranking bureaucrats, and eminent hatamoto seeking higher office. Row upon row of footwear in the vestibule was testimony to the constant parade of visitors. In the beginning, Nariaki's fond hopes for his son had planted the seed; then those hopes had spread to others, finally permeating Edo society at large.

Yet Keiki, the object of all this attention, was still only a boy whose greatest pleasure was physical exercise. Once he was out in Shinagawa Bay with a retainer, and observed a fisherman casting his net. "I should like to give that a try myself," he said, and wouldn't hear otherwise. Finally he climbed into the fisherman's boat, and cast a net under the other's bemused instruction. It was harder than it looked. The net balled up when he threw it into the air, and fell on the water in a hopeless tangle.

"You'll do naught but give the fish a good scare that-a-way," said the fisherman with a grin, never dreaming that this was the much-talked-of Hitotsubashi scion. "You've got to toss it so's it spreads wide in the air before landing splat on the water. That's the way it's done, see. Your way, it'll only sink like a stone. Well, it's asking too much of an amateur like yourself. Takes three years to get the knack."

"Three years?" repeated Keiki. He paid for the net, took it home, and set to practicing in the garden. At a month's end, after practicing like a man possessed, he had mastered the subtle body movements required for the net to billow out in the air and waft gently to the surface of the water. "Humph," he said. "That fisherman said it took three years, but I did it in a month!"

Thus the stubbornness and tenacity that were to become lifelong traits had already germinated at this early age. While net casting may seem an accomplishment of doubtful value for one in his position, it is hard to dismiss the quickness and ability of a youth able to master a complex skill attained usually by men whose livelihoods depended on it. Keiki was no ordinary boy.

Fujita Toko, a Mito scholar and one of Nariaki's ablest advisers, was known as a fine judge of character. Privately discerning Keiki to be a boy of rare gifts, he became fearful for his welfare, and wrote a letter of warning to Takahashi Taichiro, chief secretary in the Mito residence in Edo. The letter said in part:

His uncommon spirits and quickness may well bring him harm. His brilliance could provoke others to rebellion, causing them to undermine him when he least expects it. Tell him to keep his abilities to himself, and to cultivate an outward appearance of humility and deference.

Nothing was so fearful as the power of slander, he said, speaking out of a remarkable depth of understanding and experience.

At about this time, the shogun's private physician, Ito Soeki, sent a private letter to a close associate of Nariaki's. Ito, too, was unofficially on the Mito payroll, in return for which he willingly passed along bakufu secrets. Not only the Mito, but every clan resorted to this means of keeping tabs on what was afoot in the Tokugawa family and the inner circles of the shogunate.

The contents of Soeki's letter were highly unusual, consisting of a medical opinion concerning Shogun Ieyoshi's heir apparent, Iesada. In fact, in the forty years since Ieyoshi's marriage at age sixteen to Princess Sachi, Ieyoshi had sired twenty-three children in all, by his wife and consorts. Nearly all died in infancy; Iesada, his fourth child, was the sole survivor. As heir apparent, Iesada had advanced to the rank of Second Captain of the Right, and was now around twenty-five years of age; but his health was far from robust. The letter stated that Iesada had "an extremely sickly constitution." Adding delicately, "nor could he ever be described as clever." His mental capacity, in other words, was substandard. The letter continued:

> When he has a cold, and needs looking after, having too many ladies-in-waiting around upsets him, making his condition worse. For that reason, one lady-in-waiting, whom he is used to, always looks after him alone. With such a lack of interest in women, he is unlikely ever to father a child.

So Iesada displayed no interest in the opposite sex, according to his doctor, and lacked procreative power. But then Soeki went on to make an observation of great political insight: Because of the son's feeble mental powers, the bureaucrats apparently found him much easier to handle than his father the shogun.

Clearly, the castle physician chose to spell out these matters in concern for the interests of Hitotsubashi Keiki. Were Keiki to be adopted by the childless Iesada, he would be second in line to be shogun.

But it wasn't quite that simple. Hostility toward the Mito family was a bakufu tradition, and besides, the bureaucrats and the castle womenfolk alike preferred a shogun who would meekly do their bidding to one who could think and act for himself. That much was apparent. There was no guarantee that Keiki would be able to capitalize on a chance to become next in line.

One man, Yoshimichi, an outspoken monk in the shogun's family temple at Ueno, predicted a different future for Keiki. A gifted scholar and true ascetic whose one flaw was an imprudent tongue, Yoshimichi had studied with great masters, and from his youth, people predicted a great career for him as head of an important temple. He never reined in his tongue, however, but continued making fun of others' indiscretions, making harsh denunciations, and taking every opportunity to criticize until the other monks turned against him and he wound up tucked away in a minor temple office.

One day, Yoshimichi saw Hitotsubashi Keiki paying his respects at the temple, and murmured, "There's a man with a physiognomy just like mine!" He had made a hobby of reading men's character in their facial features. His conclusion regarding Keiki was that he was not the type to be a king or general, but rather an able councillor. In other words, he would not possess the greatness of a Toyotomi Hideyoshi or Tokugawa Ieyasu, the giants of Japanese history who brought about national unification, but rather the lesser role of an able steward—someone with great mental powers but lacking the physiognomy of a ruler. (For his imprudence in making this prophecy, however, Yoshimichi found himself sent packing to a remote country temple.)

Keiki himself needed an able right-hand man. Nariaki asked the faithful Fujita Toko, his grand chamberlain, to recommend a hatamoto of some education and firmness of character to serve as his son's attendant. Toko responded by naming Hiraoka Enshiro, a vassal of the shogun and a man of undisputed integrity.

Born the fourth son of an impoverished samurai named Okamoto, Hiraoka was an adopted son. He was a young man of some eccentricity, excelling at his studies but impatient with social niceties. His manners were boorish, and he was not fond of social intercourse. At the home of a superior, he refused even to bow. At the time of the offer to become page to Hitotsubashi Keiki, he was stuck in a low-ranking job with little hope for advancement. By joining the Hitotsubashi now, he might rise to dizzying heights in the event that Keiki became shogun. It seemed a position of limitless promise—and yet he turned the offer down on the spot, claiming he would feel out of place. Hiraoka's refusal caused a minor stir. Impressed by the man's rectitude, Nariaki personally intervened, and prevailed on him to accept.

In addition to a stipend, Hiraoka was given a small extra emolument, and entered into trial service with Keiki, who was now a teenager. One of his duties was to serve the rice at meals. Clumsily, he would draw the rice tub toward himself, pick up the server, and dish rice into the bowls, but it did not go smoothly, and invariably he wound up spilling a good deal of rice.

"What, Hiraoka, don't you know how to serve rice?" Keiki said with sympathy to his retainer, who was his senior by five years. Taking the bucket from Hiraoka's grasp, he picked up the server and bowls and neatly demonstrated how the task was done. It was impossible to tell who was waiting on whom.

Hiraoka was in a cold sweat at his failure. At the same time, he was horrified that Keiki would do such a thing. No daimyo but Keiki would have so casually offered his attendant instruction in the mysteries of serving rice. Keiki was a man of many gifts, to whom nothing was apparently impossible.

Another incident of a similar nature took place involving a recently promoted retainer named Watarai Ryozo, a country samurai likewise quite unaccustomed to his new surroundings. When Keiki organized an archery competition for his brothers, Ryozo was given the task of gathering up fallen arrows, but he was sadly lacking in proper form. The equipment was not combat size but smaller, with bows some two and a half feet long, and arrows under a foot; targets were at a distance of forty-five feet. That style of archery was originally a court amusement, and it had a fixed protocol. Seeing Watarai at a loss, Keiki stepped in and offered to demonstrate how to pick up the arrows for a few turns. "Watch how

I do it," he said, and proceeded to do the work of an attendant with aplomb.

It was the duty of the page Igai Katsusaburo to shave the front of Keiki's head and do up his hair in samurai style. He was a clumsy barber, however, and nicked Keiki regularly. Without losing his temper, Keiki announced he would show him how the job was done, and proceeded to sit his barber down and do a fine job of shaving his head. His skill was mysterious, as a boy of his upbringing would never have been allowed to handle a razor. Somehow, he carried it off brilliantly. Igai was simultaneously perplexed and full of admiration. Indeed, the monk Yoshimichi was right: Keiki would have made an excellent retainer or adviser, had he set out on that path. Or had he been born a merchant's son, he could have succeeded easily at a trade, for that matter.

His daily regimen since joining the Hitotsubashi family was crammed with lessons, all private. There were nine in all: calligraphy, Chinese, Japanese, classical poetry, horseback riding, archery, fencing, javelin throwing, and shooting on horseback. In each category he achieved what any able student might, but no more. It was characteristic of Keiki that he did not take well to being taught by others, much preferring to acquire knowledge and skills on his own. As a result, he scarcely applied himself to his lessons. Fujita Toko realized that that trait was actually a sign of his greatness. Later, even Keiki's enemies were to credit him with being a hero of the caliber of the great Ieyasu; whether Toko went so far is unknown.

The shogun Ieyoshi doted on Keiki so much that even his closest associates thought it remarkable. He bore himself with the mildness and dignity of a Confucian gentleman, but as a politician he was crafty and suspicious by nature, inclined particularly to be wary of Nariaki, so it seems improbable that his affection for Keiki had a political motivation. Rather, he seemed to love the sturdy youth for his personal qualities. Dissatisfied with his slow-witted son Iesada, unable to love him unconditionally, he may have attempted to satisfy unfulfilled parental longings via the quick, responsive Keiki.

An incident occurred in January 1853, when Keiki was fifteen, that forced Ieyoshi's associates to acknowledge in surprise that the shogun did evidently plan to make Keiki his son's heir. Among the shogun's special annual events was a day of falconry, after which he would present the emperor in Kyoto with game he himself had bagged. "This time I'm taking Hitotsubashi Keiki along," Ieyoshi announced suddenly to Asahina, Keiki's chief attendant. Asahina was astounded, as it was customary for the shogun to be accompanied by the heir apparent. For him to take Keiki along on such an occasion was tantamount to telling the world that he intended to make the youth Iesada's heir.

Asahina's close association with Keiki gave him a personal cause to rejoice, as his own fortunes would naturally rise along with those of his master. But what of the inner circle in the bakufu? Would not the anti-Mito elements put up fierce opposition, nipping Keiki's chances in the bud? Sensing danger, Asahina consulted with the chief senior councillor, Abe Masahiro.

For a moment, Abe's face lit up with pleasure at the good news regarding his protégé, but he soon sank into deep thought, finally shaking his head. The political situation was not without pitfalls for Keiki, he adjudged. Quickly Asahina relayed Abe's opinion back to Ieyoshi. "Too soon, is it?" said the shogun. The laconic remark clearly reconfirmed his undoubted intention to make the boy his son's heir in good time. Simple as it was, the remark was clear indication of his private thoughts on the matter. When Nariaki heard of it, he was overjoyed.

And yet, who can know the future? In a matter of months, on July 11, 1853, Ieyoshi himself died of illness, having taken no formal steps regarding the succession. His physician Ito Soeki diagnosed it initially as a mere attack of heatstroke, but three days after he fell ill, the shogun Ieyoshi lay dead.

The timing of his death was dramatic. On July 8, only days before, U.S. Commodore Matthew Perry had sailed into Edo Bay with a squadron and proceeded to issue an ultimatum to the bakufu, persuading them that he was prepared to force open the country and put an end to two and a half centuries of self-imposed isolation. The bakufu and the country alike were thrown into an uproar. The chaotic upheaval of the last days of the Tokugawa had begun. The Tokugawa would last only fifteen years more.

Perry's message was stark: "Open the country, or fight." Denouncing the soft diplomacy Western powers had used heretofore in dealings with the recalcitrant Japanese, Perry was of the belief that amenities were of no use in establishing relations with a closed-off country like Japan. Only military force would do the job. He was prepared, if necessary, to occupy the Kuril Islands.

Perry's tough approach gave the Japanese people a greater shock than he could ever have imagined. Among the citizenry, it ignited a fierce determination to protect Japan and "expel the barbarians" at any cost. In the bakufu, however, it gave rise to a defeatist foreign policy of groveling in the dirt. Friction and conflict between advocates of these two diametrically opposed ways of thinking lay at the heart of the national turmoil in the latter days of the Tokugawa era, which would last barely fifteen more years.

As for the commercial treaty that Perry also sought, the Japanese intelligentsia inferred from his attitude that granting it would constitute surrender. "Why give in without a fight?" they demanded. "Let us fight it out, and only if we are defeated should we capitulate." This was the opinion of all antiforeign nationalists, headed in the west of Japan by Emperor Komei, and in the east by Mito Nariaki.

In any case, the shogun Ieyoshi died at the height of the furor over Perry and his black ships. In conveying this circumstance to Perry, the bakufu representatives referred to the shogun in correspondence as *taikun*, or "great lord." It was a delicate problem; they could not describe him as ruler or sovereign so long as the emperor remained on the throne in Kyoto, nor could they translate the word *shogun* literally as "generalissimo," for that would imply he was a mere soldier lacking in political power. Under the circumstances, they were forced to invent a new word, one that all the foreigners, particularly the French, took initially to mean "crowned head." As far as any of the foreign powers knew, Japan's crowned head was dead—and his successor was mentally incompetent.

A Failed Opportunity

K EIKI HAD HAD A NUMBER OF AUDIENCES WITH IESADA, Japan's de facto ruler. "What sort of man is he?" Hiraoka Enshiro, Keiki's senior aide, wanted to know, but Keiki answered only "I cannot discuss the sovereign." By nature, Keiki was an eloquent and fluent speaker, but perhaps as a result of the Mito-style education he received, he had become more closemouthed.

In fact, Keiki had heard and observed some startling behavior. Before Iesada became shogun, Keiki had once called on him at the western enceinte of Edo Castle, traditionally the official residence of the heir apparent. "Who's there?" Iesada had called out, jerking his head up. His face was pale and triangular, his gaze wavering. Just in front of him sat an earthen charcoal brazier stamped with gold, and across the coals in it was an earthen pan for parching beans. Iesada was indulging in his greatest earthly pleasure—roasting beans with bamboo chopsticks.

"Oh, Hitotsubashi, it's you! Have some beans," he exclaimed, and placed a few in Keiki's palm. Just then a hawk landed in the garden before them. With a shriek, Iesada jumped down from the veranda and chased after it. It was hard to believe that this was a full-grown man, twice widowed. His first wife was the daughter of Regent Takatsukasa Sukehiro, his second the daughter of former regent Ichijo; both women had died shortly after marrying him.

Since Iesada became the thirteenth shogun, every time Keiki had an audience with him, they had met in the garden. He was there now, galumphing unsteadily around the edge of the pond with his awkward, half-limping gait. In his hands he held a bayonet rifle, the gift of a Dutchman. Iesada was very taken with the weapon, and brandished it aloft now as he chased his aides around, hobbling after them and giggling in glee as the ash-faced men ran for dear life.

In the midst of this commotion, Keiki went over by the pond and knelt with one knee on the ground to wait. Soon Iesada came charging by, but as soon as he recognized Keiki, he turned pale. Suddenly throwing aside the rifle, he looked as terrified as if he had seen a monster. On the verge of tears, he called hysterically for his nurse: "Oshige, I'm scared! Hitotsubashi is here!"

Keiki was taken aback. He had spent time with Iesada on any number of occasions, always as a trusted member of the family. Never had the sight of him caused such a reaction before. The shogun's aides felt equal consternation, and hurriedly asked Keiki to withdraw, which he of course did without protest. As he left, however, Keiki was mortified. "Am I a monster?" he asked himself. Someone must have planted the idea in the simpleminded Iesada. It could only have been the castle women.

A new shogun meant, naturally, a shift in the map of power lines in the Ooku, or "great interior," the all-female household made up of women serving the shogun. Under Iesada, the head of that household, was his natural mother, O-Mitsu. She was the daughter of a hatamoto named Atobe Yuzaemon, and had been a consort of the former shogun Ieyoshi when he was heir apparent. Her luck had been extraordinary. While falling short of the prolific standard set by his father, Ienari, the eleventh shogun (who fathered fifty-five children by forty consorts, and kept hundreds of other ladies in his castle household), Ieyoshi still managed to have relations with some fifty-six women over his lifetime, impregnating twenty of them. Virtually all of his progeny died as infants, however. His sole surviving issue was O-Mitsu's feebleminded boy.

After Ieyoshi's death and Iesada's accession to power, O-Mitsu took Buddhist vows and became known as Honju-in, but continued to exercise great influence. There was a precedent for this: Hojo Masako was called the "nun shogun" because of her lifelong involvement in and dominance of shogunate politics following the death in 1199 of her husband Minamoto no Yoritomo, founder of the Kamakura shogunate. Iesada's condition, which prevented him from communicating freely with any but his mother and nurse, meant that interpreting the will of Japan's shogun lay entirely with O-Mitsu.

Convinced that Mito Nariaki was seeking through Keiki to overthrow the Tokugawa and establish himself in power, O-Mitsu was rabidly hostile to the Mito. Nor was she far mistaken. That very scenario was likely to play out. Once Keiki became shogun, Nariaki would be *ogosho*, grand old man of the shogunate. Entering Edo Castle as regent, he would overhaul the administration and stand up heroically to the foreign powers. O-Mitsu cared nothing about what happened with foreign powers, but she knew for a certainty that the frugal Nariaki would lay an ax to the institution of the Ooku. Her position would be ruined.

"The old man of Mito is a big monster," she drilled into her son the shogun night and day. "So is his son, the young Hitotsubashi lord. Why, if you make him your heir, there's no telling what will become of you." Like a shamaness breathing life into a doll, she had kept whispering in her son's ear. Keiki saw it all in a flash of insight.

So that was it. They were against him, and he would end up banished from the main enceinte, the heart of the castle, and from the western enceinte as well, residence of the heir apparent. He was annoyed. For all the gifts he was born with, Keiki lacked one thing: ambition. Never for a moment had he entertained any desire to be the shogunal heir or the next shogun.

"How absurd!" Night after night, in the privacy of his bedroom, he would mutter this to himself. He shared his bed with a concubine named Suka. Each night, as Keiki lay on top of her repeating that word over and over—"Absurd! Absurd!"—she would cringe. To Suka, it seemed only that he was criticizing her prowess.

All his life, Keiki had an outsized appetite. The possessor of a fine physique, he matured early, and had just been assigned his first concubine that year, at the age of sixteen. This was done not at his request, but at the behest of his aides. The young woman selected for the purpose was this Suka, daughter of a Mito retainer by the name of Isshiki. (For the record, Suka stayed with Keiki for the rest of his life, even after his marriage and beyond.)

When Suka first came to him, Keiki took a keen interest in the details of her anatomy, examining them with the same intrepid spirit he had once shown for casting nets. As she lay naked on the bedding, he would draw the lantern closer, marveling, "This is completely different from a man!" He gazed on her, enthralled, with the same concentration as when he was bent on mastering a skill, experimenting and learning. Nor did his preoccupation end there. Summoning Hiraoka Enshiro, he told him, "Her body is made like this," and sketched a picture of something resembling a lily on a piece of drawing paper. Hiraoka was nonplussed, but Keiki was so intent on his sketch, without the slightest hint of a smile, that he could do nothing but bow politely.

Keiki's attention to detail took him even further. Drawing his paints over, he began to color in the outlines of his sketch, at pains to get the shading just right. After each application of pigment, he cocked his head appraisingly until he had gotten the same exact hue as his model.

Finally he announced, "This is Suka. Are they all the same?" Hiraoka was unable to answer, having never laid eyes on his own wife's private parts. "I do not know," he confessed humbly, and then for the first time, Keiki laughed. "Well then, you're a bungler."

Whether Keiki was uniquely lacking in a sense of modesty, or whether that sense was lacking generally among people of his station, Hiraoka had no idea. In any case, never in his life was he at such a loss for words.

And now, as he embraced Suka, Keiki muttered over and over again how "absurd" it all was until finally, unable to stand it any longer, she spoke up. Hands over her face, she asked nervously, "Sire, do you mean me?" Caught off guard, Keiki realized only then that he had been speaking aloud. Still, he was hardly inclined to confide in Suka his unhappiness at losing favor with the shogun Iesada and his mother.

In fact, though, he did just that, though not in so many words. "A woman is a fearful thing," he said. What if Suka, so pliant now beneath his caresses, were to conceive a son? Then if he, Keiki, were to become shogun, and that son became his heir, Suka would wield power and influence over the affairs of state equal to that of O-Mitsu—no, Honju-in—now. That was what he meant. "I tell you, it's idiotic."

"What is? Us, you mean?" Though his senior by two years, Suka could not keep up with the twists and leaps of Keiki's quick mind. He was thinking now how ludicrous it was that in this hour of crisis for Japan, the reins of power should be in the hands of a mother-and-son team as foolish and incompetent as those two. A foreign invasion was imminent, the nation's peril great—yet no one could do anything.

"Just keep me out of it," he thought. Patriots in and out of the government wanted him to become Iesada's heir, so that he could act as proxy for the shogun and take control of the affairs of state. But Keiki himself wanted no such thing. Always precocious, in this respect he had a veteran's instinct to lie low.

Yet there was one man of action on the scene who believed that no matter what the cost, it was imperative that Hitotsubashi Keiki be made heir to the shogun. There was no other way to save the nation. Failure would mean the inevitable collapse of Japan. He devoted all his means and all his human strength to the furtherance of that cause. Keiki had not, of course, requested the man's help—had indeed barely heard of him. His name was Matsudaira Yoshinaga, though people mostly called him the "major general of Echizen." Later, during the Ansei Purge of 1858, he was placed under house arrest and took the name Shungaku, the name by which he is best known to history.

This Matsudaira Shungaku was daimyo of Fukui, or Echizen, domain, with an income of 320,000 *koku*. Born into the Tayasu family, one of the three junior collateral houses of the Tokugawa, he was adopted into the powerful Matsudaira family at age seventeen. Daimyo who achieved their status by adoption were in fact generally abler and more active than those who were heirs by blood, and few daimyo in the two and a half centuries of Tokugawa rule had the wisdom and farsightedness of Shungaku. Even before the arrival of Matthew Perry and his black ships, in his domain Shungaku had embarked on a program of westernization, and was switching the local economy from dependency on rice and other grains to greater emphasis on industry. He was also a progressive civil administrator who dramatically lowered the death rate from smallpox by enforcing widespread inoculation.

In personality, he had a touch of the schoolboy, less like a daimyo, it seemed, than a student of politics burning with idealism. Enlightened ruler though he certainly was, ideologically he was an antiforeign hard-liner of the Mito school—though this would later change—filled with an acute sense of crisis over the possibility of impending foreign invasion.

This was the man who came calling at the Hitotsubashi residence late one night inside a woman's palanquin. No sooner was he inside the entryway, palanquin and all, than he emerged asking to speak to Keiki. For one daimyo to come calling on another was unheard of. Shungaku assured the flustered retainers milling about the hallway that since he had come incognito, they need not bother about fine points of protocol or hospitality. With those reassuring words, he disappeared into the house.

"I am from Echizen. We met once in front of the latrine," he said easily, and asked if Keiki remembered. His laugh was high-pitched, like a woman's. "So this is the lord of Echizen," thought Keiki. No ordinary daimyo, he represented the family next in rank after the three successor houses and the three junior collateral houses.

"Perhaps you are aware that I have been doing all I can to see that you are made the shogun's heir," said Shungaku. "However, I actually know very little about you. This won't do any longer!" And that was why he had come incognito, he explained—to get a good look at Keiki.

Shungaku spoke of Japan's looming crisis, the answer to

which was the old cry *sonno joi*, "Revere the emperor, expel the barbarians." The means of resolving the crisis were threefold: replenishment of national defense, development of Western-style weaponry, and unity of national spirit. Yet even if all those objectives were met, it would come to nothing with a simpleton like Iesada in power. Someone had to step forward, a man of boldness and vision to serve as the shogun's proxy at court and lead the domains to band together against the foreign barbarians. The only man capable of filling such a role was Hitotsubashi Keiki himself. That was why he, Shungaku, in his single-minded desire to save the nation, had focused all his efforts on the goal of seeing that Keiki became the shogun's heir. Shungaku was a mover and shaker; to ensure the success of his campaign, he had reached out in all directions, enlisting the support of the bakufu cabinet, the women of the castle, and lords of the most influential domains. He had even sent bribes, he said. "And yet," he concluded wryly, "the one thing I have neglected to do is to sit down face-to-face with the man himself, and pay him my devoted respects."

"You do me too much honor," murmured Keiki, unsure what to say.

Shungaku stayed and talked for two hours, then left in a whirl, overjoyed to have found that the hoped-for prodigy was a youth of even greater talent and ability than rumor had led him to expect.

"Now, what the devil was all that about?" Keiki found the whole idea an imposition. Funny, it was, the way people looked to him for leadership that way, even though he wished they wouldn't. Not only Matsudaira Shungaku, but all four daimyo from the leading domains of Tosa, Satsuma, Uwajima, and Echizen, as well as every patriot in the nation, it seemed, down to the most humble and obscure, devoutly wished for Hitotsubashi Keiki to become next in line to Iesada. Apparently they were all convinced that once he took a stand, the country's woes would magically evaporate.

The following anecdote will serve to illustrate this simple faith. After one apparent victory in the struggle to line up backers for Keiki, Shungaku stopped off in Tosa to share the good news with the Tosa daimyo, Yamanouchi Yodo. In response to bribes and pressure, Matsudaira Tadagata, a member of the senior council, had agreed to throw his weight behind Keiki's candidacy. The promise was worthless, but Shungaku, ever the naive schoolboy, was easily deceived. Nor was Yodo any less unsuspecting: On hearing the news, he set down his drink, jumped to his feet, and proclaimed melodramatically, "The land is saved!" Then, opening his fan, he slid into the smooth moves of a classical Japanese dance.

Another of Keiki's influential backers, Shimazu Nariakira, lord of Satsuma, went even further in his maneuvering. Of the leading daimyo in Keiki's court he was the most progressive, the most cultured, and the most politically astute, all of which showed in the remarkable stunt he was able to pull off: In an attempt to soften anti-Mito sentiment in the powerful women's quarters of the castle, he had married his own adopted daughter to the shogun Iesada. As his wife, she would naturally have a considerably free hand in steering the course she wanted the feebleminded shogun to take.

"The shogun is not a normal man. I feel for you, my dear, but you must think of your country first, and consider your

marriage a necessary sacrifice." These were the words Nariakira had spoken to the young woman, the beautiful and
bright daughter by birth of a kinsman. After spotting the
girl's potential, he had adopted her and renamed her Atsuhime, a name befitting the daughter of a daimyo. Then he
had had her adopted into the Konoe family, whose men
were eligible to serve as shogunal regent. That made it entirely appropriate for her to marry into a shogunal family.

The marriage was arranged by Abe Masahiro, the equivalent of a prime minister in the bakufu. He and Nariakira
were sworn friends. They each respected the other's intelligence—and at the same time, they each used the other. By
allying himself with Shimazu Nariakira, Abe was attempting
to break a centuries-old taboo. Ever since the days of Ieyasu,
the heart of the shogunate's internal defense plan had lain
in guarding against an eastern advance by the two powerful
western domains of Choshu and Satsuma, *tozama*, or "outside" domains, granted originally to vanquished enemies of
Tokugawa Ieyasu, the dynasty founder. The great fear was
that they might unite to occupy Kyoto in opposition to the
Edo bakufu, with the emperor on their side. That was why
Ieyasu had left explicit instructions for his body to be buried
on Mount Kuno, facing west. The same reasoning governed
the construction and placement of castles: The bakufu's pre-
sumed enemies in Choshu and Satsuma might be expected
to work their way toward the capital by attacking the road between the capital and the western provinces, along the In-
land Sea, and so enormous castles were erected at Himeji,
Osaka, and Nagoya as fortresses to hinder such an invasion.

Now the Satsuma leader was about to join forces with the

bakufu leader, Abe Masahiro. Moreover, Abe had established cordial relations with the Mito, said to be a treacherous friend to the Tokugawa, in order to use their strength to ward off foreign invasion. It was no wonder that Abe did all he could to further Atsuhime's marriage to the shogun Iesada, and the installation of Keiki as successor.

By the time of Shungaku's visit to Keiki in a woman's palanquin, Atsuhime was already installed as Iesada's third wife. "Apparently, it's been far from easy for her," Shungaku revealed to Keiki, alluding to the intimacies of married life. With normal conjugal relations impossible, Iesada had no cause to warm to the woman, whose presence he found an intrusion. His powerful mother, Honju-in, was wary of Atsuhime and did all in her power to keep her at bay.

"Still," said Shungaku, "now I have the advantage of knowing exactly what goes on inside the walls of the women's quarters." Confidential communication took place between Atsuhime and him, or his representative, at his Edo residence. Nariakira then shared with Shungaku any information he was able to glean.

These political intrigues were as yet a mystery to Keiki. Despite Shungaku's assertions that only he could save Japan, it was impossible for Keiki to see how someone as young as himself could have much influence. "Isn't that so, Hiraoka?" he commented one day to Hiraoka Enshiro, who had matured considerably since the old days. After that inauspicious beginning, when he was unable even to serve rice, by now his managerial style had won him the respect of all patriots and men of influence who called at the Hitotsubashi residence. Hiraoka never admitted it to Keiki, but in fact he was a central figure in the drive to support his master's candidacy. At Shungaku's request, he had compiled a record of Keiki's daily life under the title *A Chronicle of the Sayings and Doings of Hitotsubashi Keiki.* Shungaku had his retainers copy it and distribute it to influential leaders in the bakufu and around the country so that Keiki's clear-sightedness might become a matter of common public knowledge. It was Shungaku's intent to make a hero of the youth, and Hiraoka believed his publicity campaign was bound to work.

"Sire," he said, "it seems to me that a man's influence is often created by self-confidence. That is what you need now. If I may say so, you are the greatest genius our country has known since Ieyasu himself. You and no one else can keep out the barbarian invaders, restore the peace and prosperity of our country, and so fulfill the wishes of the emperor in Kyoto."

"No, surely that is a task for my father," said Keiki with a wry smile. No one could have enjoyed greater public confidence than Nariaki. Many of the patriots regarded him as all but superhuman. Keiki's Confucian training had taught him to revere his father, and yet it was slowly dawning on him that Nariaki was not all the man he was cracked up to be, that it was in fact the power and ability of his grand chamberlain Fujita Toko and the other attendants behind the scenes that made him seem such a giant among men. To Keiki it seemed that his father's public image was largely a fiction, an idea he found vaguely displeasing.

"I want no part of it," he announced. Surprised, Hiraoka understood in a flash of insight that Keiki was disabled by an utter lack of ambition, the result perhaps of his aristocratic upbringing. Men of similar background who were the illegitimate offspring of a powerful man's concubine tended to harbor strong ambition, but Keiki had been born to his father's official wife. As an aristocrat of impeccable standing, he had always been accorded certain privileges, which he took for granted, so he had none of the common man's desire for self-betterment, nor any apparent need for it either.

"Something must be done," thought Hiraoka. Once noted for an honest simplicity worthy of the sages of old, Hiraoka had lately undergone a personal awakening to ambition. Should Keiki become shogun, he, Hiraoka, would be entrusted with the day-to-day running of the country. Even apart from the satisfaction of attaining such a responsible position, nothing could provide greater pleasure for a man than to promulgate his own ideas. But for this tempting vision to become reality, it was first necessary to ensure that Keiki become the successor.

Not only Shungaku, but the entire house of Mito was engaged in relentless behind-the-scenes maneuvering to jockey Keiki into a position to be named successor. On the surface, Nariaki declared it was none of his affair. Beneath the surface, however, the movement had become a full-blown conspiracy. Nariaki himself had the makings of a master conspirator. He had put Fujita Toko and another man in charge of the actual wire pulling, and even worked out a secret code for them to use in all their spoken and written communications.

Keiki's code name was "Amiisa," possibly a veiled reference to his fondness for fishing with a net (*ami*). Keiki, who had no idea that he had been assigned any such name, found out about the code when he caught Hiraoka in the act of consulting a small notebook while jotting down what seemed to be random *katakana* characters.

"What's this?" he inquired, picking up the notebook. Hiraoka was momentarily flustered, but quickly recovered, answering boldly with the truth. "Sire," he added, "you must prepare yourself for what is coming."

Keiki blanched, and said in disgust, "These are the actions of a traitor." Livid, he charged to his room and dashed off an angry letter to his father. "There is a rumor afloat that I am to be made the shogun's successor, a notion which is extremely distasteful to me," he wrote. "If there is anything to it, I want you to issue an immediate denial."

He entrusted the letter not to a man but to a woman named Karahashi, someone with no political leanings whatever, lest the letter be captured and read on the way. Karahashi was the daughter of a Kyoto nobleman; though described by most historians as an "old woman," she was in fact barely twenty-two.

When Keiki's wife, Mikako, the adopted daughter of Regent Ichijo Tadaka, had made her bridal journey to Edo from the capital, Karahashi had attended her. She was the chief administrator of household affairs in the Hitotsubashi family, and if and when Keiki became shogun, she would rise automatically to a rank of *churo* or better—the equivalent of daimyo for a man.

Hiraoka Enshiro had often warned Keiki to "keep Karahashi pure." Had Keiki ever been intimate with her, she would have been unqualified to manage the household af-

fairs when he became shogun. That Hiraoka Enshiro, his senior aide, felt called upon to issue this warning now shows
he was secretly rather appalled by the extent of Keiki's philandering. "His Lordship has a strong libido," he mused.
That in itself was by no means a bad thing for a man, particularly a daimyo, but it pained him that this extraordinary vital-
ity of Keiki's was never transmuted into public ambition.
Above all, he felt, Keiki must not end up a tranquil daimyo
put out to stud, devoted solely to preservation of the family
line.

When reminded of the need to refrain from intimacies
with Karahashi, Keiki would agree: "I know, I know." But the
woman was certainly far too beautiful for comfort. Her height
was a flaw, but she had delicate hands with long, elegant fingers as narrow as chopsticks. It fascinated Keiki that a woman
with fingers so narrow could perform her work with such energy and skill. How was she put together, he wondered, what
did the rest of her look like? The sight of her always set his
mind throbbing, filling him with an overpowering curiosity. It
was an obsession akin to love. For a man in Keiki's position,
physical desires were always satisfied easily at that initial stage,
without a chance to develop into the more tortured longings
of romantic love. Virtually all of the women who waited on
Keiki became objects of his passing curiosity. Hiraoka saw this
behavior as licentious.

"I want you to let me borrow Karahashi," Keiki announced
to his wife. Since Karahashi was his wife's retainer, the order
would have to come from her.

Mikako's instructions to take a letter to the Mito mansion
in Komagome ringing in her ears, Karahashi set off in a

44

woman's palanquin with silver trim. She returned in the evening and reported back to Mikako, but there was something odd about her. Her breathing became painful and she was in evident distress. When her mistress asked her what had happened, Karahashi only shook her head like a child, and wouldn't look up. She was weeping.

Then it all became clear. Keiki had told her that as the letter was not for others' eyes, she was to ask permission to be admitted personally into his father's presence, and see that he opened it before her eyes. This had been done.

Nariaki had received her in the teahouse. After perusing the letter, he thanked Karahashi—and then suddenly embraced her. "It's in the letter," he murmured. "You're to do as I say." He contrived to make it seem that Keiki had written a letter handing Karahashi over to him, and then entrusted the letter to Karahashi for her to deliver herself. Later, in answer to Mikako's questions, Karahashi revealed that she had struggled, but to no avail. Had she been violated for no reason, she would have said nothing, setting it down to her own lack of experience. But the facts were otherwise. Apparently, Keiki had turned her over to his father with a letter attached. She felt betrayed. "How could this happen!" she raged in her Kyoto drawl, and wept. To her, Keiki had seemed the noblest man in the world; in fact, she had secretly been in love with him. Never had she dreamed that her trust in him would be so brutally repaid.

After hearing the story from his wife, it was Keiki's turn to be amazed at being betrayed. He and Nariaki were fellow daimyo as well as father and son. For one daimyo to violate the woman of another was beyond belief. "So that's the kind of man my father is," thought Keiki in disgust. That his father was a notorious lecher struck him as unimportant. But what could it mean that he would resort to such a subterfuge to seduce a woman? Keiki was as uncomfortable as if he had caught a whiff of his father's viscera. He struggled to overcome his feelings. Had he been a rash daimyo in the rough-and-tumble age of the warring states, he would have felt no compunction in expressing his revulsion directly. But Keiki was born at the very end of the Tokugawa regime, when the teachings of Confucianism with their emphasis on filial devotion were widely taught and accepted. All his education had been deeply imbued with Confucian thought. Moreover, it was an era in which education determined action. For Keiki, keeping a tight lid on his emotions was the only possible course.

"Father is a military strategist," he explained to his wife, forced to come up with an explanation. There were times even now, he went on, when military strategy took precedence over ethics, just as it had for the generals of the Warring States period.

"Anyway, believe me," he concluded. "There was nothing in that letter to trap Karahashi." To himself he thought, "I must be on guard against my father." And he was right: Nariaki was not a man to be taken lightly. After receiving Keiki's letter, he wrote to his fellow conspirators, Toda and Fujita, as follows: "Amiisa [Keiki] has sent me a letter to this effect. If such reports have reached even his ears, we have cause to rejoice. This is proof that the movement to establish him as heir is not confined to a few scattered conspirators, but has acquired the backing of public opinion." He ended on a hopeful note: "Even the slightest rumors can be taken as such evidence."

Within the walls of Edo Castle, however, the movement to push the candidacy of little Tokugawa Yoshitomi of the collateral house of Kii seemed more likely to succeed in the end, all the more so as it was wrapped in an eerie silence. Common sense said that Yoshitomi, a boy of twelve, could not possibly lead three hundred daimyo safely through this time of national peril. Moreover, if he took over as head of the Tokugawa family, the Kii family would be left without any head. Either way, Yoshitomi was not an appropriate candidate for the office of shogun.

Yet there were political realists determined that the next shogun should be Yoshitomi, and none other. Men who now gripped the reins of power were free to govern as they saw fit with a feebleminded man as shogun. They had no desire for a quick-witted, able, reform-minded ruler if their careers were to survive into the next age. A child suited their designs perfectly. Besides, Hitotsubashi Keiki stank too much of politics. Even if he himself were innocent of ambition, behind him was the Mito family, and Mito Nariaki could be expected to take an active role. The Kii faction called Nariaki the "Evil Dragon." The Evil Dragon would come out on top, taking national power into his own hands.

In any event, final approval rested with the shogun Iesada, whose mother, Honju-in, was reported to be whispering in his ear, "If you choose Lord Hitotsubashi as your successor, I will stab myself in the throat and die. Will you choose him anyway, knowing that?" To her, Keiki was nothing but the son of the Evil Dragon.

The one ray of hope for the pro-Keiki faction was that Abe Masahiro was on their side. "When the right opportunity presents itself, I will speak with the shogun," Abe Masahiro told Shungaku and the rest. The right opportunity, however, never seemed to come along. Iesada was scarcely able to comprehend human speech, and communicated directly only with his mother and his nurse. The "opportunity" of which Masahiro spoke may have been an oblique reference to the likelihood that the shogun would die young.

And yet it was Abe Masahiro himself who died a sudden death, before Iesada. He was only thirty-eight years old. It was the fourth year of Ansei, 1857, and Keiki was twenty. The death of Abe Masahiro meant a virtual end to Keiki's chances of becoming the fourteenth shogun. It would be another ten years before his chance came around again.

Ii Naosuke and the Ansei Purge

Keiki's supporters were stubborn enough not to lose hope even after the death of Abe Masahiro. Since they were motivated by patriotic zeal, not personal interest, their opposing faction could not attack them openly. Not only did a group of young and able administrators within the bakufu offer Keiki their unanimous support, but most of the daimyo had fastened their hopes on him as well. In Kyoto, even the court nobles and imperial princes in holy orders longed for Keiki's day to come. And yet, of all these enthusiasts, only a scant few had ever set eyes on the man, let alone spoken with him. Moreover, Keiki's youth meant that he had no record of significant achievements, nor had he written anything substantial enough to shed light on his abilities.

There was only rumor. Word of the prodigy's brilliance, courage, and resourcefulness had spread far and wide, exciting the popular imagination. Loyalists in the lower echelons of society saw him as a heroic figure destined to save the nation, holding him up as their model and carrying on frenzied campaigns of support. It is questionable whether any man in history has ever achieved the status of public hero in such a fashion. Keiki himself was completely taken aback.

"Total nonsense," he told himself. Perspicacious as always, he saw what was happening. Faced with the prospect of imminent foreign invasion, the nation was trembling in fear with premonitions of the downfall of Japan. Overwhelmed by tension, terror, and an angry sense of foreboding, people longed for a hero to come along and shoulder their burdens, and thus provide a measure of relief. Under the illusion that such a champion was bound to appear, they had latched on to him, Keiki, as the man of the hour, allowing their fantasies to control them. It was damned inconvenient.

"Even if I did become a great barbarian-quelling generalissimo, there's not a damn thing I could do," he would say to Hiraoka Enshiro.

But his supporters paid no heed to such talk, finally, in desperation, carrying their campaign to the imperial palace in Kyoto, where they sought to have Keiki designated the shogunal successor by imperial edict. Such an irregularity was of course utterly without precedent.

Yet change was under way. New to the bakufu cabinet was a man named Ii Naosuke, daimyo of the powerful Hikone domain, yet still a virtual unknown. His relative obscurity was perhaps natural; as the fourteenth son of the previous lord of Hikone, he had remained dependent on his parents until well into his thirties, living quietly on a modest stipend, and occupying himself with the study of classical poetry, tea ceremony, and other artistic pursuits. He was also a learned scholar of Japanese able to write elegant prose. Naosuke had attempted several times to marry into other daimyo families, but talks had always broken down. Next he had attempted to become the adopted son-in-law of a Buddhist priest at a temple in Nagahama, near Hikone, but that plan also fell through.

It took a series of deaths to bring luck to Ii Naosuke. First the son of his elder brother Naoaki, previous head of the Hikone domain, collapsed and died, causing his brother to name him, Naosuke, as heir. Then Naoaki had died as well, leaving thirty-five-year-old Naosuke head of the Ii family, with a magnificent stipend of 350,000 *koku*. When he sent thirty pieces of gold to Matsudaira Tadagata on the shogunal council of elders in a bid to enter Edo politics, councillors thought of him dismissively as an idler fond of the tea ceremony and flower arranging. That same Ii Naosuke climaxed his dramatic leap to power on the twenty-third day of the fourth month in 1858, when he was named to the traditional post of tairo ("great elder")—an office he took full advantage of, functioning thereafter as virtual dictator of Japan.

Before and after his rise to power, Ii Naosuke was deeply involved with the Kii faction. Together with key figures in the Kii family and palace insiders, he devised a secret plan to push the candidacy of twelve-year-old Tokugawa Yoshitomi, who was born to the Kii branch of the Tokugawa in the Wakayama domain. Naosuke had conceived an intense dislike for the Mito, and for Keiki's father, Nariaki, in particular. He was a resolute traditionalist. There was no need to select an enlightened ruler, he felt. Not all the shoguns thus far had been enlightened, and yet Tokugawa rule had continued unbroken well into its third century, an illustrious achievement. That was because the daimyo and vassals of the shogun held Tokugawa blood in awe. Yoshitomi, grandson of the eleventh Tokugawa shogun, Ienari, had closer blood ties to the Tokugawa than did Hitotsubashi Keiki. That fact alone determined which of the two was better qualified to be shogun. If the man with the more tenuous claim to kinship were made heir, the Tokugawa house would lose its mystique. Besides, the masses were clamoring for Keiki simply because he was a man of enlightened intellect. Nothing could be more inimical to the interests of the shogunal families than this tendency for people to clamor for such rulers, and thus pass judgment on their sovereigns. For the lower classes to take it upon themselves to choose a sovereign could lead only to civil unrest.

Following this conservative line of reasoning, Naosuke was a firm supporter of Yoshitomi, but he kept his thoughts to himself and promoted Yoshitomi's cause only from behind the scenes. Matsudaira Shungaku met with the new tairo without realizing where he stood, and attempted to recruit his support for Keiki. Results of their talk were inconclusive, however, and Shungaku was left with an impression of a man who was arrogant and overbearing, a vulgar fellow lacking a scrap of ideals where his country was concerned.

Tairo Ii Naosuke would periodically send all others out of earshot and have a private audience with the shogun Iesada, in an endeavor to sound out his opinions regarding the crucial succession issue. "All right now, tell me which you like better, Lord Kii or Lord Hitotsubashi?" he would ask patiently, as if speaking to a little child. Each time, Iesada would lisp in reply, "I like Kii. Don't like Hitotsubashi." Naosuke contended that twice, once on June 18 and again on the twenty-third, the shogun voiced that opinion. Naturally, there were no other witnesses.

Ii Naosuke refrained from making an official proclamation, instead leaking the information that the shogun had indicated his preference. At the same time, he set about gradually demoting all those favoring Keiki, many of them among the ablest men in the bakufu. The balance of power was shifting.

Meanwhile, negotiations moved forward on the signing of a commercial treaty with U.S. consul Townsend Harris, a momentous issue interwoven with that of the shogunal succession. Harris's dire threats of imminent naval action had the desired effect. Ii was convinced swift action was necessary to stave off military attack by a vastly superior opponent, and on July 29, 1858, five years after Perry's arrival and only weeks after Ii's appointment as tairo, the treaty was signed—without imperial sanction.

The following day, Ii refrained from reporting to Edo Castle, remaining at home on a pretext of illness, waiting nervously to see which way public opinion would go. On finding an unexpected tide of opposition, he went to the castle and summarily dismissed the two ministers who had worked out details of the signing. One was Matsudaira Tadakata, who had recommended him for the post of tairo. It is hard to escape the impression that Ii meant to pass off responsibility for the unpopular deed on his subordinates.

"That is an outrage!" cried the twenty-one-year-old Keiki. Now he set out on his first positive action of a political nature. He was armed with the Mito theory of the state, that the true ruler of Japan was the emperor, from whom the bakufu's power to conduct the nation's affairs derived. Ieyasu had not of course had any such arrangement in mind when he founded the Tokugawa bakufu, but the theory had since been fostered and refined by the Mito and others, and was now fast becoming an article of faith among those most radicalized by the threat of Western invasion.

"Lord Ii must face the results of flouting the imperial will," Keiki declared. By ignoring the will of the emperor, Ii had demonstrated that the leader of the bakufu himself was wrong in his interpretation of the national polity. If the matter were allowed to rest without censure, people would come to think such lapses acceptable, and the Mito theory of delegated power would be discredited.

"I am going to the castle. Inform Lord Ii," he ordered Hiraoka Enshiro, who also notified the bakufu officials and made all the necessary arrangements. The day Keiki would go to the castle was set for August 2, the fourth day after the signing of the treaty.

Rumors that Hitotsubashi Keiki was going to denounce the tairo soon spread everywhere, in and out of the bakufu. The news was reported in a highly sensational manner. Ii himself was said to be "thunderstruck." The shogunal families were supposed to be above politics, without any overt voice or influence. What could be the meaning of this, for

Keiki to come marching into the castle and seek an audience? Ii found it disconcerting.

On the appointed day, Keiki went to the castle. After resting in an antechamber, where he was served tea, he was summoned into the corridor and ushered into an inner room by a castle "priest." Inside, Tairo Ii Naosuke was kneeling formally; he bowed low, forehead to the floor, and stayed that way a long while before raising his head. Thereupon the youth announced, "I am Keiki." At that, Naosuke prostrated himself once again and then sat back up, thinking to himself, "Well, well. An obstinate young fellow."

Keiki, for his part, studied the massive face of the corpulent Ii, set with eyes that seemed disproportionately narrow and slanting, and thought that he looked less like an important daimyo than a fishermen's boss from some village.

For generations the house of Ii had been chief among the shogunal families. Ever since the epic battles of Sekigahara and Osaka, men of Ii had had the honor of serving as advance guard on the battlefield, and only men of Ii or Sakai were qualified to become tairo. Ii Naosuke had suddenly become head of the Ii family and stepped into a life of unexpected ease as a wealthy daimyo; the situation in which he found himself was fresh and exciting, both for its glamour and its power, and he was burning with callow ambitions and desires. Doubtless he entertained the ridiculous notion that as head of the Ii, it was up to him and him alone to defend the house of Tokugawa. That was why he was hostile to the Mito, thought Keiki.

As far as Naosuke was concerned, the excessive proimperial bias of the Mito was nothing short of treasonous. In fact, looking at Keiki now, Naosuke could think only of the power of the Mito behind him. So this was their Keiki, was it, he thought, taking a good look at the youth. The face was as intelligent as he had heard, the bearing genuinely aristocratic. Still, he was only a kid. Nothing serious could possibly come from this encounter.

As Ii Naosuke was thinking these thoughts, Keiki began to speak. To the other's amazement, he began with words of formal praise: "Recently Your Excellency was awarded the post of tairo, senior minister to the shogun. In these difficult times your extreme dedication is highly appreciated." Despite the stiffness of the words, his voice had a lilt, and he spoke with an ease and a carrying power that might have served him well as lead actor onstage.

Out of courtesy, Ii was forced to bow as if highly moved by this tribute.

Keiki went on. "For generations the Ii clan has borne a special relationship to the house of Tokugawa, and it is heartening to all of us to see your lordship serving now with the same faithfulness as his worthy ancestors."

Naosuke relaxed. The pleased look he bestowed on Keiki as he replied was perhaps the indication of a surprisingly simple nature. "I am unworthy of the heavy responsibility which has most unexpectedly fallen upon me, but I shall be unremitting in my efforts to carry out my duties." He was inwardly astonished at the elegance and political precocity of the youngster's greeting.

Keiki then entered into his main theme. Now his tone took on the iciness of autumn frost. His rebuke was tightly logical, and delivered with a rapidity that left his listener scarcely time to draw breath. He reproached Naosuke for the enormous crime of going against the emperor's will, as well as for a brazen failure even to see or admit his wrong, so that the fact of the signing of the treaty had been reported in Kyoto with as little ceremony as a bill of delivery. What could Lord Ii have been thinking? "Was that deference?" Keiki lashed out. "I think not. Am I right? Well?"

This went on for some time. Keiki did not construct airy, abstract arguments, but laid out an array of concrete, specific facts, seeking a reply from Naosuke at every juncture.

Naosuke's response to all this was peculiar. Twisting his huge body, he only repeated, "I beg your pardon. I humbly beg your pardon." He never delivered himself of any speech longer than this, and his voice was oddly gentle, in contrast to his fierce appearance, sounding something like a mewing kitten. Despite his literary gifts, Naosuke was not adept at the rigors of logical debate, and could not develop or sustain a coherent argument; that may well have accounted, at least in part, for his reticence on this occasion.

Still, there could be no doubt that in comparison to Keiki's white-hot excitement, Ii Naosuke's bearing was the more controlled and statesmanlike. It was crucial that he remain noncommittal. Behind Keiki were the Mito clan and the extremist daimyo. It was too risky to say anything, however simple, that might later be held against him. Besides, what advantage could there be in out-arguing a young and inexperienced child of privilege like Keiki?

In the face of Naosuke's calm, Keiki gradually fell silent. The other's meek tone of voice was also rather unnerving, and finally Keiki changed the topic.

"Concerning the matter of the shogun's adoption of an heir..." Hearing himself say the words, Keiki became disconcerted at having introduced such an incongruous topic. Still, having once begun, he could not very well leave off in mid-sentence. Summoning the power of eloquence that was a lifelong gift, he went on in a richly resonant voice, his tone direct yet deferential: "I should like to ask you this. What decision has the shogun made?"

Records of the interview state that here "the tairo suddenly turned red." Apparently he could not conceal his agitation at being asked such a question by Keiki of all people. Yet he only bowed low and said again, "I beg your pardon."

Keiki smiled wryly. "Come, no need to be abashed. I am asking you in strictest confidence," he pressed, but Naosuke's answer was again the same. "Has he made no decision yet?" queried Keiki, deliberately nonchalant, but again his only reply was a low bow and the same formulaic reply. Keiki was stymied.

Finally he summoned his resolve and said, "Rumor has it that he has settled on the lord of Kii as his heir. Is it true?"

At this, Naosuke glanced up slightly and studied Keiki's expression before he finally nodded and admitted that it was so.

It was a delicate moment for Keiki, but he was a born actor with the ability to rise to any occasion. All at once his face brightened, his voice conveying intense pleasure as he said with ease, "Wonderful. That is cause for rejoicing indeed." Rumors on the topic were rife, he went on, some of them apparently even involving himself, so that he had been extremely concerned, but nothing could please him more than to know it had all been safely settled. Splendid. Incidentally, he had been told that the young lord suffered from epilepsy, but the other day when he happened to run into him at the castle, he had not appeared in the least ill, and had in fact struck Keiki as quite strapping for his age. This, too, was splendid. Some people were evidently of the opinion that a child barely twelve years old was too young for the job, but with Tairo Ii Naosuke on hand to guide him, everything would certainly be all right.

"And," Keiki concluded on a changed note, "be assured that I, too, will be at his service in any way possible, for as long as possible." Thus he wound up his speech with a statement of intention to be the new shogun's most faithful vassal in the realm.

Listening to the torrent of gracious words, for a moment Naosuke was lost in admiration, but then he quickly came to himself, all smiles, and chatted amiably with his guest. During the course of their desultory conversation, Keiki asked idly who was to take over the headship of the Kii family, which would, of course, now be vacant.

Apparently Ii had not yet given thought to the question of a successor. He stuttered, then tilted his head to one side and smiled with the coquettish air of an old cat, looking up at Keiki all the while. Keiki gave an inward shudder. For the rest of his life he never forgot that smile, half coaxing, half fawning.

"Have you no such inclination yourself?" Ii asked. Would Keiki consider becoming the daimyo of Kii, in other words. As he himself had been forced to spend most of his life living off others, due to his mother's low rank, Ii doubtless considered this an irresistible offer. Should Keiki be interested, he would gladly see what he could do, he said insinuatingly, all but tapping the other on the knee as he spoke with great familiarity.

This was too much for Keiki. For a moment he was speechless, but then he firmly declined. "I have no desire to leave the Hitotsubashi," he stated flatly, choosing his words carefully. "That is why I announced I would not be adopted into the house of Tokugawa, much less the house of Kii!"

Keiki left the castle. At home, he reverted to his usual taciturnity, but Hiraoka Enshiro pressed him so insistently for his impression of the tairo that he finally relented and answered honestly, "A man of decision, but lacking in wisdom." This was his actual feeling. Ii Naosuke had been transparently fawning toward him, but Keiki had heard that toward anyone lower in rank than the senior elders of the bakufu he spoke with unconcealed arrogance. Anyone who toadies to those above him and treats those below him with hauteur lacks confidence in his own resources and competence, he had learned years before from his old tutor, Inoue Kanzaburo.

"I'd say he is a man of little significance," he summed up.

Yet it was soon brought painfully home to Keiki that a man's estimation must be based not on his ideas or intellect but on the degree of power he holds. Soon after his encounter with Ii Naosuke, the tairo masterminded the infamous coup that came to be known as the Ansei Purge, after the era name of the time. A more scathing, ruthless, and cold-blooded political oppression never occurred in Japanese history.

No, not political oppression. There was no direct connection to politics. Naosuke's motivation was far simpler: sheer malevolence. As he saw it, Tokugawa Nariaki had for years been plotting an overthrow of the shogunal families, promoting it by one devious means after another. This was his considered opinion, but without evidence it was only an abstract and nebulous theory. The one who fleshed it out and gave it brilliant color was Naosuke's vassal Nagano Shuzen.

Shuzen engaged in constant espionage, based on certain assumptions, and when he reported his findings, he dressed them up with various romantic flourishes. His assumptions were on this order: 1) that Nariaki sought to have his son made shogun in order that he, Nariaki, might seize control of the bakufu; 2) that to further this scheme, he used Matsudaira Shungaku, who had already been promised the position of chief senior councillor as reward for his efforts; 3) that Nariaki was attempting to influence the imperial court in Kyoto to back his son as the next shogun, and had in particular incited Prince Shoren'in, a close confidant of the emperor, promising him as reward that he would be next to ascend the throne. And so on. It was Nagano Shuzen's opinion that Mito Nariaki was a would-be usurper plotting to take over the country.

Ii sent Nagano Shuzen out in search of corroborating evidence. His policy was to begin by arresting ronin loyalists, masterless samurai active in Kyoto, torture them, and force confessions from them. He began with the ronin scholar Umeda Umpin from Wakasa, but turned up not a scrap of incriminating evidence. He then proceeded to seize other suspects, one after another, until the list of those he had taken into custody included the retainers and advisers of court nobles and daimyo. Ultimately, the scope of his investigation and convictions reached even higher, affecting court nobles and daimyo themselves, as he sought to round up every patriot activist in the land.

Not even Keiki was immune. Two months before the arrest in Kyoto of Umeda Umpin, Keiki was banned from the castle grounds. It was barely a fortnight since Ii Naosuke had spoken so insinuatingly to him, catlike, within Edo Castle. The official notification of the banishment contained the phrase "in accordance with the shogun's wishes." In other words, it was claimed to be a direct shogunal order. Yet the shogun Iesada had lain near death for some time, and according to Keiki's informants, had breathed his last inside the castle on August 13, one day before the notice of Keiki's banishment. The death had not been made public, however, and Naosuke was guarding the secret closely. If word of the shogun's death should leak out, Nariaki would seize the opportunity to launch who-knew-what sort of insurrection. In the tairo's mistaken judgment, Nariaki was already spearhead of a plot to wrest power from the bakufu, and Shungaku and his cohort Prince Shoren'in, active supporters of the plot, were like two sly buffoons in a *kyogen* farce. The prince's code name in Naosuke's letters was "the actor."

Keiki sensed that Ii Naosuke was about to make his move. Why else hide the death of the shogun and issue an order of this sort, intended to create the illusion that he was still alive?

The injunction did not stop at banning Keiki from the castle premises. He was also expressly forbidden from using the main entrance, rear entrance, and kitchen entrance of the

Hitotsubashi residence. Only the gate of his wife's quarters was open to him.

"We can't tell what's going on this way," murmured Hiraoka Enshiro, and he secretly asked merchants who came to ply their trade to go check on the Mito residence. Sure enough, Nariaki and Shungaku had also been charged and convicted. Nariaki was placed under house arrest, his authority in domain personnel matters was revoked, and he was forbidden from corresponding with anyone. Shungaku was to enter forced retirement.

As time went on, the number of casualties swelled. The Ansei Purge began with the arrest of ronin patriots on June 20, 1858, soon after Ii became tairo, and lasted till early 1860. Shungaku's adviser, Hashimoto Sanai, was executed; Saigo Takamori, a Satsuma leader in the anti-Tokugawa movement who had traveled discreetly around Kyoto and Edo on various assignments for his countryman Shimazu Nariakira, escaped home with a comrade; Nariaki's messenger Ugai Kokichi was decapitated, and the head displayed on the prison gates. The purge reached even to a man like Yoshida Shoin of Choshu, a teacher full of rage against the shogunate's apparent sub-servience to foreigners, disrespect to the court, and arrogance toward Japanese citizens, but innocent of any participation in the movement to select Keiki: He was investigated by bakufu agents, extradited to Edo in a cage, and beheaded in 1859. In all, untold numbers were executed or banished.

Besides ronin, priests, and daimyo retainers, those caught in the crackdown included ten court nobles, ten daimyo, and fourteen hatamoto. Of these, the one dealt with most harshly was, hardly surprisingly, Mito Nariaki. His original sentence

of house arrest in his Edo mansion was changed to one of
lifetime imprisonment in Mito. Tokugawa Yoshikumi, the
lord of Owari, had backed Keiki's succession and was also
placed under house arrest, as were Matsudaira Shungaku
of Echizen, Yamanouchi Yodo of Tosa, and Date Munenari
of Uwajima (now part of Ehime). Of the "reform-minded"
daimyo, Shimazu Nariakira alone escaped incarceration—
only because he fell ill at home in Satsuma and died during
the roundup.

Keiki's punishment was subsequently increased from banishment from the castle to house arrest. "What is the meaning of this!" he exclaimed on hearing the news, and then was
silent. He had no choice. Ii engaged in government by spy-
ing, and his agents were everywhere in Edo and Kyoto. The
saying that "walls have ears" was on the lips of every trouba-
dour monk. Had Keiki let slip the slightest complaint, word
would surely have gotten back to Ii Naosuke, who would
have announced, "Here's the real culprit!" pounced, and
sent Keiki off to his death.

A sentence of house arrest meant the imprisonment of
everyone in the household. All gates were shut. Keiki himself
was confined to his quarters, where the shutters were kept
constantly closed save for an inch or two to let the sunlight
in. He was forbidden even to keep his head properly shaved.
The order from the bakufu stipulated that he was to wear his
hair long. Soon his unshaven head gave him the scruffy appearance of a ronin.

Under ordinary circumstances, his retainers would come
every morning to the antechamber or corridor to inquire
after him, but that too was now strictly forbidden. All com-

munication between them and the outside world was cut off; even in case of an earthquake, they could not so much as send a messenger to find out if Edo Castle was still intact.

Keiki spent all his time in his shuttered room, dressed formally in a hempen *kamishimo*; sitting bolt upright, he devoted himself to reading. There was no one to talk to. Even his trusty aide Hiraoka Enshiro had been implicated, and told not to report for work. Keiki regretted Hiraoka's loss. He thought of him as a real friend. Though he teased him now and then for his roundabout way of doing things, his simplicity, and his obstinacy, the truth was that through his dealings with men of distinction from around the country as they strove together to promote Keiki's succession, Hiraoka Enshiro had matured rapidly.

Hashimoto Sanai, Shungaku's adviser and reportedly one of the cleverest men of his day, was one of the men with whom Hiraoka had had especially close dealings. Nakane Sekko, another prominent man from Echizen, heard a conversation between the two that he described this way: "Hiraoka Enshiro is a man of superlative wit and eloquence, universally censorious. Hashimoto Sanai has superior wisdom and insight, and amazing clarity of understanding. As I sat alongside them, I was intoxicated by the one and sobered by the other."

Hiraoka had not been an effective speaker in the beginning. This change was unquestionably the influence of Keiki, who, though normally closemouthed, was capable of flights of stunning eloquence. Constant exposure to his young master's gift for fluent and persuasive speech had apparently enabled Hiraoka to cultivate his own powers of communication until he achieved a reputation for "superlative wit and eloquence."

The fate in store for him was sadder still. When his initial punishment was lifted, he was assigned maintenance duty in Kai Castle, Yamanashi. For a hatamoto, or "bannerman" in service to the shogun, transfer to such a position was tantamount to exile, for the transferee rarely made it back to Edo. "Poor Hiraoka, his life is as good as over," thought Keiki sadly. He had no way of knowing that just as he himself was to experience a comeback to public life, so too would Hiraoka, building a reputation as one of the wisest leaders of the day.

Keiki's sole sympathizer in the shogunate cabinet, Matsudaira Noritake, sent a private messenger with the comforting words "A man's destiny cannot be told from his present situation." Keiki, of course, took this as nothing more than a conventional bromide.

Day after day, he had nothing to do but read. Chiefly he read Chinese historical works like the monumental *Tzu-chih t'ung-chien* ("Comprehensive Mirror for Aid in Government") of Ssu-ma Kuang and *Shih-chi* ("Historical Records") of Ssu-ma Ch'ien, endeavoring to learn the laws governing the rise and fall of nations. Never in his life did he accomplish as much reading as he did during the years of house arrest. Late in life, he was to remark that such book learning as he had acquired, he owed to Ii Naosuke.

The days went by. Eighteen months after Keiki's banishment from the castle, in 1860, the era name changed from Ansei to Man'en. Around that time, he began hearing rumors that the Mito were up to something, but under the circumstances he was naturally unable to find out any details. His life went on without change. The sheer length of his sentence at last began to tell on him: He was despondent, and passed much of the time staring vacantly.

"What manner of man am I," he thought wretchedly, unable to keep from self-pity over the laughable, miserable turn his life had taken. What crime was he guilty of, after all? He had never once made any official act, yet here he was, treated like a criminal, locked inside his shuttered house. The fault lay in the old rumors—rumors of his brilliance.

"They weren't even rumors that I started," he mused. Come to think of it, from as early as he could remember, his father, Nariaki, had sung his praises to one and all. One day his son would be on top, in command, his father had said, and people had listened and believed. The legend of the promise had swept the land. And had ended by making him a criminal. "Stupid nonsense," he muttered.

Keiki searched histories of China and Japan, seeking examples of other fathers and sons with fates similar to his, but found none. That meant he really was in a peculiar position—and heaven only knew what further troubles might lie ahead.

March came. It was the month of the spring festival, when all the daimyo in Edo assembled in the castle before the shogun in celebration. In ordinary times, as the highest-ranking of the lords Keiki would have urged the procession on and appeared before the shogun himself—the fourteenth Tokugawa shogun, Iemochi, as the Kii boy had been renamed. But for the second year in a row, he was excluded.

"Looks like snow," Keiki murmured that morning in his bedroom. He had slept late, a rarity for him. His wife, Mikako, was already up. He could hear the rustling of silk behind the screen. The previous summer, she had given birth to a girl. Keiki could not think of that time without a heavy heart. Cut off from the world, he had been helpless either to celebrate or officially announce his daughter's birth. The baby had lived for a few days, her existence unremarked, and on the fifth day she had died.

"Spring snow is falling," he said again, listening hard for the muffled sound of it beyond his shutters, his voice purposefully loud so his wife could hear him as she made her toilet behind the screen. Once she had remarked, with typical Kyoto grace, how she missed seeing spring snow since coming to Edo. He remembered it well.

After his second remark, she responded from the shadow of the screen with a tiny cough. It was her signal that she had heard him. Not until she was properly dressed and seated would she answer him in words.

Keiki got up. When he stepped out into the corridor on his way to the latrine, he discovered snow as far as his eyes could reach. The ground beyond the edge of the eaves was completely white, and snow was still falling so heavily, he could hear the swish of the flakes. Snowstorms in late March as heavy as this were unheard of in Edo.

Just then, from the castle tower came a single beat on a hand drum, followed by five booming drumbeats on the large *taiko*, signaling eight A.M. and the daimyos' entrance into the castle. He little suspected that at that exact moment, outside Sakurada Gate, an event was taking place that would drastically alter the course of his life. He learned about it at three that afternoon, just seven hours after it was all over, when a Mito loyalist disguised as a fishmonger sneaked through the back way, summoned his old tutor Inoue Kanzaburo in private, and briefly related the facts.

Ii Naosuke was dead.

Keiki heard the details the following day. Ii had been ambushed in a procession on his way to the castle. The ambush party had included seventeen loyalists from Mito and one from Satsuma. Ii had first been stabbed from outside his palanquin, then dragged out into the snow and stabbed repeatedly. Every time a sword had penetrated the flesh, there had been a soft sound like the sound made by hitting a rubber ball. Someone from a neighboring residence who had witnessed the incident from a small window had described it that way, according to a member of the Hitotsubashi household.

"Like hitting a rubber ball," repeated Keiki.

He brought a ball into the room, raised a fan, and hit the ball into the air with it several times, listening intently each time to the light, percussive sound.

Entering the Pantheon

ANOTHER CYCLE OF THE SEASONS WENT AROUND IN EDO. A year after the assassination of Ii Naosuke at Sakurada Gate, the fate of Hitotsubashi Keiki had not been affected in the slightest. Just as before, he was still held prisoner in the Hitotsubashi residence for crimes against the state. In fact, none of the nobles, daimyo, or loyalists convicted in the Ansei Purge had been released, though it was widely held that new administrative measures were but a matter of time.

"You must be patient a little longer," the youth's aides encouraged him.

"What do you mean?" he would invariably say.

"Why, there is bound to be an amnesty. Then you will be set free."

"Nonsense," he would snort. Keiki was an eccentric. At such times he never failed to declare with a scowl, "There ought not to be any amnesty." He ought not to be pardoned, in other words. The victims of the purge ought to continue to be imprisoned or confined to their homes. At first surprised, little by little Keiki's attendants came to understand his thought process. Above all, he respected logic. To release yesterday's criminals simply because Ii had been killed would have made a mockery of the law, destroying the integrity of the bakufu then and ensuring its future collapse.

Keiki was eccentric not only in his devotion to logic, but in the extent to which it afforded him day-to-day serenity and peace. "How dull this must be for you," well-meaning people would say sympathetically, but their commiseration was completely off the mark. Keiki was incapable of remaining bored for long. A man of many facets, he found endless ways of keeping busy. He painted. He studied the physiology of the horse. He conducted secret observations of the anatomy of women in the house, comparing his findings with Dutch texts on female anatomy. Now and then he would even bring out a plane and saw and go to work doing repairs around the house. Only the necessity of forgoing his favorite sport, polo, caused him a twinge of pain.

As word of his versatility got around, his supporters whispered that here, too, he resembled the great Ieyasu. According to legend, while unskilled in fine arts, the founder of the Tokugawa dynasty had possessed far more than a layman's knowledge of medicine, and had excelled at muscular pursuits such as swordsmanship, horseback riding, and falconry. Yet not even Ieyasu had been capable of home repairs. When

Keiki, his tenth-generation descendant, planed a board, the shavings were as thin as smoke, and the surface of the wood shone like a mirror.

A full two years after Ii's assassination, on May 23, 1862, Keiki was granted permission to receive visitors and engage in correspondence. He continued to lie low, however, refraining from outside activities. His very quiescence only added to the luster of his image. Kyoto nobles and loyalists from Satsuma and Choshu, the two strongest realms in southwestern Japan, had all heard his reputation. His name was on everyone's lips. There were even those who touted him as a possible savior of the country. The triumvirate of reform-minded daimyo who supported him (Matsudaira Shungaku, Yamanouchi Yodo, and Date Munenari) also sang his praises. Yodo, who had a penchant for grandiloquence, declared solemnly, "Unless he steps forward, what is to become of the Tokugawa state?"

And yet Yodo's knowledge of Keiki was limited to what he had heard from Shungaku. As Keiki had never held any office, his political accomplishments were nil, and there was no way to judge his political weight from his actions. In short, an image of the man quite unconnected to reality, based solely on hearsay, was fast developing in the public mind.

Following the opening of the ports in 1859, based on the Harris Treaty and similar treaties subsequently signed with other nations, a burgeoning foreign presence in Japan provided increased provocation for the xenophobes and gave new meaning to the slogan *joi* ("expel the barbarians"). Among rank-and-file loyalists, adulation of Keiki acquired the fervor of religious faith. Once he took control, they swore, he would bypass the shogunal emissary to enforce the expulsion of all foreigners, chasing out the aliens and restoring the purity of the land of the gods. Within the bakufu cabinet and the palace, however, anti-Keiki sentiment remained strong, and he was shunned as an enemy of the shogun. This personal misfortune for Keiki was construed by patriots as a disaster for the nation, fanning their impatience.

At the court in Kyoto, prevailing opinion held that the only way for Keiki to have his day was for the emperor to apply pressure on the bakufu. Finally, on June 27, 1862, an imperial messenger was sent to Edo in the person of Ohara Shigetomi, an elderly court noble and die-hard exponent of the antiforeign cause. Shimazu Hisamatsu of Satsuma, father of the young Satsuma daimyo, escorted him with a large and well-armed body of troops, his display of military might reinforcing Ohara's proposals. In essence, these called for reforming the bakufu and driving out the foreigners, to be accomplished by giving high shogunal office to two men: Hitotsubashi Keiki and Matsudaira Shungaku. Keiki was to be made shogunal guardian, and Shungaku a ranking member of the cabinet.

To shogunal officials, such talk was anathema. What could be more ill omened than for the court to interfere in matters of bakufu personnel? To make matters worse, pressure was being applied by antishogunate loyalists from Satsuma—one of the *tozama,* or "outside" domains, those whose original lords were erstwhile rivals or enemies of the Tokugawa house. To yield would be to surrender authority and suffer a possibly fatal loss of prestige.

Besides the total inappropriateness of the request, the officials had severe objections to Hitotsubashi Keiki. He was the son of the Mito firebrand Nariaki, for whom the bakufu had long felt great antipathy. True, Nariaki had fallen ill and died in 1860, shortly after Ii's assassination, but who was to say what designs his son might not have on the house of Tokugawa? Keiki's very maturity and ability only increased the threat.

If Hitotsubashi became shogunal guardian, it would mean the end of the Tokugawa: This was the hysterical consensus in Edo Castle, shared alike by everyone from senior councillors down to the shogun's tea servers and maids. Keiki's eloquence, courage, and resourcefulness would overwhelm the youthful shogun, and the senior councillors as well; he would be egged on by loyalists in Satsuma and Choshu, and this would arouse the indignation of the fudai daimyo, the inner circle of those closest to the Tokugawa, who would then do battle to protect the shogunal families. It would all end in civil war. Hitotsubashi would then jump in and make himself master of the country. Even the Ohara-Shimazu mission, it was rumored, was the product of Keiki's rebellious spirit.

Yet in the end, the bakufu bowed to the imperial will.

On hearing word of this development, Keiki told his aides, "This is the beginning of the end for the bakufu." A fatal weakness had been displayed. From now on, anytime the tozama daimyo sought an imperial order, backed by a strong army, the bakufu would again have no choice but to cave in. "The government has lost the high ground," he sighed.

In due time a formal letter of appointment was delivered to Keiki. "In accordance with the wishes of His Majesty the

Emperor," it read, "you are hereby appointed shogunal guardian." The overt reference to the emperor's wishes—unprecedented in any such letter from the bakufu—was doubtless meant to imply that it was contrary to the wishes of the shogun; the senior councillors were apparently miffed. The wording was identical on Matsudaira Shungaku's notice of his appointment as political director.

Unlike the position of shogunal guardian, that of political director was new. It would put Shungaku in command of the bakufu administration, with authority exceeding that of the council of elders. He would have been in effect prime minister, or tairo. But while Keiki accepted his appointment, Shungaku turned his down. His retainers were equally opposed to the idea, seeing it as an insult to the shogunal families. Ever since the days of the founder, Ieyasu, the administration of the Tokugawa family had been handled by fudai daimyo. They were the equivalent of clerks in a merchant family. But the head of the estimable house of Matsudaira was head of the major line of the Tokugawa family itself, not a "clerk" like the Ii, Honda, or Sakai daimyo. For Shungaku to become political director would be a considerable comedown, equivalent to the master of the house assuming humble clerical duties. Shungaku repeatedly turned the appointment down, but in the end his resistance wore down, and he too accepted.

The new bakufu appointments sent people into raptures. It seemed hopeful that as long as these two men held positions of central power in the government, Japan would manage to escape a fate of ruination under foreign oppressors—as neighboring China, for one, had not. Even a man as level-headed as Okubo Ichizo, a Satsuma official who became one of the strongest leaders of modern Japan, fairly babbled on hearing the news: "My joy is so extreme that I fear I must be dreaming." Nor was he alone; a wave of relief and excitement swept the country.

Keiki went to the castle to meet with the boy shogun, Iemochi, and pay his respects in accordance with convention. His expression remained purely formal throughout, and Iemochi for his part betrayed no sign of intimacy but followed strict protocol as befitted the head of the Tokugawa. He was still a boy of sixteen, handsome and modest almost to a fault. How he had acquired his touching reverence for the imperial court in Kyoto was a mystery. Ieyasu had made himself supreme ruler of Japan by his own efforts, taking command as shogun and placing the emperor under great pressure, restricting the imperial family by law to the pursuit of "scholarship and poetry." Later, Arai Hakuseki, a Confucian scholar and adviser to the shoguns in the second decade of the eighteenth century, would supply a rationale for shogunal supremacy by declaring the emperor to be a purely regional figure, sacrosanct in Yamashiro, a district of Kyoto, and nowhere else. With Perry's arrival, the Mito theory that the authority of the shogun was delegated to him by the emperor took on prevalence, especially among the tozama daimyo of southwestern Japan. Daimyo from eastern Japan were not so quick to follow along. Yet Iemochi, perhaps because of his youth, appeared to fit naturally into the mainstream of the new understanding.

Besides his trusting and unquestioning nature, Iemochi also had the virtue of impartiality in his dealings with people. Bakufu officials and the women in the Ooku alike marveled at his sweet, unspoiled disposition, and declared that never was any master easier to serve. The one man on earth Iemochi did deal with unfairly was Hitotsubashi Keiki, whom he had been taught to despise. Never lower your guard around Keiki, he was constantly warned, and so came naturally to regard Keiki as something of a beast in human form. Unlike his lunatic predecessor, however, he was able to suppress his feelings under cover of perfectly correct behavior.

It was not only the young shogun Iemochi who looked on Keiki with suspicion as an unknown quantity. Soon after he became shogunal guardian, Matsudaira Shungaku realized that he didn't know him well either. Shungaku had stood behind Keiki since the beginning of the succession dispute, his enthusiastic support even landing him in jail at the hands of Ii Naosuke. Yet he was in for a shock.

That autumn, the bakufu would have to settle once and for all on a foreign policy. The choice was stark: either adhere to the commercial treaty signed by Ii Naosuke under military threat from the Western powers, or carry out what amounted to a supreme command from the emperor to "expel the barbarians"—i.e., unilaterally abrogate the treaty and fearlessly wage the ensuing war. Neither option seemed acceptable. Going with the first option and opening the country to international intercourse would make the bakufu loyal to international society and disloyal to the emperor, as well as vulnerable to concerted attack from all xenophobic loyalists. The second option would lead almost certainly to military attack by the outraged foreign powers, with subsequent partitioning and eventual colonization of Japan.

Matsudaira Shungaku placed a high value on the opinion

of the people, and in order to avoid a deep internal split, he chose to go with the second option, that of abrogating the treaty and chasing out the foreigners. Entrusted with the task of respectfully soliciting the opinions of the other councillors was Okubo Tadahiro, the shogun's private secretary. The councillors unanimously disagreed with Shungaku's decision. Okubo carefully wrote down their opinions before going to see Keiki to ask where he stood as shogunal guardian.

He had no doubt that Keiki would go along with Shungaku's plan. After all, Keiki was by birth a Mito, a member of the clan where the rabid antiforeigner doctrine of *sonno joi*, "revere the emperor and expel the barbarian," had originated. Moreover, he was Nariaki's heir, the repository of the hopes of every loyalist in the realm, Shungaku's own confrere—how could such a man possibly come down against Shungaku's plan to oppose the foreigners?

And yet as Okubo Tadahiro knelt prostrate awaiting Keiki's reply, the first words to pass over his head were these: "So Shungaku is another fool."

Okubo caught his breath. "I beg your pardon, sire."

"Expelling the foreigners can't be done."

Okubo could not believe his ears. With all his powers of eloquence, Keiki now launched into a cogent and impassioned defense of opening the country.

"In this day when nations the world over enjoy bonds of friendship based on universal justice, it is inconceivable for Japan alone to carry on in the old way, in isolation. Yes, it is true that Ii Naosuke, himself a believer in ridding the country of foreigners, was intimidated by the Americans' bluster into signing the agreement on his own authority, without waiting for the emperor's approval. There is no denying he acted improperly. But the impropriety of his action is purely domestic, a matter of no concern to other countries. To abrogate the treaty now on those grounds would be an act of perfidy bringing worldwide censure to bear on Japan. War would be inevitable. Even if we managed to emerge the victor, no honor would be ours; we would be the laughingstock of future generations. And if we lost, the shame would be that much greater. Given all that, is Shungaku still determined to stay this course?"

Surprised, Okubo replied that the plan did not reflect Shungaku's true intentions, that at heart he, too, supported the goal of opening the country. But given the opposing views held by the court, the powerful tozama domains, and public opinion, he explained, Shungaku thought it best to go along, for now witches were crying out for expulsion of the foreigners, thus mollifying the opposition and uniting popular sentiment. Afterward, he assured Keiki, Shungaku would slowly draw up new plans as the occasion arose.

"That's a cheap trick," said Keiki immediately. The thing to do was argue down the emperor and his supporters, convince and enlighten them.

On hearing Keiki's opinion as reported back to him by Okubo, Matsudaira Shungaku pondered in silence for a while. It amazed him to think that Keiki was not, after all, an exclusionist. At the same time, he was outraged at being called a fool. All his life people had lauded his ability, society had respected his judgments, and his retainers had esteemed his benevolence. He took no great pride in such

79

things, but to be called a fool! Perhaps Keiki was after all not fit to be shogun, no matter what his political opinions, Shungaku contemplated, forced to revise his estimation of the young man.

Besides, Keiki failed to appreciate the pains he, Shungaku, had taken: Like other men of discernment, he had moved beyond the old, simpleminded impulse to banish all foreigners; opening the country to foreign intercourse was unavoidable, he knew. But unless he came out now ostensibly on the side of banishing foreigners, neither the imperial court nor public opinion could well be assuaged. His exclusionism was purely technical, a means to the end of ultimately opening the country.

Shungaku went straight to the castle, entered Keiki's chamber, and set forth his views. Keiki responded by recounting the injurious effects of such double-dealing. In the end, Shungaku yielded.

"Very well, I will follow your advice," he said, switching his allegiance then and there in favor of opening the country. But as leader of the bakufu, he was faced with an urgent practical problem: A pair of messengers were on their way from Kyoto even then, bearing an imperial order urging the immediate expulsion of foreigners from the land. One messenger was Sanjo Sanetomi, the other Anegakoji Kintomo—two of the most radical opponents of establishing ties with foreign countries. If he refused to obey the imperial command they brought, then the bakufu and Shungaku alike would be guilty of failing to show proper reverence for the emperor. "Matters are out of my control," he declared.

Keiki assured him that there was no cause for worry. No

matter what the extremists said, he need only ignore them. The sole issue that mattered was what Emperor Komei thought. The thing to do was awaken him, open his eyes. "I will go to Kyoto, obtain an audience, and explain things to His Majesty in person," said Keiki confidently. But what he proposed was a practical impossibility. With messengers already on their way to Edo bearing urgent orders from the emperor to throw the foreigners out, for Keiki to pass them in the opposite direction with a contrary message for His Majesty would create instant chaos. Plans for the trip were quietly dropped.

Shungaku feared public opinion no less than the imperial messengers, however, and so despite his conversation with Keiki, he quickly reverted to his antiforeigner stance, humbly accepting the imperial order when it arrived and proceeding to shape bakufu policy to that end. His conversion had apparently been skin deep, mere camouflage.

"Shungaku is a weakling," thought Keiki in some surprise. Without another word of dissent, he submitted to the official bakufu line. Not long after, as he was talking casually with Shungaku, Keiki seemed to remember something. "Oh, see here, Shungaku," he said. "About that business the other day."

"I beg your pardon?"

"That business about my being in favor of opening the country up. I have no doubt you realize this, but you've got to keep it under your hat."

At his words, Shungaku felt a spine-tingling chill.

According to Keiki, due to his Mito origins, everyone in the land saw him as their best hope for driving away the foreigners, and his appointment as shogunal guardian had therefore helped to revive the popularity of the bakufu. Once it became known that Keiki was no advocate of exclusionism, but in fact adamantly in favor of opening the country to foreign trade, there would be hell to pay.

"I know that," said Shungaku.

In fact, Yamanouchi Yodo, another wise man and longtime supporter of Keiki, had already warned Shungaku that under no circumstances was Keiki's true position on this all-important matter to be leaked to anyone. The consequences would be dire. He had also warned Keiki, telling him, "The morning that the messengers arrive, whatever you do, don't say anything to them about opening the country. They are both young and headstrong, and they would be so incensed that they would jump up and run straight back to Kyoto."

Everyone knew that the messengers were backed by the powerful Choshu domain, ruled by antishogunate, antiforeign forces. If the messengers went back and told the emperor of Keiki's supposed perfidy, the men of Choshu would raise an alarm; then, gaining the ear of the emperor and the nobles, they might well seize the chance to have an edict issued overthrowing the shogunate. Listening, Keiki had nodded in understanding and thanked Yodo for the warning.

In the end, the bakufu responded to the imperial messengers with assurances of driving away the foreigners as commanded. Public opinion ran as follows: "So the bakufu finally has quit its shilly-shallying and come out clearly and forcefully on the side of getting rid of the foreigners. About time! This is surely a big difference from Ii Naosuke's day. It

can be only because we have Hitotsubashi Keiki, son of Nariaki, as shogunal guardian."

The reverence and awe of the loyalists toward the Mito
family in general, and Mito Nariaki in particular, bordered
on religious faith. Keiki was more and more a part of their
pantheon.

"Know Your Enemy and Know Yourself, and You Will Be Invincible in a Hundred Battles"

There was at this time a young farmer whose anti-foreign zeal led him to contemplate seizing Takasaki Castle, outside Edo, in an attempt to shake up the bakufu. He was Shibusawa Eijiro, eldest son of a wealthy farmer in the village of Chiaraijima in Musashi Province (modern Saitama and Tokyo). Later he would change his name to Eiichi, and become known as the founder of Japanese capitalism.

Besides farming, the family also ran a profitable business selling indigo balls, clusters of fermented leaves of the indigo plant that were pressed into balls and used in dyeing. In fact, they had become one of the wealthiest families in those parts, and were granted permission in the father's generation to use a surname and bear swords, the prerogatives of samurai. Eijiro was a small, round-faced youth with glossy black hair that looked its best when he wore it in a samurai queue. He was in full samurai regalia when he came calling one day at the home of Hiraoka Enshiro, Keiki's trusted vassal, at about this moment in Keiki's career.

Around the time Keiki was absolved of wrongdoing and made shogunal guardian, Hiraoka had been recalled from exile and reinstated as his adviser and right-hand man. As such, he had achieved a considerable reputation. "The only way to reach Lord Hitotsubashi," the youth from Chiaraijima decided, "is to go through Hiraoka Enshiro."

From earliest boyhood, Eijiro had helped with the family business of making and selling indigo balls, often traveling as far as Shinshu in search of indigo leaves. On trips to Edo for instruction in swordsmanship, however, he shed his merchant's attire in favor of samurai garb. He studied under Kaiho Honpei, master of the North Star Lone Blade school.

"In order to raise up an army," he thought, "I'll need the unofficial backing of the Hitotsubashi." It was an indication of Keiki's widespread popularity. Shibusawa Eijiro was now twenty-three years old, Keiki twenty-five.

The farmers of Musashi were a hot-tempered lot who reveled in a fight, and farmers though they were, nearly all could handle a sword. Some put that knowledge to good use, like Kondo Isami and Hijikata Toshizo, who went on to become founding members of the Shinsengumi, an elite corps of swordsmen in the service of the shogunate.

But Shibusawa had the grandest plan of all. It was his ambition to gather young hotheads like himself and launch an attack on Takasaki Castle that year, 1862, on the night of the winter solstice. Then, with the castle as base, they could muster soldiers from the eight eastern provinces of Kanto and raise an army devoted to expelling the foreigners. Together they would charge down the Kamakura Road and attack the open seaport of Yokohama, slaughtering foreigners on sight and forcing the bakufu to take a stand against the odious foreign presence on Japanese soil once and for all.

Shibusawa was not alone in his plan. A country scholar named Momonoi Gihachi in the neighboring village of Nakase maintained a close liaison with him, while recruiting volunteers with whom to launch a same-day attack on Numata Castle in Kozuke (modern Gunma).

Shibusawa made frequent trips to Edo to procure necessary arms and muster men under his banner. Umedaya Shinnosuke, a merchant of fencing equipment in Kanda, Edo, provided swords, spears, and coats of mail.

On hearing young Shibusawa's plans, Hiraoka Enshiro cried out, "Are you mad?"

"Not in the least," replied Shibusawa. "I have confided this secret to you despite the certainty of my arrest if the bakufu finds out, for one reason: I trust you. It is the same reason I want you to make us retainers of the Hitotsubashi lord. We ask no stipends. It would be enough if you accepted us as retainers in name only. I have at my command a band of four or five dozen brave warriors. Should anything happen to Hitotsubashi Keiki, we will give our lives to avenge him."

"Wait," said Hiraoka. He had already ceased to believe that merely expelling the foreigners was the answer, and like Keiki was an advocate of opening the country. But if he debated with this zealot the follies of antiforeigner fanaticism, he might well be cut down on the spot. Knowing this, he pretended to agree with his caller. "Everything has its proper time," he cautioned in an attempt to calm the youth. "Wait awhile."

Shibusawa was naturally dissatisfied. "So Hiraoka has joined ranks with the temporizers after all."

"What are you saying?"

"What all Edo says. That the reason Lord Hitotsubashi has done so little even after becoming shogunal guardian is that you take exception to him; that you are in fact a believer in opening the country, and are clouding his vision."

"That is not true," Hiraoka assured him, and urged him to come again, treating him with all the courtesy and respect due *shishi*, or "men of high purpose"—loyalist patriots prepared to die for their country. At the same time, he mused, "I'd sure like to have him on our side."

There were reasons that a man like Shibusawa was needed. Soon Keiki would be stationed permanently in Kyoto; he would need men. Even though the Hitotsubashi family received a stipend of 100,000 *koku* from the bakufu, it was not a domain proper but a collateral branch of the Tokugawa. There were a number of family retainers like Hiraoka himself, but unlike daimyo vassals who pledged loyalty to one lord, they were hatamoto on loan from the shogun, and the work they did was not military in nature but administrative.

In Kyoto, Keiki would have immediate need for a retainer of unquestioned loyalty and ability, someone who could mingle with other retainers and discuss national affairs. Otherwise, in Kyoto the Hitotsubashi would become isolated from the movements of the various domains.

"A hot-blooded fellow like that is just the ticket," Hiraoka thought.

The nation was aboil with tension. Hiraoka recalled words penned by his acquaintance Kiyokawa Hachiro to memorialize the formation of a ronin corps: "Extraordinary times require the use of extraordinary men to seize the victory."

Keiki left for Kyoto. He was scheduled at first to travel in the shogun's entourage, but then there was a change in plans: Go on ahead of the others, he was told. The reason was the tinderbox situation in the eastern capital, concerning which Nagai Naomune, the Kyoto magistrate, had written to the senior council in desperation. The imperial capital had become virtually an independent political entity and was now under the domination of Satsuma and Choshu. Under the circumstances, a lowly magistrate like himself was insufficient to represent the shogunal authority, so it was urgent for the survival of the bakufu that Lord Hitotsubashi come swiftly. "Edo influence wanes here day by day," warned Nagai. "There is a growing gulf between the court and the bakufu, with communication all but impossible. Satsuma, Choshu, and the other tozama domains take the side of the court, and have power to make it do their bidding. Unless Lord Hitotsubashi and others in high office come speedily to Kyoto and demonstrate their sincere reverence for the emperor, the situation will be lost."

This communication sent Edo Castle into a frenzy. The senior councillors unanimously urged Keiki to leave at once. He was willing, but lacked able samurai to serve him reliably. Not being a Tokugawa by birth, Keiki felt some compunction in asking the bakufu to supply him with the men he needed, and decided instead to make a personal request of the Mito domain. He invited Takeda Kounsai, chief retainer of the Mito family, to his home and told him, "I would like to borrow ten men who are informed on current affairs, firm of character, able to offer me good counsel, and willing to die for me if need be."

Takeda agreed to the request and, after a rigorous search, selected eight men. Among them were several who would become Keiki's chief strategists, including Hara Ichinoshin, Umezawa Magotaro, and Kaji Seijiemon.

At the moment when the hotheaded Shibusawa Eijiro was meeting with Hiraoka Enshiro, Keiki was no longer in Edo. He was on his way overland to Kyoto.

Shortly after New Year's in 1863, Keiki—now the Minister of the Center—entered Kyoto. His lodging was provided by the temple Higashi Hongan-ji. Three days later he set out to call at the homes of Konoe, chief adviser to the emperor, and other high court officials. The procession he led was a jolting break with tradition for the people of Kyoto. He traveled not in a conveyance, but on horseback. Moreover, he made blatant use of a Western saddle—anathema to exclusionists—and led a corps of the bakufu's newly formed Western-style cavalry with a full suite of attendants on horseback as well, even the junior councillors and housekeepers. In all there must have been fifty men on horseback. The thunder of their hooves created an instant sensation along the main thoroughfare of the city. "This is no ordinary lord," thought the city residents, while the daimyo and court nobles wondered what to think.

Before ever setting foot in Kyoto, Keiki had achieved a reputation there based on the words of his father's adviser, the illustrious Mito scholar Fujita Toko, who was crushed to death in the Ansei earthquake of 1855. As reported by Mito retainers quartered in the temple Honkoku-ji, Fujita had said of Keiki, "He is a superior man to his father, and few his equal will ever come again. Because the nation now lacks men, even if things are left to chance, the day will surely come when the reins of government will be entrusted to his hands."

Since Fujita Toko was idealized by antiforeign radicals, this encomium had a special impact on the loyalist ronin gathered in Kyoto. Soon after Keiki's arrival, in the mansion of the Choshu domain, one young man slapped his knee with enthusiasm. It was Kusaka Genzui, a leader of the most radical faction in Choshu. "All right," he announced, "I'll go see and hear for myself what stuff the man is made of."

Terajima Chuzaburo of Choshu, Todoroki Buhei of Higo, and Kawakami Gensai, also of Higo, leapt to their feet and declared their desire to go with him. Gensai was known as "Killer Gensai," and not even he could have told how many supporters of the shogun and advocates of opening the country he had slain during the past year.

With a clatter of wooden clogs, the vermilion scabbards of their long swords bright at their waists, Kusaka and the others arrived at the temple where Keiki was staying and demanded an audience, offering their cards to the samurai who met them there. Their doing so was in itself clear evidence of Kyoto's chaotic state. Ordinarily, rear vassals such as they could never have hoped to meet directly with someone in the highest echelon of the shogunate like Keiki. Yet here they made rounds of calls at the homes of court nobles, threatening, cajoling them, and in general treating the nobility like personal adornments or familiars of theirs. They had lost all sense of propriety, of place. They did have great sway at court. It often happened that a ronin's drunken arguments would be spread about the following day as an imperial order. Given that the bakufu was forced to tremble these days at any expression of imperial wishes, it was scarcely surprising that an upstart like Genzui should boldly walk up to Keiki's door and demand to see him.

This could never happen in Edo, thought Keiki. Only in Kyoto. And it had hardly taken long for him to receive his induction to the realities of life there in the capital either.

"Show them in," he ordered. Now twenty-six years old, at the peak of his physical and mental vigor, he had no fear of getting the worst of an argument with them. Rather, he relished the prospect of tearing their arguments to shreds, and thus neutralizing their poison.

But his adviser stopped him. Inspector General Okabe of the bakufu, having come along as Keiki's aide, argued so convincingly against a confrontation that Keiki thought better of the idea and ended up sending word that he was ill.

The visitors refused to leave. Finally, Okabe himself agreed to receive them, and they were shown into a small room adjacent to the entryway.

Kusaka Genzui launched into a harangue. "At the present hour, the debate over whether or not to open the country remains unclear," he declaimed. Twenty-three years old, Kusaka was full of ardor, and when he delivered an opinion he spoke with a peculiarly ponderous quality, as if reading aloud from a page of classical Chinese. The gist of his remarks that day was that the bakufu should decide expeditiously on a time to carry out the expulsion of foreigners from Japan, in accordance with His Majesty's clear wishes. If they did not, they would earn universal contempt as traitors who dared to oppose an imperial mandate.

When this was reported back to Keiki, he nodded to himself in satisfaction. It was just as he had always thought: Their inflamed antiforeign rhetoric was antishogunate radicalism in disguise. "It is impossible to carry on a rational dialogue with them," he said, and through Okabe conveyed a noncommittal reply that served only to further inflame his guests.

"We did not come to hear such palaver," declared Kusaka, and remained stubbornly in place until nightfall in a vain attempt to force Keiki to set a date then and there for the expulsion of foreigners. Finally taking his leave, he delivered a parting shot: "I had heard that Lord Hitotsubashi was the hope of the nation, enjoying both high position and the esteem of all. And what do I find! The evasions and equivocations he spouts are no different from those of any mediocre official. If this is what Lord Hitotsubashi is like, it is plain that the shogun himself could come to Kyoto, and the bakufu still would have no intention of expelling the foreigners. They have nothing but contempt for the imperial court!"

Keiki knew the source of the arrogance of these *shishi*, men of high purpose. It was the Gakushuin, or Peers' School. Ever since the days of the Muromachi shogunate, which ended in 1573, the court had lacked an institution for debate of political affairs. The previous month, in light of the ongoing crisis, twenty-nine nobles had been selected for the purpose, meeting in rooms in the Gakushuin buildings. Nearly all were in sympathy with Choshu, the hotbed of anti-foreign fanaticism, and their leaders were Sanjo Sanetomi and Anegakoji Kintomo. Those two in turn were controlled by Kusaka Genzui and his men, who continually passed bogus "imperial orders" along to them. When the loyalist Ogawa Yaemon of Oka domain was disciplined and placed under house arrest, the daimyo received an imperial order from Kyoto with instructions to free Yaemon— and did so, in great astonishment. The document was a forgery, the joint work of the nobles and *shishi* based in the Gakushuin.

On his eighth day in Kyoto, Keiki ordered the horses saddled for a visit to the Gakushuin. The recent incident involving Kusaka at his lodgings had been more than he could stomach. Vowing to put an end to such insolence once and for all, he made sure the cavalry carried new-style rifles, headed north in a cloud of dust, and entered the Gakushuin. Ostensibly it was a courtesy call, yet even when noon came he did not leave, but took out the lunch he had brought with him and ate, continuing to engage in desultory conversation.

"Since the emperor wishes it, the expulsion of the foreigners must be carried out," he stated. "As it is said, know your enemy and know yourself, and you will be invincible in a hundred battles. Today I would like to talk about the enemy." With this introduction, he proceeded to discuss world affairs, but the nobles, entirely ignorant of such matters, could only listen in dazed silence.

Finally, he told them, "I am a military retainer. I will apply myself with all my might to getting rid of the foreign presence in our country. Because this means making an enemy of the whole world, the crack of gunfire and the roar of cannonfire are bound to echo over hill and dale across every inch of Japan. You men are from Choshu, where the cry 'Expel the barbarians!' first arose. When the time comes, see that the roar of guns does not cause you to take flight in alarm." Tight-lipped, he looked around at every man in the room. Overawed by his fieriness, not a man uttered a word. They were amazed to think that among the pusillanimous officials of the bakufu there should be one capable of such an intimidating speech.

Keiki was careful, however, to make no overt criticism of the essential idea of exclusionism. He knew well that if he did, the cry would go up instantly that he was disloyal to the emperor, putting him and the shogun alike in an untenable position and leading inevitably to the end of the Tokugawa bakufu.

Drastic Action

KEIKI'S ONLY SUPPORTERS IN KYOTO WERE HIS LONGTIME comrades, the progressive daimyo triumvirate known as the "three sages": Yamanouchi Yodo of Tosa, Matsudaira Shungaku of Echizen, and Date Munenari of Uwajima. Yodo and Munenari had both been named by the court to the ambiguous post of "consultant on national affairs." Opinion had it in the capital, however, that the three were no longer to be trusted—that they were turncoats who had abandoned the holy antiforeigner cause and now espoused the treacherous course of opening the country and kowtowing to Western military might.

After Keiki's arrival in Kyoto, this sentiment rose to a peak among the loyalist *shishi* encamped in the capital. "Even a daimyo, if he is a rascal, will be treated like a rascal and cut down!" they boasted, and on the door of the temple where Date Munenari was lodging they stuck a paper on which was boldly written in dark ink these words:

To the great traitor, lord of Iyo [Munenari]:
    Your statements are a monstrous outrage. If you do not repent of your ways, in punishment for the crime of violating an imperial edict we will attack your lodging and make of you a blood offering to the cause of expelling the barbarians!

That was on the tenth day of the new year. Exactly three weekes later, on the balcony of the drumtower in the Higashi Hongan-ji, where Keiki was staying, someone placed a small offering stand of plain wood. Upon it was the severed head of a man with hair in the style of a high steward and a sign, OFFERED TO LORD HITOTSUBASHI.

Keiki had the dead man's identity confirmed. It was an antibakufu nobleman of the Chigusa family, High Steward Kagawa Hajime. Formerly, he had participated in preparations for the Ansei Purge with Nagano Shuzen, Ii Naosuke's tactician. Two nights earlier, a number of ronin had burst into his residence, threatened the maid, and tried to force her to reveal her master's whereabouts. When she refused to divulge anything, one of the ronin grabbed Kagawa's son and made as if to slay him. At that, Kagawa had leapt out from behind a double wall in the alcove, where he was hiding, and begged them to take his life instead. Before the eyes of his sobbing child, the ronin severed Kagawa's head. After that they threw his left arm into the home of Iwakura Tomomi, the emperor's chamberlain, who was in disfavor with the more extremist antishogunate samurai for supporting a movement to bring the court and the shogunate together. Finally, they presented the decapitated head to Keiki. The message was unmistakable: Fail to honor the imperial command to purge the country of foreigners, and you will meet with the same fate.

The following day, Keiki called on Konoe, the chief adviser to the emperor and representative of the court nobles, a man known for his meekness and pusillanimity. "Everything is by imperial command, they say," Keiki fumed. "Does His Majesty have any idea of the violence these people are perpetrating in his name?"

"He knows nothing of it," Konoe replied. Far from approving, His Majesty loathed the radical extremists and the Choshu loyalists who manipulated them, and made a point of distancing himself from them. All the talk of imperial edicts, commands, mandates, and the rest was sheer fabrication and forgery on the part of Sanjo Sanetomi, Anegakoji Kintomo, and their cohorts. The loyalists had nicknamed Sanjo "White Bean" and Anegakoji "Black Bean," and were using them as their tools.

Hearing this, the hot-tempered Yamanouchi Yodo of Tosa grabbed his sword, drained a sake cup, and went to see Sanjo Sanetomi at his home, full of fighting spirit. His family was related to the Sanjo family by marriage, and seizing Sanetomi by the sleeve, he demanded to know, for the sake of their familial bond, the truth. "You people accuse others of going against His Majesty's orders. Now I want to know: Has His Majesty directly said these things or not?"

Frightened, Sanetomi finally confessed that there was no imperial mandate. Yodo pressed further.

"The Western powers are vastly superior in military strength to Japan, and to force them to leave our country will be exceedingly difficult. Does His Majesty know this?"

"No."

"Then why in God's name don't you tell him the truth? You're the adviser to the throne—isn't it your duty?"

Sanjo crumpled and said with a sob, "Lord Yodo! If I did such a thing, the loyalists would kill me!" It seemed that Sanjo, too, was being persecuted by the fearsome men of Choshu, and forced to adopt a hard line. He ended with his own appeal: "Please, instead of taking me to task, try to understand the situation I'm in."

When Keiki heard this, he decided that his first priority must be to take charge of the ronin loyalists encamped in Kyoto and restore order among them. Summoning Matsudaira Katamori, lord of Aizu and Protector of Kyoto, he advised him of the need to crack down, telling him to send out ruthless armed patrols on daily rounds of the city.

Katamori listened to the suggestion and tilted his head delicately to one side, considering. "I don't believe that will be possible," he said finally. A mild-tempered man, no doubt he found the tactics of oppression little to his taste. Despite his opposition, Keiki continued doggedly to recommend a crackdown, finally prodding Katamori into forming the Shinsengumi, ronin troops of the bakufu charged with maintaining order in the city. The result would be a bloodbath.

* * *

In the meantime, the recklessness of Kyoto activists had continued unabated, reaching its zenith on the fourth day of the third month with the entrance into the capital of the shogun Iemochi. They had a plan: They would persuade the emperor to make a pilgrimage to Iwashimizu Hachiman Shrine in southern Kyoto to issue an antiforeigner proclamation and offer prayers for the Westerners' expulsion. Naturally, the shogun Iemochi would be obliged to attend such a ceremony. He would have to mount the long stone steps of the shrine, and at the top, within the shrine precincts, be presented by the Son of Heaven himself with a barbarian-quelling sword. After that the bakufu would no longer be able to vacillate, but would have to take immediate steps to expel the foreigners. If he dared to disobey the emperor's direct command, the shogun would be branded an enemy of the throne, subject to universal condemnation. It was a ruse, thought Keiki, a clever trap.

"They have a clever man on their side," commented Hiraoka Enshiro, Keiki's strategist, who had finished up his remaining business in Edo and come to Kyoto to aid Keiki. According to Hiraoka's sources, the plan was the brainchild of a Shinto priest called Maki Izumi, from Kurume. Kusaka Genzui and the other Choshu extremists all followed his bidding. He was also the author of the dubious imperial proclamations being promulgated by Sanjo Sanetomi and the rest. "He is a man of extraordinary resourcefulness," concluded Hiraoka.

"Resourcefulness, is it?" muttered Keiki, irked by that description. In Edo, members of the cabinet had made numer-

ous criticisms of Keiki, most of them emotional, anti-Mito di-
atribes he had largely ignored. The criticism of one man,
however, had hit home. Councillor Kuze Hirochika, then
Keiki's sole supporter in the cabinet, had said, "There are
those who assert that he [Keiki] is Tokugawa Ieyasu reincar-
nate, but it appears to me that such a statement goes overboard. I suspect that he is merely a man of some resources."
Lacking in fiber, in other words.

"Hmmph. What does a man like Kuze know about me?"
That was what Keiki thought, vaguely put out, when the comment was relayed to him. Now here was Hiraoka declaring
Maki Izumi to be a man of superior resourcefulness. No
priest from Kurume was going to get the better of him on
that score, thought Keiki defiantly.

But the men of Choshu and their sympathizers in the
court pushed ahead with their plan, bringing it to fruition.
At the same time, a rumor spread that on the day of the ceremony, the shogun Iemochi was to be assassinated. As proof,
among the courtiers in the extremist ranks, a chamberlain
named Tadamitsu had suddenly disappeared from Kyoto.
Rumor had it that he was to assume command of the loyalists
of Choshu and Tosa, cut into the imperial procession, and
capture the emperor's carriage; then he would beg for an
immediate mandate to bring down heaven's punishment on
the shogun, which his troops would carry out by slaying him
on the spot. It was all too plausible a scenario.

Hearing this, Keiki schemed to have the emperor's visit to
the shrine called off, but failed. Then he went to Nijo Castle
in Kyoto and obtained an audience with the shogun, telling
him, "For the sake of the country, give up your plans to ac-

company the emperor on his pilgrimage." Lowering his voice, he explained the circumstances. Iemochi was an earnest youth who took no pleasure in this sort of maneuvering. His cheeks flaming, he protested, "But that would be disloyal!" Keiki continued to press his case. Finally, ministers of the cabinet were won over, and it was decided that none of them would leave the castle grounds on the day in question, pleading a sudden outbreak of illness.

One who opposed their counterplan was Matsudaira Katamori, Protector of Kyoto. Going to Nijo Castle, he declared, "No matter what rumors there may be, I will protect His Majesty and Your Lordship with my life. You and your families are pillars of the warrior class. If you allow fear of idle rumors to keep you here at the castle, the military prestige of the bakufu will be severely compromised." But Keiki argued successfully for his plan, and eventually carried the day.

Soon the day of the pilgrimage arrived: May 28, 1863. At six A.M., the imperial carriage left from the gate of the Gosho Imperial Palace in Sakai-cho. At the head of the cavalry were Yokoyama Chikara, elder of Aizu domain, with the rear brought up by Katakura Shojuro, elder of Sendai domain. Over ten thousand men marched in the procession, including court aristocrats and officials, with Keiki and the various daimyo also in attendance. The shogun Iemochi and Tokugawa Yoshikatsu, lord of Owari, each stayed in with a fever. Keiki attended as their proxy. The procession wound down Tobe Road and across Yodo Bridge, arriving in the foothills of Iwashimizu after eight P.M. The emperor stayed the night in monk's quarters at the foot of the mountain.

At another monk's hut nearby, Keiki loosened his ceremonial robes and lay down. The plan was to get a few hours of rest and then, at half past midnight, to climb the mountain bearing torches. As the shogun's stand-in, there was no doubt that he would end up being presented with the sword. It was the very sword that the emperor carried on military expeditions, returning it after his triumphal reentry to the capital in accordance with an ancient Chinese custom introduced to Japan during the Heian period (794–1185). Keiki's acceptance of the sword would commit the bakufu first to using military force to expel every Westerner from the open ports, then to doing battle with the allied forces of the West that would surely descend on Japan in retaliation.

Suddenly Keiki sat up in bed and called for his adviser and guard, Nakane Chojuro, a man who had been with the Hitotsubashi family since the days of his father. "Chojuro! I have a fever. My head aches. Fetch a doctor," he ordered. He was nauseated and could not possibly climb the mountain. Chojuro was to send immediate word of his illness to the appropriate officials.

Quick to catch on, Chojuro beamed as if to say "Good for you, sir!" Then he nodded, withdrew, and swiftly set about carrying out Keiki's instructions. Pandemonium broke out among the court nobles in their rude lodgings scattered through the area. Keiki's declaration of illness at such a time was a bombshell. Whether feigned or genuine, his illness could be seen only as a political act with major consequences. The radical loyalists swiftly sent a messenger to his quarters, informing him, "The emperor commands you to call on him immediately."

Keiki sent a reply via his aide Chojuro: "Whoever may

command me, right now I am physically unable to call on anyone."

The first messenger was replaced by another with the identical message. Keiki sent him away with the same reply, then turned to Chojuro and said, "Let's get out of here." If he lingered, the court nobles might well carry him up the mountain by sheer force. Keiki had a palanquin readied. So sudden was his flight that he had no escort or retinue. "Let anyone who happens to be in the vicinity come along," he said, and set off in the dark of night from his monk's hut in the foothills, borne swiftly along the ink-black road.

As they traveled, more and more of Keiki's attendants caught up with them, until by the time they reached Jonan Shrine, their company numbered over two hundred. Keiki decided to spend the rest of the night there.

Keiki's abrupt flight threw the Kyoto loyalists into a frenzy. Six days later, on June 4, someone posted this announcement on the approach to Sanjo Ohashi Bridge: "Concerning the imperial visit to Hachiman Shrine in Iwashimizu, the shogun's feigned illness and Minister Hitotsubashi's decampment are both unpardonable! Let justice be meted out without delay!"

The residents of Kyoto, accustomed to strife though they were, rubbed their eyes in disbelief. Over the last year or so, graffiti calling for heaven's punishment on malefactors had appeared countless times, but never before had anyone explicitly named the shogun or Keiki. No one knew who was responsible, but immediately after the sign was posted, the lord of Choshu left the city to return home. It could only have been the handiwork of Choshu extremists.

Keiki was incensed. The text of the notice read in part, "These scoundrels posture and temporize, holding the emperor in contempt." Never before had he been so reviled.

"If the court nobles are so hell-bent on expelling the foreigners, I ought to go ahead and do it!" he said slowly, spitting out the words with venom. Let the irresponsible men of the court see with their own eyes what war would do to the country. Keiki's pride could take no more beating. Let them find out if he was a posturing blowhard or not.

A few days later, the court sent an urgent letter demanding to know if he was going to expel the foreigners, and challenging him to set a firm date for action.

"Certainly. June the twenty-fifth," Keiki replied. It was then June 6. There were only three weeks left before the battle would begin. After the imperial messenger had left, all the bakufu officials in Kyoto gathered around Keiki in fear and wonder and asked, "Are you sure that will be all right?"

Keiki gave a scornful laugh. "The whole idea of expelling the foreigners is a fantasy. Since it can never be done anyway, our only course is to set a date that allows no time for any sort of preparation."

"The court will think you mean it."

"Let them."

Another imperial messenger soon arrived. "The deadline you have set is splendid. Will the bakufu issue the order to the daimyos, or should it come directly from the court?"

"Let it come from the court."

Exclusionism was the court's idea, so the order might as well come from there. That way, responsibility for defeat and the destruction of the country would rest squarely with the court as well. "Under the circumstances," he added, "I must hurry back to Kanto to begin preparations." The messenger was instructed to inform all the high court officials of Keiki's imminent departure from the capital.

Iemochi stayed on in Kyoto, but Keiki left. Voices of protest were heard among the retainers in Nijo Castle: "Why does the shogunal guardian go off and leave the teenaged shogun here alone?" Keiki countered that he had a perfectly good reason: "The shogun should remain in Kyoto. I must leave to supervise the ousting of the foreigners." If the policy of expulsion of foreigners were to be carried out, Keiki would have to assume command of the Japanese forces. As commander-in-chief, his place was in Edo Castle, the center of Japanese military and political affairs, preparing without delay for war.

Not even the chief senior councillor, Itakura Katsukiyo—the equivalent of today's prime minister—who was stationed permanently in Kyoto, could fathom Keiki's motives. Could it be that Lord Hitotsubashi was seriously planning to carry out the bidding of the court and declare war on foreigners? he wondered.

The consensus was that Keiki was indeed serious. For one thing, on the occasion of his departure for Edo, he took with him senior councillor Takeda of Iga, leader of the Mito *joi* faction. Takeda was fond of boasting that he was the spiritual heir of Tokugawa Nariaki of Mito—and, in general, the public concurred. If Keiki had taken that prominent exclusionist back east with him, who could doubt his intentions?

They took the overland route back to Edo, leaving Kyoto on June 6 and stopping overnight in the Tsuchiyama Inn on the Eastern Sea Road. The inn was one officially designated as lodging for daimyo. Keiki's companion, Inspector General Okabe of Suruga, stayed in a travelers' inn. That night, ten assassins stole into the inn garden, threw rocks at the wooden shutters to break them down, and burst inside, yelling "Where is the villain Okabe of Suruga?" While Okabe's retainers fought off the would-be assassins, Okabe fled out the back way, barely escaping with his life. Later gossip had it that the band of assassins had been sent by Anegakoji Kintomo, a court noble who sided with the loyalists.

They went by sea from Kuwana, stopping overnight in Atsuda, Owari. That night, Keiki did something rather peculiar. Holed up in a back room of the inn, he got out his inkstone and composed two letters, one long and one short. The long one was to the senior councillors in Edo. Beginning politely with a conventional phrase or two describing the warming weather and expressing his fond hope that all of them were enjoying good health, he went on to inform them in detail of the imperial order he had received, and directed them to take the appropriate steps.

The short letter was a terse note addressed to Regent Takatsukasa Sukehiro, tendering his resignation. "It is not my place to act as the shogun's proxy," he wrote. Thus, even as he sent orders to Edo to begin preparations for a battle expelling foreigners, he effectively fired himself for having issued those very orders. "It's the only way," he told himself. He had proved himself a master tactician. He'd had this plan in mind all along, and had left Kyoto prepared to step down.

After that Keiki made his way down the Eastern Sea Road in a leisurely fashion. This, too, was part of his plan. He would spend sixteen or seventeen days traversing the three hundred miles between Kyoto and Edo, arriving in Edo on the evening of June 23.

The following day he reported to the castle. The day when they were to declare war on the Western powers was the very next day, June 25. With so little time remaining, nothing could be done. Nevertheless, with full assurance Keiki summoned together the senior councillors, junior councillors, and foreign magistrate and conveyed to them the imperial order. Then he said, "This is the emperor's command. Let every man prepare himself and do all he can to see that the expulsion of the foreigners is carried out."

That was all. Not a word about particulars or how-tos. Without taking any questions, he got up and went home to his wife. The cabinet members were in shock, until finally it began to sink in that it was all a clever ruse.

"It's a way to avoid having to carry out the expulsion," they told themselves, but the more they thought about it, the more they realized that the show had only just begun. More was to come.

Four days later Keiki returned to Edo Castle and reassembled the cabinet. "After much thought I have decided to resign my position as shogunal guardian," he announced. "See that a letter is sent to that address." Stupefied by this decision coming on the heels of the order to attack foreigners and drive them out of Japan, his listeners were silent.

Inwardly, they thought, "Aha, so that's what he was up to!" To satisfy his duty to Kyoto, he'd issued a nominal order without a word as to how it should be carried out. That left the bakufu hamstrung, unable to take appropriate action;

then, as the officials sat flabbergasted, the very one who had handed them the order took his leave with a flourish. This way Keiki and the bakufu alike came out of a sticky situation unscathed, with no hard feelings all around.

Oh, the uncanny cleverness of the man! After this tour de force, the men in the bakufu and the women in the Ooku were struck alike with renewed awe of Keiki. He had brought them out of the crisis; now, thought the bakufu officials, it was over.

But the script Keiki was authoring had still not played out. After resigning, he submitted to cross-examination, and then summoned a castle priest and had him fetch his writing things. When the castle priest began to grind the ink for him, Keiki took the inkstone out of his hands, insisting on doing it himself. That was always his way; whatever he did, he preferred to do it himself, and even the ink he used came out darker if he ground it.

Finally he picked up the brush and began to compose a letter to senior councillor Takatsukasa in Kyoto. The letter contained his resignation and an explanation. He had already written a similar letter to Takatsukasa from Atsuda, in Owari, but now, in order to clarify what his little charade had all been about, he included a fuller explanation.

In formal epistolary style, he wrote, "I, your humble servant, having received a sacred order from His Majesty the emperor to expel the barbarians, returned east to carry it out, but there is in fact no prospect of winning such a war." Even so, he added, the emperor's words, once given, were not to be rescinded.

"For that reason, I came to Edo prepared to die in battle

alongside the other bakufu officials, but none of the council elders, or any of the other officials, great or small, consented to expel the foreigners. Rather, they doubted my motives. They appeared to speculate that I planned to take advantage of the confusion surrounding the current debate to seize control of the country. Under the circumstances, I cannot possibly carry out the emperor's stated will. I can only offer my deepest apologies to the emperor and the imperial court, and step aside. I humbly request that you convey this information to His Majesty."

After retiring to his home in Koishikawa, he gathered Nakane Chojuro, Hiraoka Enshiro, Kurokawa Kibei, and his other closest associates to explain to them where he now stood. "And that is what I have done. Take it under advisement, will you?"

8

Keiki's Charade

THOSE WHO SUFFERED THE MOST IMMEDIATE INCONVENIENCE
due to Keiki's virtuoso performance were his personal attendants, Hiraoka Enshiro and the rest. Every antiforeign,
proimperial *shishi* in Edo came rushing to their residences,
hand on scabbard, demanding to know if they had gone
against the order to expel the foreigners. Shibusawa Eijiro,
now a close friend of Hiraoka's, was among them.

"Every loyalist in the prefecture is furious," he said.

"With the Minister of the Center?" asked Hiraoka.

No, said Shibusawa, with Hiraoka and his other attendants. Faith in Keiki was strong among the antiforeign *shishi*;
they could not accept that he could have done such a thing.
Instead, they assumed that his trusted vassals must be cloud-

ing his judgment by urging a course of pettifogging and delay. "Some of them are calling for your head," Shibusawa added, meaning not to inform on his friends, but rather to attempt to use public opinion as a lever to influence Hiraoka and get him to toughen his stance on foreign policy.

Before he came into power, Hiraoka had been an ardent exclusionist, like the other patriots, but once allied with the powerful Hitotsubashi and given his own influence on the edges of national politics, it appeared to Shibusawa that Hiraoka had gone soft. He had seemingly cast aside the purity of *sakoku joi*, "close the country and expel the barbarians," in favor of a doctrine of *kaikoku haigai*, "open the country and venerate the foreigners."

"Be careful," Shibusawa warned.

As a result of this conversation, Hiraoka became extremely cautious, refraining from going out after dark and shunning company. Still, he was unable to turn away old friends and longtime companions, whom he would receive as always. His guests grilled him. One time, cornered, he burst out with angry bravado, "Look here, I'm no advocate of a wait-and-see policy. I am and always have been a believer in exclusionism. The spirit of Tokugawa Nariaki runs deep in my veins!"

"Then who is feeding the minister with such ideas?" his inquisitors pressed.

"That would be, ah, Nakane Chojuro," he replied under the pressure of the moment. Of course, no such thing was true. Nakane Chojuro had no political opinions one way or the other; content merely to handle business affairs for the Hitotsubashi family, he was Hiraoka's senior official. Hiraoka came up with his name on the spur of the moment in self-protection, confident that a stick-in-the-mud like Nakane would provide excellent cover. For Nakane, it proved a most unfortunate choice.

Several days later, it rained. On his way home in the evening, Nakane Chojuro went through Kijibashi Gate. As he stepped outside the castle grounds, he tipped his umbrella back and came under sudden attack, umbrella and all. As he crumpled forward, a flurry of sword thrusts caught him about the head, face, and shoulders, leaving him dead with more than two dozen stab wounds.

When Keiki heard what had happened, he ordered an immediate search for the perpetrators, but to no avail. Then Hiraoka Enshiro came to him and said, "Please listen to me. I am to blame." He then confessed all that he could remember of what had transpired.

Keiki listened in silence, staring at Hiraoka with his head cocked slightly, as was his habit, before replying, "No, it is the times that are to blame." But to be precise, the blame lay with Keiki's own overelaborate political schemes. Nakane had been the victim of Keiki's all-too-clever charade, a fact of which Hiraoka was dimly cognizant—for had Nakane not been killed, he, Hiraoka, would have been. Of such niceties, however, Keiki was unaware. He was to that extent a true aristocrat.

In the meantime, Keiki's solo performance in this self-authored script went right on. There was the matter of his resignation, over which Kyoto was understandably up in arms. As far as the imperial court was concerned, and the shogun in Nijo Castle as well, exclusionism was possible only with Keiki's participation. No one else had the position or popularity required to lead Japanese forces against the foreign powers. Messengers from Kyoto arrived one after another, bearing urgent appeals for him to remain in office. By special order of the bakufu, Keiki's elder brother came by to persuade him to change his mind, and even the senior bakufu official in Edo, never a fan of Keiki's to begin with, came to him on the same errand in evident distress. Finally word came from Regent Takatsukasa in Kyoto that the emperor himself commanded Keiki to reconsider. Ever since Keiki's resignation, it seemed, His Majesty had scarcely been able to eat or sleep.

"But His Majesty's determination to expel the foreigners is unswerving. I must remind you that there can be no turning back. He is fully willing to pay the price—even if that price be reducing the empire to scorched earth."

Keiki's heart sank. He had an inkling that the emperor Komei was a man of uncommon fortitude, wisdom, and ability, but because he was surrounded by extremists who kept him in the dark regarding foreign affairs, his grasp of international politics was that of a child. Unbelievably, after Perry's ships arrived, all the emperor ever saw of the event was a single, fanciful portrait of Perry drawn freehand by an Edo *ukiyo-e* artist. In it, Perry had the face of a bull devil, more beast than man. To allow such people near the emperor's domain would defile the land of the gods and insult the ancestors; the military retainers must be prevailed upon to drive the interlopers off. This was the emperor's sole political stance. Yet, unlike court radicals, the emperor was no opponent of the bakufu, but a firm supporter, relying on the bakufu and seeking to use it to set the court at ease. In that sense, he was perhaps more conservative even than the bakufu's own senior councillors.

The emperor's thinking was not likely to undergo a change. Keiki gave up that hope, but otherwise, he was satisfied. After this, now that the court nobles realized how highly the emperor thought of him, his work would surely be easier. That applied equally to the shogunal cabinet, who had all but clung to his sleeves, pleading with him to remain in office; perhaps now he would be able to effect changes making the bakufu more manageable. His little charade had achieved its goal.

"I can no longer in good conscience refuse," Keiki said, replying to one and all that he would make plans to return to Kyoto. His charade had worked—and yet he kept it up, now more than ever, showing consummate skill. He would no doubt die in the coming war, he said, and set about immediately adopting an heir. (He chose his younger brother, Yokumaro.) Not only that, he attempted to remove his wife, Mikako, and his father's widow, Tokushin-in, from the Koishikawa residence. For safety's sake they would be sent away from the fires of war. Nor did he stop there, but encouraged the wives and children of all Hitotsubashi retainers to evacuate as well. People were astonished, but Hitotsubashi appeared quite sane and sober.

"Edo will become a battlefield," he said seriously. These actions of Keiki's (although in fact his family never did flee, since no suitable residence could be found for them in the countryside) deeply impressed the radical exponents of *joi*. "Hitotsubashi is our only hope," they said fervently, relieved that their faith in him had not been misplaced after all. Now if for any reason he failed to carry out his mission, they would know for certain that he had been foiled by the evil machinations of his aides.

9

The Wheel of Fate

On December 6, 1863, Keiki sailed west aboard the bakufu steamer *Hando-maru* on his second visit to Kyoto. Recent events were developing somewhat in his favor. As a result of political turmoil in September during his stay in Edo, the Choshu units had been driven from the capital, along with seven loyalist court nobles, leaving the court empty of reckless proimperial extremists. Another headache had arisen, however: Satsuma, having joined with units from the Aizu domain to drive Choshu from the capital, was now the dominant force in capital politics, in what seemed a virtual reenactment of the ancient turnabout in fortunes of the Genji and Heike. (After being supplanted by the Heike family, their influence in the capital at low ebb, the Genji swept back to power in 1180–1185 under the inspired leadership of Minamoto no Yoritomo. In the end, he subjugated all of eastern Japan and established a military government, inaugurating nearly seven hundred years of warrior rule in Japan.)

Soon after Keiki's departure, Shibusawa Eijiro and his cousin Kisaku called at the home of Hiraoka Enshiro, who was then in Kyoto. Having failed in their attempt to raise an antiforeign army, they were now determined to go to Kyoto to judge the situation for themselves. They wished for convenience sake to make the journey as temporary vassals of Hiraoka Enshiro. Hiraoka had already given his consent, and left word that if they came in his absence, they were to be accommodated. Arrangements were soon made, and the cousins set out for Kyoto overland.

As soon as they arrived, they took lodgings near the temple Higashi Hongan-ji, where Keiki and the rest of his contingent were encamped, and quickly sent word to Hiraoka.

From that day on, the two men frequented the Higashi Hongan-ji temple grounds as if they were full-fledged Hitotsubashi retainers. Hiraoka began to urge them to enter into permanent samurai service with the family. Lacking a daimyo, the Hitotsubashi had few retainers to speak of, he told them; they had brought with them from Edo only two hundred soldiers from the shogunate's military training camp, along with a dozen men borrowed from the Mito, and Hitotsubashi officials. "We lack soldiers, and we lack talented men," said Hiraoka.

These were troubled times, thought Shibusawa. For them to recruit a former farmer like himself, a man who had

planned an armed uprising to bring about the expulsion of
the foreigners and the overthrow of the bakufu, was proof of
that.

Hiraoka told Shibusawa about Keiki's daily regimen. His
favorite food was pork. Was it possible that a man who insisted on having pork sent daily for his delectation from the
open harbor of Yokohama could qualify as a true antiforeign
loyalist, one who would return sanity to the land of the gods?

"Does that shock you?" asked Hiraoka, peering at the
youth, whom he evidently wanted to enlighten, to train to
think as Keiki and he did. "He is particularly fond of riding
horseback," Hiraoka went on. Before dawn every morning
he put a Western saddle on his favorite steed, Lightning
Bolt, and ran it through its paces for two or three hours. He
was fascinated by Western-style horsemanship, and after the
head of the bakufu cavalry in Kyoto, Lord Takashi of Osumi,
came to give him pointers, he picked up the knack so quickly
that he soon surpassed his teacher. At least where pigs and
horses were concerned, Keiki was clearly a man of Western
tastes—anathema to die-hard loyalists.

He liked having his photograph taken too. To commemo-
rate his second entrance into Kyoto, he had had a picture of
himself taken seated formally on a cushion against a background of a dozen rifles standing on end. Hiraoka explained: "If the loyalists find out about this they will raise
hell, but he swears that the rifle and the four-pound howitzer
are the weapons that will save our country."

Hiraoka summed up by saying of his revered master, "Well,
is he not a man of heroic qualities?" Shibusawa realized the
inherent contradiction in swearing fealty to the Hitotsubashi

after having tried to launch a movement to expel the foreigners and overthrow the bakufu—and yet, the things he heard Hiraoka say about Keiki gradually won him over. Whatever his position on opening the country, Keiki, it seemed to him, might well be the national savior who could lead the country out of its current state of confusion. And there was another consideration. By acquiring the status of a retainer of the Hitotsubashi, on whom the eyes and ears of the world were now focused, he might be able to accomplish something important in life. Shibusawa decided to accept Hiraoka's advice.

There was only one problem: His present status of farmer stood in the way of a formal interview with Keiki. Never mind, counseled Hiraoka, he had an idea. He, Hiraoka, would speak of Shibusawa to Keiki beforehand. Then, early some morning when Keiki was out exercising his horse, Shibusawa was to wait at Matsugasaki and run out when he came by, to make a direct appeal.

Shibusawa laughed. "Sounds like a scene from the life of Toyotomi Hideyoshi!" he declared, mentioning one of the great warlords of the medieval era.

The following morning, Shibusawa put the plan into action. Located to the north of Kyoto, Matsugasaki, or Cape Pines, took its name from the red pines whose green branches covered the hills there. Every morning Keiki rode on horseback from the southern part of Kyoto through the city center, all the way north to Matsugasaki, accompanied by fifty cavalry and twenty men on foot. The cavalry consisted of bakufu riflemen as well as top-ranking instructors in swordsmanship in the bakufu version of a military academy. It was undoubtedly the most formidable security corps in all Japan, apart from the Shinsengumi, the bakufu's crack ronin troops in Kyoto.

Before dawn Shibusawa and his cousin Kisaku concealed themselves in a bamboo thicket, waiting for Keiki and his entourage to pass by. Finally, just as the sky grew light in the east, they heard an earth-shaking thunder of hooves, and Shibusawa ran forward. The entourage galloped right past him. "What fast horses!" he marveled to Kisaku.

Twice they failed. The third time they ran doggedly in pursuit of the cavalry. The security corps was soon in an uproar and came wheeling back, encircling the two men. Shibusawa drew out his unsheathed sword and tossed it on the ground, then knelt down and bowed in Keiki's direction. Keiki drew on his reins and beckoned to Shibusawa with his whip. His figure appeared to Shibusawa to be enveloped in radiance, that of a man destined to play a major role in history.

As in a dream, Shibusawa approached him; as in a dream, he spoke to him. He made an earnest summation of his appraisal of the times, but afterward could not remember a word he had said. When he had finished, Keiki nodded slightly and said shortly that he would speak to Hiraoka. Then he turned his horse around and rode off. That was all; and yet Shibusawa thought fervently that for such a noble man he could gladly give his life.

The next day, Shibusawa went to see Hiraoka and found that the punctilious Keiki had already seen to details, including the matter of his status. He was to be an inner guard with a stipend of four *koku*, enough for two. There would be a small additional allowance to support his residence in Kyoto.

Early in the following year he was promoted, becoming able for the first time to ride in a long-poled palanquin on journeys, and commanding spearmen of his own. The signs all pointed to an era of endemic war not very different from the Age of the Warring States.

With his second return to Kyoto, Keiki sought to establish absolute authority over the political world, with the court, the nobles, and the daimyo all in his control. There seemed no other way to disentangle the chaos.

Soon after arriving, Keiki moved out of the Higashi Hongan-ji and into an empty house belonging to the Sakai of Wakasa. To his new, more permanent quarters he summoned for frequent conference his three ever-faithful cronies Matsudaira Shungaku of Echizen, Date Munenari of Uwajima, and Shimazu Hisamitsu, the regent lord of Satsuma. Yamanouchi Yodo of Tosa was another of their number, but he was a man of shifting and unpredictable moods whose appearances were rare.

"Let's call these the 'meetings at the home of the shogunal guardian,'" suggested Keiki.

Each of the men assembled there was leader of a great domain; no other members of the military elite were as well versed in the affairs of the realm as they. Keiki sought to use these meetings to forge a political nexus with which to oversee both the court and the bakufu. And yet they were all four of them stubborn and willful men. There was immediate discord. Even Shungaku, the most easygoing among them, had begun to harbor doubts about Keiki.

"Does he think that ingenuity alone is enough to rule the

country?" he grumbled. "He comes up with too many devious plans; you can never take the man at his word."

Keiki, for his part, had never placed any faith in Shimazu Hisamitsu. Satsuma intended to use the power of the court to abolish the Tokugawa bakufu and set up a government of its own, he suspected. It was the suspicion harbored by every member of the bakufu, one that went a long way to explain the political maneuverings of the Satsuma loyalists. At the moment, they had the court in their pocket. The emperor's three most trusted aides (Prince Nakagawa, former regent Konoe Tadahiro, and Regent Nijo Nariyuki) were virtual puppets of Satsuma, which paid the bulk of their living expenses—and those had lately undergone a dramatic surge. Satsuma's vast outpouring of energy, money, and grain on Kyoto was certainly uncommon. Before long, the "meetings at the home of the shogunal guardian" broke off due to internal dissension, while Satsuma Hisamitsu and his followers were preaching to the emperor and the nobles, beginning to make them unlikely converts to throwing open the doors of Japan.

At first Keiki was unaware of this development. He took occasion one day to tell senior councillor Sakai Tadashige and other bakufu officials, "ridding the country of foreigners is no longer a viable option. Rather than allow a rift between the court and the bakufu based on such an unenforceable policy, why not issue an unequivocal order now for opening the country?"

No one responded.

"Why are you silent?" Keiki was incredulous. Suffering under constant pressure from foreign countries as they were, the cabinet members would be quick to see the merit of his plan, he had assumed.

Finally Sakai spoke up: "Sir, are you aware of the recent doings of the Satsuma?"

It seemed that the behind-the-scenes maneuvering by the Satsuma elements had succeeded in converting the emperor's aides to a position in favor of opening the country to foreign trade.

The senior council was of the opinion that to side with Choshu exclusionism one day, and Satsuma moderation and readiness to accommodate foreigners the next, would leave the bakufu shorn of all dignity. Moreover, a change in policy now would cause Satsuma prestige to soar beyond recall. If Keiki insisted on carrying out this plan, the entire cabinet was prepared to resign forthwith.

Hearing this, Keiki dropped his fan and sat in stunned silence. Ordinarily, he would have laughed at them as a bunch of stubborn old fogies, foolish and narrow-minded, and declared, "This is why the authority of the Tokugawa bakufu is in such decline!" But he was in no position to speak his mind. He was aware that he stood at a crucial crossroads. If he spoke up in favor of opening the country, siding with Satsuma, those who had always been suspicious of him would feel vindicated. Rumors that he was in league with Satsuma, seeking to grab power for himself, would swirl around him and he would be ostracized as a traitor. If he opposed Satsuma, on the other hand, and appeared to stand up for antiforeign feeling, he would gain the trust and confidence of the bakufu. Although their representative, Keiki had never been taken into their bosom. He chose what was politically

the wisest and most expedient course: to firm up his standing with his base of power, casting his principles aside.

"Very well. Let Yokohama be closed," he declared, his
mind racing. The closing of Yokohama Harbor had been a
pet demand of antiforeign extremists in the court ever since
the rise of Choshu. Time and again, the bakufu had been
pressed. The closing of an open harbor, effectively dumping
foreign consuls and trading houses into the sea, would
doubtless provoke foreign armies into action. In that case,
said Keiki, he would not back away from war. The enemy
now was Satsuma.

They would need the court on their side. Keiki sought the
thinking of Matsudaira Shungaku and Date Munenari, hoping to gain their sympathy, but found to his surprise that Satsuma elements had gotten to both of them already,
converting them to their way of thinking. Keiki knew he was
defeated.

Then he sent Hiraoka Enshiro and Hara Ichinoshin to
sound out the views of Prince Nakagawa and others in the
court, and learned it was only a matter of time before the issuing of an imperial edict. Again he found himself outmaneuvered and isolated.

First Choshu, now Satsuma, was issuing its own imperial
edicts, he thought, covering up his sense of personal defeat
in a wave of indignation. It was an outrage. For all practical
purposes, Japan had no official government at all.

Keiki mounted a countercampaign. First he won over
Prince Nakagawa, a Satsuma lobbyist, and succeeded eventu-
ally in getting a directive issued to close Yokohama. Shimazu
Hisamitsu, Matsudaira Shungaku, and Date Munenari

protested vigorously, and Shungaku was so incensed that he privately declared Lord Hitotsubashi had lost his mind. The three met with Keiki and grilled him, only to find themselves immediately on the defensive.

"You are wrong," he told them bluntly. "You of all people, Shungaku—why, you know very well that when you were political director, you wanted the harbor closed! But let us leave the past alone. Let me speak rather of the present situation. The opening of Yokohama and the other harbors has caused prices to soar, bringing great suffering to the people. Clearly, the open harbors have done harm. If only one of the three, Yokohama, were to be closed, why should anyone raise a fuss?" He adopted an extreme antiforeign stance, surpassing even the Choshu radicals of old.

The three men exchanged glances, astonished at Keiki's apparent volte-face, and left without a word. Shimazu Hisamitsu, however, embarked on a plan of his own to upset Keiki's design. His goal was to see that Prince Nakagawa used his influence to have the order to close Yokohama rescinded. The prince, obligingly changing sides yet again, lent Shimazu his support, and the Satsuma maneuverings succeeded. The court officials were men of no settled convictions.

By this time the shogun Iemochi had returned to Kyoto, and was settled in Nijo Castle. As Keiki was sitting in the business office of the castle, Iemochi entered and proposed a drink. Matsudaira Shungaku, Date Munenari, and Shimazu Hisamitsu were also summoned, and Iemochi himself poured drinks all around. After the shogun had retired to his private quarters, Shimazu drew close to Keiki and began to speak in a confidential tone.

That morning his retainer, Takasaki Chotaro, had been in-vited to the residence of Prince Nakagawa, where he had been told that the order to close Yokohama Harbor was is-sued mistakenly, that it was not in fact the emperor's wish, and that it should therefore be regarded as a dead letter. "I thought you ought to know," concluded Shimazu.

Keiki stared at the three men, at a loss for words. Never had he suffered such a gross insult. It was insulting not only to him personally, but to the entire bakufu as well. An impe-rial directive issued via Prince Nakagawa was genuine insofar as the men of Satsuma were concerned, wasn't it, and yet false where he came in?

He couldn't let this pass. Now was the time to stop such meddling in affairs of state. Unless he could cut those peo-ple off and take personal charge of presenting any and all imperial orders to the bakufu, the nation's ills would be im-possible to cure.

He got up and said, "I'll go call on the prince immediately. Come with me. We'll have it out with him." Reluctantly, the other men also stood up, and together they left the castle, Keiki half dragging the others to Prince Nakagawa's house.

In years past, the prince—then known as the Lion—had been a radical exponent of exclusionist thinking. After the Ansei Purge, he had become a supporter of the bakufu, and was now a ringleader of the pro-Satsuma elements in the court. It took him no time to figure out the meaning of this unexpected visit. Sensing a need to lighten the mood of the gathering, he sent out a hasty order for drinks and snacks, playing the gracious host. Keiki, seeing what he was up to, used the ploy to his own advantage.

"These cups are too small," he said, and had the page pour his drink into the inverted lid of his soup bowl instead. Keiki, not a drinker at this stage of his life, astonished his companions that evening with the quantity of sake he consumed. Soon even his arms and legs were bright red, and he was the very picture of a drunk. His eyes glared.

"Is it true, what I have heard?" he said, alluding to the announced retraction of the imperial directive.

Cornered, the prince tried to talk his way out of it by saying that he had no memory of ever having said such a thing to men of Satsuma, but the presence of Shimazu Hisamitsu made that story untenable. After a while, he fell silent.

"This is unpardonable!" Keiki thundered. "Does Your Highness mean to toy with the nation of Japan?" The full tide of his eloquence was turned on the hapless prince. His voice always rang enough to shake the dust on the rafters, yet possessed subtle cadences that had a dramatic effect. He was a born actor. After a while, he raised his voice yet a notch higher, lashing out, "The sinister plans of the Satsuma are known across the land."

All present turned pale. Shimazu Hisamitsu gripped his formal *hakama* so hard that the blood vessels on the backs of his hands appeared to tremble. Shungaku and Munenari suffered Keiki's wrath as well, having been involved like Hisamitsu in the "sinister plans" in question. As he always did when excited, Shungaku moistened his lower lip by chewing on it sideways. Date Munenari, whose hair was already grizzled at age thirty-eight, seemed unsure how to receive the stinging rebuke of a man ten years his junior. Setting his sake cup down, he assumed a stony look, directing his gaze at the darkened ornament over the nail head in the side of the alcove pillar. It bore a floral design, that of a sixteen-petaled chrysanthemum.

Keiki paid no attention to the general shock caused by his harsh words. "All because Your Highness gave ear to the wicked designs of Satsuma, you went back on your word, and brought about this terrible misdeed. If the word of a Satsuma retainer is to be accepted, and that of the shogunal guardian ignored, the nation of Japan is finished. In that case, I meant to cut you down for the good of the nation and then take my own life, and for that purpose I brought with me a blunt sword. But now it seems you have indicated that the actual circumstances are different. So be it. I will pursue it no further. Let me say only that when the august pronouncements, orders, and personal missives of the emperor are countermanded so that a single court official can use them as a vehicle for the expression of his personal opinion, offered casually on his own authority to a daimyo's vassal, the country cannot stand. Let it be understood that from now on, the bakufu will no longer seek the emperor's approval or permission on any matter, but will conduct the nation's business as it sees fit. Is that clear?"

Keiki paused. The prince sat with shoulders drooping, unable to speak. Keiki watched him steadily, biding his time, then turned to the three men behind him and spat out, "As for you three, you are the biggest fools and the worst villains in all Japan."

The three looked up in disbelief. In all the centuries of Tokugawa rule, no other daimyo ever received such a harsh dressing-down as they. Keiki was not being ironical or clever;

he was speaking straight from his gut, out of deep conviction. The three men may have prided themselves on their wisdom and patriotism, and no doubt their intentions were the best, but they had trampled on the great principle that authority for the affairs of the nation must reside with the bakufu, getting in with foolish members of the highest court aristocracy and seeking to use them to promote their own views, thereby confounding the nation's course. Their intelligence made them dangerous. At the same time, their failure to comprehend that even though they were not outright opponents of the bakufu, their actions could only lower Tokugawa prestige made them great dunces. To Keiki, Japan's only hope lay in unifying the theory and administration of the state. In that sense, these three men posed a worse threat to the nation's future than any Choshu radical. Nor were they the only ones.

Keiki lifted his head and looked straight at Prince Nakagawa. This man, the emperor's favorite at court, was the greatest obstacle of all. Keiki had prepared to give bitter vent to his anger and contempt, but wound up speaking ironically.

"Tell me," he said, "just what was it that made you place your confidence in these three? Eh? Oh, of course, Shimazu Hisamitsu, here, is in charge of financial affairs. That must be what makes you so tractable."

The implication was clear: Because he was receiving money from Satsuma, he allowed himself to be ordered around. The prince mustered a protest.

"Don't try to defend yourself," said Keiki. "Starting tomorrow, I'll be offering *you* treasure money instead of him, so from now on, you do what I say." With scathing irony he indicated that the prince was an unprincipled villain, motivated solely by greed. "So from now on," Keiki repeated, his speech more and more slurred, "don' ever turn up your nose at me, the shogunal guardian, again. Don' ever mix me up with these three horses' asses. Make sure ya don't forget it."

With that, Keiki fell forward heavily, collapsing on the small table in front of him. Dishes smashed, soy sauce spattered, and the sake holder fell over. Keiki lay motionless on the floor, dead drunk, oblivious. He had to demonstrate in this way how very drunk he was. Should his harsh language come back later to haunt him, he could always say that he had spoken under the influence of too much strong drink, that he had no memory of anything he had said.

The sight of Keiki lying passed out cold on the floor took the others aback. "What should we do?" asked Shungaku in a low voice. Keiki would have to be carried to the front door. They could have their retainers do the job, but for a man of Keiki's importance to be physically manhandled by men of such low ranking would be unseemly. No, the three of them, whom Keiki had only now called horse's asses, had no choice but to tote him out themselves.

"Don't ask me to do it," declared Shimazu Hisamitsu, unable to conceal his anger. Though not a strong man, Shungaku was forced to bend down beside the unconscious figure, take hold of an arm, and drape it across his shoulders. Date Munenari supported the torso, his long, stern face even longer and sterner than usual.

This incident left Keiki isolated from his supporters. Yet Keiki had never been one to fear isolation. He devoted himself to strengthening his political position in Kyoto, without regard for the feelings of others.

Soon after this Keiki chanced to learn that Shimazu had petitioned the regent on a matter of vital importance: defense of Osaka Bay. He proposed to erect batteries along the shore and station large numbers of soldiers there so that when foreign battleships came up and attempted to occupy the capital, Satsuma forces would be ready to fight them off. But both the bakufu and the other domains interpreted Satsuma's intentions differently. As they saw it, the only real reason for Satsuma to position an army in Osaka, so near the capital, was to watch and wait for a chance to occupy Kyoto themselves in a sweeping coup d'état. Nijo Castle buzzed with rumors.

Probably it was true, Keiki admitted to himself. Satsuma no doubt did have some such plan in mind. He sought by taking the initiative to destroy their hopes of succeeding. For that reason his retainer Hiraoka Enshiro approached the court, negotiating particularly with Prince Nakagawa. Since the Hitotsubashi had taken over the handling of financial affairs ever since that night when Keiki administered a tongue-lashing, the prince had yielded to their request and obtained a direct imperial order from the emperor, about which not even the regent knew anything. At the same time, to head off a Satsuma coup, Keiki asked to be named to a new post to guard the security of the palace, and this too was done. Officially, Keiki was now "Commander of Sea Defense and Governor of Palace Security," thus shoring up his position in Kyoto and Osaka alike. Public opinion, however, did not follow along.

Voices in the bakufu were heard to say, "There's no telling what he's up to. After all, Kyoto already has a protector—Matsudaira Katamori, lord of Aizu." In Edo, Lord Hitotsubashi's planned "rebellion" was openly discussed, sparking such antipathy toward Keiki that people avoided saying his name. Instead, they called him "Two-faced One," because (they said) he meant to overthrow the shogunate and make himself Son of Heaven.

Another name they called him by was "Swine-eater." That appellation was particularly offensive, for it implied not only that he had a revolting taste for the flesh of beasts, but also that a man of such unnatural proclivities was a strange creature capable of God-knew-what perfidy. In fact, no one in the bakufu was favorably disposed toward Keiki. With the single exception of chief councillor Itakura Katsukiyo, they were all his enemies.

Even the men of Satsuma spread false rumors that he was an ambitious malcontent, a "crafty schemer the likes of which has never been seen." For some, it went beyond rumormongering. There were those, like the Satsuma leader in Kyoto, Okubo Ichizo, who did not doubt it to be so.

No sooner had Keiki taken over his new office than he summoned Hiraoka and ordered him to muster an armed force. The Hitotsubashi family, too, had need of soldiers. Keiki's new duties required him to have at least as many soldiers under his command as there were in the troops of the large domains stationed in Kyoto. Eventually, a major recruitment would have to be undertaken, but in the meantime Hiraoka borrowed two hundred men from Mito. In so doing, he inadvertently deepened popular suspicions. Keiki was thought to be in league with antiforeign elements in the Mito domain, bent on occupying Kyoto and seizing national power for himself. Even Prince Nakagawa, who was in league with Keiki, warned Hiraoka that allowing a large body of antiforeign, radical Mito troops to camp in Kyoto would only sow distrust.

One after another, various daimyo in Kyoto began to leave. By early summer Shungaku, Munenari, and Hisamitsu had all returned to their home fiefs, and in the capital the tension of the past few years began to wane, yielding to a sense of the impermanence of all things. This suited Keiki very well, but voices in Satsuma whispered, "Kyoto is all but deserted. This is just what Choshu will be wanting." Men of Choshu who had been lying low at home ever since the previous year's political disaster were now engaged in secret maneuverings to recover their lost ground in the capital. Disguised as ronin, peddlers, and the like, they infiltrated the city in large numbers, responsible for citywide acts of carnage. Among the best known of their victims were Matsuda Kanae of Aizu and Takahashi Kennojo, Prince Nakagawa's retainer, felled by unknown offenders out to wreak heaven's revenge.

The bakufu also conducted its own investigation. On July 8, 1864, when it was learned that the spy ronin were to assemble at the Ikedaya, an inn in central Kyoto, the Shinsengumi were sent in ambush, killing and capturing many.

This incident enraged extremist *shishi* across the country, who assumed that Keiki was behind it, and therefore they concentrated their full malevolence against him. Posters went up all around the city denouncing Keiki as instigator.

"Lord Hitotsubashi used evil designs to capture and kill men who were loyal to the emperor and lovers of justice. His lodgings should be torched!" declared one. Another said, "Recent events are all his doing. Hitotsubashi is the greatest offender in the empire, and must have his divine punishment meted out soon."

Some ten days later Hiraoka Enshiro set out from Keiki's inn, turning east. Despite the blistering summer heat, he was neatly and properly dressed, and he walked along erect, his fan unopened in one hand. With him were two attendants and a subordinate, Kawamura Keijuro, the son of a country samurai with whom Hiraoka had become familiar while on exile in Kai. When Hiraoka returned from political exile, he had recommended this youth for a post with the Hitotsubashi family as well. More swordsman than scholar, Kawamura accompanied Hiraoka wherever he went.

When they came to the Horikawa Bridge, a voice called out to Hiraoka from an alleyway to the right, and Hiraoka made the mistake of turning and looking that way. Thugs leapt out and blocked his path. With lightning speed one of them slashed his sword down, slantwise, from Hiraoka's right shoulder across to the ribs on his left. The wooden fence around the building on Hiraoka's left was sprayed red with his blood. That one blow proved fatal.

Instantly, Kawamura Keijuro flashed his sword crosswise at the assassin, cutting him down, then raised his sword over his head and brought it slicing down on the head of another man. As he did so, the rest of the gang killed Hiraoka's two attendants and then split up, fleeing in all directions. The streets were dark. Wounded, Kawamura chased after two of the men before he was forced to give up. The two thugs escaped down Horikawa Avenue, finally stopping exhausted before a flower shop. There, one disemboweled himself with his sword, and the other held his blade upside down and stabbed himself in the throat. They lay together, lifeless, in the street. For assassins, they died magnificent deaths, and the incident was long remembered in that neighborhood.

It was past midnight when Keiki heard the news. With him in his room that night was a sloe-eyed girl from Edo called O-Yoshi. Hearing excited cries, Keiki threw on his clothes inside the mosquito netting and put on his sword. He was nimble. Few men of his background could have moved with such alacrity.

"Sanmi-sama," said O-Yoshi, calling Keiki by the name she and the other women reserved for him. She too had quickly dressed, careful to make no noise. "What is it?"

Keiki said nothing. The spate of posters in the streets calling for his demise left little doubt in his mind as to the nature of this disturbance. He assumed that a band of assassins had burst into the building. Finally, however, in another room he found out the truth: Hiraoka was dead.

"Who did it?" he demanded, but no one knew yet. In the morning an examination of the bodies would no doubt yield information.

Keiki returned to his chamber, but he was still breathing hard. To calm himself down, he lit two candles. O-Yoshi, feeling extraneous, started to leave, but he implored her to stay, turning to this young daughter of an Edo tradesman a look of vulnerability and fear such as he had never shown anyone in the daytime.

"Hiraoka died in my stead," he said, and wept, burying his face in his hands. But his next words showed his aristocratic upbringing: "He died as he would have wished to die." It was the duty of a samurai to die for his master, and so this was as it should be. Still, the question remained: Who had done it, and whose side were they on?

There was no dearth of people antagonistic to Keiki and Hiraoka on either side of the great debate. They included hatamoto loyal to the bakufu who looked on Keiki as a traitor; political adversaries in Satsuma; and now military adversaries in Choshu. Keiki no longer had any friend in the whole realm. About the only person who would follow him blindly anymore was O-Yoshi. Or perhaps her father, a member of the Edo fire-fighting brigade.

Before leaving Edo, Keiki had told Hiraoka and another man, Kurokawa Kahei, that to keep from getting homesick while he was away, he wanted to take an Edo woman with him. To make such requests of them was unusual, but Keiki knew he had no choice. His wife, Mikako, was jealous by nature; if he had asked one of the other women in the household to see to it, she would have been sure to find out, and then there was no telling what she might have done.

Keiki could not sleep if he went so much as one night without a woman. It was no doubt a legacy from his father, Nariaki. And yet he was particular about women, having no use for any from Kyoto. This was in part because his wife was from there; he had his fill of Kyoto women through her. Keiki had once specified a preference for daughters of Edo tradesmen, so Kurokawa had already set up an arrangement with his friend the firefighter, Shinmon Tatsugoro. That was how Keiki and Tatsugoro came to know each other.

In Kyoto, Keiki felt the need for a firefighter, and sent for Tatsugoro. The firefighter jumped at the chance, declaring himself determined to serve Keiki for the rest of his life. Choosing a company of two hundred men to go with him, he boarded the bakufu steamer and headed west. Currently he was responsible for guarding Keiki's residence, supplying manpower, and handpicking twenty of his followers for training in Western-style infantry.

Morning broke, and an official came to report the identities of the bodies. To everyone's astonishment, they proved to be Mito retainers named Hayashi Chugoro and Ebata Teishichiro, two of the most radical members of the antiforeign faction.

"Mito men, were they?" Keiki was stupefied. If even retainers of the Mito family, which he had been born into, had started turning against him, then in all the sixty-plus provinces of Japan there was no longer anywhere he could turn for succor.

After Hiraoka's death, a rumor circulated among Hitotsubashi retainers that it had all started when a gang of exclusionists, acting on the assumption that someone in the Hitotsubashi family was a villain, called first at the home of Hara Ichinoshin. Hara had once modeled himself after the senior councillor Takeda Kounsai, and was known as a diehard, fanatical believer in *joi*. Keiki took a liking to his mettle and intelligence, and received permission from the Mito family to make him his personal strategist.

In point of fact, however, it was Keiki who became the

other's teacher. Hara Ichinoshin did not become Keiki's adviser so much as he was baptized into Keiki's beliefs, casting aside his own stubborn opposition to foreigners on the tenth day of his new position. Opposition to foreigners had a certain ideological purity, but it was certainly not practical politics. Without fanfare Hara became an advocate of opening the country. Mito patriots in Kyoto were quick to detect his conversion. "Ichinoshin is a foxy fellow," they said, and accused him of taking possession of Keiki with his foxy wiles. These were the only terms on which they could make sense of Keiki's inscrutable, quick-change political acrobatics. Together they trooped to Hara's house and censured their old comrade. Finally, aggravated at their accusations, Hara announced that he was not the traitor. All right, then, who was? demanded his fanatical accusers. Had he given them no name, Hara himself would doubtless have been slain on the spot. Pushed for an answer, Hara had yelled, "It is Hiraoka Enshiro!"

The day after Hiraoka was cut down, an ancient *waka* was copied out in a woman's hand on a slip of paper and hung from the branch of a tree in the garden of Keiki's residence:

The world is a wheel of fate
Turning without fail.
Good and bad alike
Each has its turn and
Comes around again.

Once before, a similar indiscretion on Hiraoka's part had led to the death of Nakane Chojuro outside Kijibashi Gate by Edo Castle. Hiraoka had now paid for that indiscretion, in full. Just as Nakane's death had paved the way for Hiraoka, so now that of Hiraoka would do the same to Hara. Written purposely in a woman's hand by an anonymous family retainer, the poem was a pointed reminder that nothing guaranteed Hara himself would not meet the same fate.

"Fate, is it?" murmured Keiki to himself, gazing at the message in his garden and wondering whether it was meant as a slander of himself. He then dismissed it from his mind. For a liege lord, there could be neither weakness nor defeat. All blame for weakness and defeat went, rather, to his advisers. This was a defining principle of the relationship between lord and retainer, comprising the chief glory of the feudal age. Having been born and raised a feudal lord, even Keiki, a man of unparalleled sensitivity, was dense in this one matter. That his acrobatics in the political arena cost lives, leaving the road littered with the bodies of his loyal strategists, was something he never understood.

The Skirmish at Hamaguri Gate

I<small>F</small> K<small>EIKI</small> <small>BE</small> <small>REGARDED</small> <small>AS</small> <small>AN</small> <small>ACTOR</small>—<small>WHICH</small> <small>HE</small> <small>WAS</small>, <small>AND</small> <small>A</small> very good one, too—his was a stage where the curtain never came down.

The raid on the Ikedaya Inn and the assassination of Hiraoka in Horikawa both occurred in the same month, July 1864. Then, at the end of that month, Choshu units were transferred to the Osaka area by ship, landing at Osaka Bay and proceeding to the capital; there they cut off access to three main roads and encircled the city, leaving only the northern road open. A heated debate broke out among the court nobles as to whether or not the emperor should be taken out by that road and deposited on Mount Hiei for safekeeping. Courtiers and ladies-in-waiting scurried back and forth through the palace, while flying rumors caused unheard-of chaos.

As governor of palace security, Keiki had the job of leading the troops of the various domains in quelling disturbances in Kyoto. Moreover, he was attracted to military affairs. His cultural hero at this time was not the civilian president George Washington, founding father of the United States, but Napoleon I—a military man who imposed order in France and was invincible in battle against foreign powers before becoming emperor. Still, for the time being Keiki kept his troops stationed around the imperial palace, reluctant to make a move. Instead, he sought determinedly to persuade Choshu to withdraw of its own volition. For three weeks, the face-off continued. At night the sky burned flame red with campfires of Choshu soldiers to the west and south, sending shivers through those at court.

Rumors that Keiki was in league with Choshu abounded, not only there but in the bakufu, as well as among the men of Aizu and Satsuma. Keiki the Machiavellian schemer had secretly joined hands with Choshu and would use this incident to overthrow the empire, people said. *Sonno joi*—revere the emperor, expel the barbarians—was the old Mito rallying cry, and the current heirs and executors of that philosophy were men of Choshu. Why should Keiki despise them, after all? This was how people reasoned.

In fact, Keiki was not free of bias in his relations with the two domains. Satsuma he hated till his dying days, but against the ultranationalistic Choshu he never bore any grudge. In old age he explained the difference this way:

Choshu had a kind of innocence. From the first, they held high their anti-Tokugawa banner, making it clear that they were our enemy. That's what I liked about them. Satsuma was different. Until the very end, they were touting *kobu-gattai* [union of the imperial court and the shogunate], making out that they were my ally, and adopting a conciliatory tone—only to turn at the last possible moment, draw out a gleaming dagger, and stab the bakufu in the heart. Such craftiness is an abomination.

It was the same now. Seeing a chance to annihilate the Choshu forces, Satsuma advisers urged attack with such rabidity—surpassing even the staunchly proshogunate Aizu in their zeal—that they seemed on the verge of launching a sortie of their own. The Satsuma leader Saigo Takamori sent an urgent letter home warning of rampant rumors that Hitotsubashi might strike a deal with Choshu. Satsuma had every reason to be concerned. The sight of the Choshu forces encircling the city left Prince Nakagawa and former regent Konoe frightened and distraught, seemingly on the point of switching allegiance. Should that happen, Satsuma influence at court would vanish overnight. If Hitotsubashi Keiki did join forces with Choshu, court officials would be bound to follow suit. Satsuma would then find itself given the gate by an alliance of bakufu and Choshu troops.

"Do you realize that Satsuma is getting impatient?" said the newly ensconced Hara Ichinoshin to Keiki. Keiki nodded. Satsuma's mounting agitation was well known to him. That was all the more reason why he refrained from issuing a declaration of war, in order to rouse Satsuma nervousness to fever pitch—a sign of his underlying spitefulness toward that domain. He still had the upper hand over Satsuma, and his strategy was winning out.

"In the end, what will you do, sire?" asked Hara.

"Strike."

Hara slapped his knee, apparently delighted to find that Keiki's intentions paralleled his own. In any case, this attack by Choshu forces had brought Keiki the blessed relief of rain after a long drought. Until then, he had been cast aside by one and all, friend and foe alike, horribly isolated. Now, however, people were uniting against their common foe, Choshu, and at least temporarily, they all were under Keiki's command. The courtiers, too, had only Keiki's military powers to fall back on. Even the armies of Choshu bore Keiki no particular grudge. The reason for their advance was, as their flag declared, to fight the probakufu forces of Satsuma and Aizu. Their other flag bore the motto *sonno joi*. To Keiki, their sincerity and ingenuousness were palpable.

"What are our prospects?" asked Hara.

"Oh, it will be easy. We will wipe them out in a single action."

It would have been hard to disagree. Protecting the court was an allied force consisting of troops of twenty-five domains stationed in Kyoto; the core of its strength were the Satsuma and Aizu forces, strongest in the land. Choshu had embarked on a battle it had no prayer of winning.

"Poor Choshu," sighed Hara Ichinoshin later to Kurokawa Kibei and Shibusawa Eijiro after leaving Keiki's presence and returning to the business office. Hara customarily referred to the men of Satsuma as "sweet potatoes," after the crop for which their province was known. "Choshu is falling into the trap of those sweet potatoes. Four times now they've been warned to withdraw, but they foolishly refuse. If they would only withdraw their soldiers, Satsuma would be disappointed, and all its scheming would come to nothing. If Choshu refuses to listen and opens hostilities, the only winners will be the sweet potatoes."

Keiki had no interest in using the allied troops to further beef up Satsuma's military might, and therefore put off issuing a declaration of war as long as he could. But on August 20, the Choshu loyalist army surrounding Kyoto on three sides swung into action, one unit reaching the area of the palace at just past five in the morning. By six they had stormed the gates and opened an artillery engagement, thus officially inciting a revolt.

Around four-thirty A.M., Keiki learned that the Choshu troops had started their drive toward the capital. O-Yoshi was with him that night. When a retainer outside the cedar door announced the movements of enemy troops, Keiki sprang up and said out loud, "This is it." Yet he still had the presence of mind to say to O-Yoshi through the darkness, "O-Yoshi, are you ready?" Forgetting herself, she answered in the down-to-earth vernacular of an Edo firefighter's wife, "Sure am!" Keiki laughed. His question had meant was she ready to die at her own hand, as befitted a member of a samurai household.

Keiki went to another room to don full ceremonial court dress for a palace visit, issuing a barrage of commands as he did so. The swiftness of his orders and his overall composure impressed his aides, making them think that even if he had lived during the turbulent Warring States period, he would have made himself master of the realm.

No sooner had Keiki left the gate than he leapt astride his horse, raised his whip, and set off at a gallop. In this, too, he set himself apart from other feudal lords of the day. He rode alone, followed by no more than four or five men on horseback. It was still dark out. In Takeya-cho he came upon a pair of foot soldiers running down the narrow street. They wore white headbands and light armor, and ran with lances at the ready. After going another short distance, he passed another pair of soldiers, similarly garbed. As he went by, cracking his whip, he thought with admiration, "Must be Aizu scouts. They run like the wind." Later he learned that they were in fact scouts sent out by the Choshu army's advance guard. The Choshu soldiers, seeing Keiki in his ceremonial dress, had apparently assumed he was a court noble and thought nothing further of it.

Keiki entered the palace. After being received by the regent, he was granted permission to approach the emperor's throne, behind a bamboo screen. "Begin a punitive expedition at once," came the command in the emperor's own voice. It was a low and husky voice, difficult to catch. Until then Keiki's messages from the throne had always come falsified and embellished by court nobles who served as intermediaries—or they had been outright forgeries—so this was for him a singular experience. The divine being had committed the indiscretion of speaking in his own voice, without any intermediary. It was a clear sign of the panic at court.

After Keiki had withdrawn from the emperor's presence

and was making his way down the palace corridors, the regent came running up behind him, accompanied by several
young courtiers.

"Lord Hitotsubashi, Lord Hitotsubashi!" he called. "How
is the war situation? Should the throne be moved?" Should
the emperor be transported to the safety of Mount Hiei, he
meant. The two young men at his side wore ceremonial dress
with their long sleeves bound up as if for work, a very queer
combination.

Keiki spun around. "As long as I, Keiki, am here, and as
long as I am the protector of His Majesty's person, you may
be assured there is no need for alarm." He spoke with his
customary theatrical flair. Given the circumstances, the
courtiers found the grandness of his tone and cadence reassuring.

Keiki left by the back gate and went to change into his
armor and helmet. When he finished dressing, he was a
grand sight. On his head was an *eboshi*, the tall headgear
worn by noblemen, edged with a band of lavender twill,
while over a stomacher of lavender, shaded deeper at the
hem, he wore a *haori* of white wool with a small hollyhock
crest in black. Slung at his hips was a gold-mounted sword
encased in a bearskin sheath. In his hand he held a golden
baton. Thus attired, he made his way out, mounted Lightning Bolt, and rode from the Kuge Gate to the Hamaguri
Gate. His horse bore a tall pole hung with silver-colored
Shinto offerings. Behind him rode ten attendants, including
Hara Ichinoshin; a camp squadron of one hundred; fifty
men of the bakufu-trained rifle corps; one commando unit
of one hundred and fifty men and another of one hundred;

and in the rear, one hundred infantrymen, two hundred men of lowly birth, and twelve artillerymen.

Battle got under way after six A.M. At Hamaguri Gate, Choshu troops prevailed for a time. Eventually, both sides commenced a cannonade, as in and out of the palace soldiers met in fierce hand-to-hand combat. The Aizu troops were frequently put to rout. Troops from Fukuoka abandoned their guard position and stampeded back through the palace entrance for vehicles. Keiki personally bawled them out and sent them back to face the enemy. Strongest of all were the Satsuma troops under Saigo Takamori. Their highly disciplined, controlled movements set them entirely apart from the rest. Midway through the battle they made an enormous advance, finally dealing the Choshu troops a devastating blow and putting them to rout.

By noon it was over, with only mop-up operations in the city, and Keiki went back to the imperial palace to rest. While he rested, Hara Ichinoshin went about listening to the gossip of the court nobles, which he found dealt mostly with Keiki's brilliant generalship and the bravery of the Satsuma troops. If those whispers would go on to shape public opinion, increasing in strength, then, in Hara's view, Hitotsubashi Keiki and Satsuma would reap equal rewards.

The Death of Iemochi

Back in Edo, the shogun Iemochi would be eighteen this year. Told of Keiki's victory by cabinet members, he declared "Splendid!" and beamed with innocent pleasure. When Iemochi declared himself satisfied with Lord Hitotsubashi's accomplishment, members of the senior council instantly assured him that Keiki had succeeded only as a result of Iemochi's own influence. Thus they attempted to discount what Hitotsubashi Keiki had done. His temporary rise in popularity in Kyoto only worsened their own reputations in Edo. To those in Kyoto, suspicions that Keiki would take advantage of his newfound fame and popularity to dominate the court and lead the western daimyo against the bakufu seemed farfetched; in Edo, they were accepted as gospel.

There was no end of circumstantial evidence against him. Mito people were all like that; this, at any rate, was the assumption of shogunal vassals, who saw Mito as a nest of insurrectionist heresy and scheming. Why, it was common knowledge among them that the secret teachings of the Mito actually contained a clause to that effect. And what was one to make of Keiki's recent brandishing of power? History books taught that it was practically a law of nature: A man whose glorious achievements set his lord trembling would seek in time to unseat his lord. Keiki, moreover, was a man who might have been the fourteenth shogun, but for Iemochi.

Once the seed of doubt was sown in Edo, nearly three hundred miles from Kyoto, other doubts continued to surface and grow. Keiki did in fact send a written opinion that this victory should be followed up by pursuing the fleeing Choshu troops, leading allied forces into Choshu territory, and securing a decisive victory in the castle town of Hagi. This was, however, not Keiki's own opinion, but that of Komatsu Tatewaki, a Satsuma elder; the opinion paper had been rather in the nature of a report on the present political climate of the capital, but the cabinet members took a different view.

"O-ho, now it's clear what the Two-faced One is up to," they thought. He covers up his real intention of bringing all of western Japan under his domination by craftily presenting this as Satsuma's opinion, using it to sound out Edo's reaction.

Based on that assumption, they showed the missive to Iemochi and explained it in plain terms. They were not intentionally slandering Keiki; convinced that what they said was true, they were attempting to protect the innocent Iemochi from the man they believed to be the greatest Machiavellian schemer of all time. They loved Iemochi for his gentleness of temper with a love exceeding what was expected of retainers; and the greater their love of Iemochi, the greater their hatred of Keiki. Even among the tea servers at the shogun's camp, it was now commonly accepted that the real danger to the shogun came from neither Choshu nor Satsuma, but from Hitotsubashi Keiki. Ulterior motives were read into every report he sent, however trifling.

For instance, not long after the skirmish at Hamaguri Gate, Keiki petitioned for the shogun to come to Kyoto and lead a campaign against the insurgents in person, adding at the end that the opinion was "shared by everyone at court, from the emperor on down." Unable to take even such a memorial at face value, the bakufu was convinced that Keiki must have some underhanded purpose. They reported to Iemochi that it was not an imperial rescript, but probably represented Keiki's own selfish motives. No answer was sent.

With the new year, the era name changed again. It was now the first year of Keio, 1865. The Choshu issue was becoming ever more entangled. On the one hand, the insurgents gave every appearance of courtesy and allegiance in their relations with the bakufu; on the other, they clearly were preparing rapidly for war. The only way for the bakufu to recover its authority was to attack. The other domains, however, were not eager to fight a useless civil war at a time when drains on their finances were many. Further, they sympathized with Choshu's adverse fortune, and reacted with scant concern to the bakufu's order to mobilize. Even Satsuma, once so eager to cooperate, declared that a second punitive expedition was now impossible. "Even if a war council is held," Satsuma leaders seemed to say, "we will dispatch no troops."

Under the circumstances, it was necessary for the shogun Iemochi himself to take the field. Far from Kyoto, the members of the Edo bakufu surmised that the daimyo would then be stirred to action. Keiki, in Kyoto, knew better. "They will do nothing," he concluded. But to Edo he wisely said nothing of his conviction, all too aware that where Choshu was concerned, opening his mouth served only to deepen suspicions about him.

On June 14, Iemochi entered Kyoto.

Later he went to Osaka, and stayed in Osaka Castle. The castle was to be the bakufu's main headquarters in its campaign against Choshu. The bakufu had no war funds, however, and the daimyo came to no agreement, so the rest of the year went by without the dispatch of a single soldier.

During that time, when Matsudaira Katamori happened to stop by one day to pay his respects, Iemochi remarked, "I've heard that Lord Hitotsubashi harbors rebellious designs against the bakufu. Is it true?"

Never before had the shogun voiced any such suspicions; his statement in itself was a political incident. Taken by surprise, Katamori vociferously denied the rumors, giving example after example of Keiki's blameless conduct. Nor was he simply making excuses on Keiki's behalf—he was convinced that at heart Keiki was indeed loyal to the Tokugawa. He knew that Keiki was both brilliant and wily. Keiki could think faster than most people, and because the logic of his actions was not immediately apparent, and he was so good at playacting, lesser men saw him as a hobgoblin. On hearing Katamori's explanation, Iemochi was ashamed that he had ever doubted Keiki, and with reddened face he took back his words.

When word of this exchange got back to Keiki, he knew for the first time what the gentle shogun thought of him. Rather than displeasure, he felt a deep unworthiness, and shame at his failings. His reaction was a mark of the upbringing he had received as a bulwark of the house of Tokugawa, and also of the ineradicable weakness that that training had created in him.

To some extent, chief senior councillor Itakura Katsukiyo understood that surprising weakness of Keiki's, but the bakufu cabinet members and officials saw him as a figure larger than life, and imagined him driven by the strong, greedy ambition peculiar to giants. Such imaginings reduced his popularity drastically.

Around this time, an incident took place that drove the shogun and the bakufu into a corner regarding the opening of Hyogo (present-day Kobe). The Western powers were urging the opening of the harbor with the pressure of gunboats, and the court was stoutly resisting. Caught in the middle, Iemochi was hard-pressed for a solution. Finally, in desperation, he called his councillors together in the great hall of Osaka Castle and announced his intention to resign: "I hereby resign as barbarian-quelling generalissimo. I intend to inform the court of my decision as soon as possible. Now Hitotsubashi can step in and take over." He asked an aide to write a rough draft of his resignation. This step was a heavy blow to supporters of the bakufu in Osaka, Kyoto, and Edo. One eyewitness wrote, "It was as if everyone in the castles had gone mad."

Keiki, in Kyoto, was told nothing of these developments. Hatamoto, in Osaka Castle, assuming that his nefarious schemes had forced the shogun into this act of desperation, roundly condemned him. One band threatened to set off en masse for the capital, storm Keiki's residence, and cut him down as a traitor. The shogun's bodyguards appointed Captain of the Great Guard Muroga to convey this message to the senior council: "We are of course required to protect a new shogun, but at this time we cannot do so. In the event that we are called upon to do so, we all are prepared to lay down our lives by storming the Hitotsubashi house. Of that you should have no doubt."

On hearing this, Iemochi scowled but at the same time let it be known that he was pleased. Upon receipt of this urgent message, Edo Castle broke into pandemonium. Women ran weeping through the corridors. One even cried out, "If the son of Mito Nariaki enters this place by evil schemes, life will no longer be worth living!" She then jumped down the well with a dagger clenched in her teeth.

Responding in amazement to the shogun's tendering of his resignation over the Hyogo issue, Keiki resolved the situation by calling together everyone at court from the regent on down and arguing with his usual forcefulness and skill, finally resorting to threats and intimidation to get imperial sanction for the treaty. He told the court nobles, "If, after all I have said and done, the court's approval is still not forthcoming, I will have no choice but to take the blame for my failure to serve the shogun adequately, and disembowel myself here and now. If I take my life, there is no telling what my retainers may do to the members of the court in revenge. Are you prepared to face those consequences? If so, then go ahead and do as you like."

With those words he would have stomped out of the room, but the nobles hurriedly stopped him, overturned their disapproval, and voted to accept the treaty. Afterward, Keiki learned just how serious was the plunge in his popularity as a man of Mito among the bakufu officials. He heard about the uproar in the castle, including the commotion in the ladies' quarters, in a letter from the Mito residence in Koishikawa. Even if events moved in such a way that he had a chance of becoming shogun, it seemed to Keiki that as a practical matter, taking the helm of the house of Tokugawa and the bakufu would be well-nigh impossible.

He also gave thought to his current situation, wondering if he still had to go on working for the bakufu despite the cloud of suspicion he was under. He had good reason to be indignant. What surprised even Hara Ichinoshin, who knew Keiki so well, was that he never let slip a word concerning his pent-up grievances. The only sign of emotion he gave was a single remark: He felt "fear and dread," he said, to think that his own existence should be a source of pain to the shogun. Unbelievably to Hara, Keiki said this not to mask his true feelings but apparently in all sincerity. He even seemed to derive a certain keen pleasure in dissipating his emptiness and dissatisfaction by transforming it into "fear and dread."

As far as Hara could tell, the only possible explanation for

Keiki's measured response was his upbringing. Having received a daimyo's education, perhaps he had developed an internal emotional framework that led him to respond that way. Keiki tendered his resignation from the post of commander of naval defense. However, Iemochi withheld permission for him to resign. Next he offered to quit the post of governmental adviser, but again his offer was rejected.

Iemochi remained encamped in Osaka Castle. The year drew to a close, and then it was the new year, 1866, but still no troops were sent to Choshu, despite loud calls for a punitive expedition. Not until July was an advance guard sent west. The following month saw bakufu troops engaged in battle with Choshu forces along the Choshu border, but the military power of the Choshu forces proved overwhelming, and the bakufu troops were routed. News of their defeat was kept from Iemochi in Osaka Castle, his health having seriously deteriorated. Always weak of constitution, the shogun had fallen seriously ill in early August. His condition worsened, and he was diagnosed by his attending physicians as suffering from acute beriberi. Word of his illness was kept a guarded secret. Not even Keiki in Kyoto was informed.

Keiki was at first informed that Iemochi had taken to his bed from light fatigue. The extent of the shogun's illness was not made known to him until August 26. Then he found out that for the past week Iemochi had been unable to keep anything down, and that he had been sleepless for nearly five days. He suffered from endless cramps and convulsions, and his suffering was pitiful in the extreme.

In consternation, Keiki went straight to Osaka, asked at the castle for an audience with the shogun, and was ushered immediately into the sickroom. Iemochi lay in bed, wasted in appearance but looking more fit than Keiki had expected. In response to Keiki's expression of concern, he mustered a smile and spoke a few words, his voice barely audible.

"Just until recently, I could sit up in bed," he rasped, "but today I cannot even do that. Have the doctor fill you in." How was Kyoto? he wanted to know, apparently full of concern despite the gravity of his condition.

Moved, Keiki sought to reassure him. "Things are quiet. That is why I am here now in Osaka, taking things easy for a change." As he said this, he slowly raised the covers at the foot of the futon and massaged Iemochi's legs with both hands. The legs were swollen. After thirty minutes of this, Iemochi dozed off, and Keiki slipped out of the room. He returned to Kyoto after that, but the following night Iemochi's condition suddenly worsened, and shortly thereafter he died. He was twenty years old.

He died without issue.

But he had left instructions about his successor. On leaving Edo, he had turned to his attendants and said, "If I am to take the field, there is no guarantee that I will not fall in battle, or die of illness. If anything happens to me, make Tayasu Kamenosuke the next shogun." Kamenosuke was the son of Tayasu Yoshiyori, head of another collateral branch of the Tokugawa. An elderly woman named Takiyama was entrusted with the shogun's request, and the day that Iemochi left Edo, she reported it to Iemochi's wife, Princess Kazu. The ladies in the Ooku were overjoyed that Keiki had not been chosen, but the bakufu was dismayed.

Tayasu Kamenosuke was barely two years old. That such a

baby could help the shogunate survive this difficult time, with news of defeats in battles against Choshu arriving one on top of another, was unthinkable.

Feeling they had little choice, the shogunal cabinet gained the approval of the court and the leading daimyo to recommend Keiki for shogun. Chief senior councillor Itakura Katsukiyo hurried to Kyoto to persuade Keiki to accept the offer.

Keiki refused. Itakura did his best, but Keiki told him flatly, "It is no use. I have no such intention." He was speaking from the heart. Even if he had accepted the offer, he knew he had no chance of succeeding, saddled with a group of men who bore him such intense ill will. "Let Kamenosuke be the next shogun," he said. "I would gladly be his guardian."

Undaunted, Itakura remained in Kyoto and called on Keiki daily, arguing his case with tenacity. Keiki, equally determined, finally refused to see him. Iemochi's death was being kept secret in the meantime, but rumors were rife. The office of shogun was vacant, people said. In Kyoto, it began to be common knowledge even among the children of merchants. Still, Keiki was resolute, refusing to accede.

"Even if it be of no use," he said over and over again—knowing very well that over the course of time, the act of refusal itself could create a certain political magnetism.

The Arm-twist Drinker

KEIKI WAS A RELUCTANT SHOGUN.

It was August 29, 1866. The previous shogun, Iemochi, lay dead in Osaka. Filled with consternation at Iemochi's sudden demise, the bakufu kept his death secret, and surreptitiously nominated Keiki as successor. The imperial court accepted the nomination as a matter of course, and Matsudaira Shungaku and other leading daimyo entreated Keiki to acquiesce. But Keiki was unyielding.

The days went by without resolution.

On the face of things, Iemochi remained shogun, and official documents continued to be put out in his name, but the actual Iemochi was a corpse tucked away in the recesses of

Osaka Castle, in sweltering heat. The Tokugawa bakufu was ruled by a dead body.

"What are we to do?" exclaimed the emperor Komei, grief-stricken and angry. A man of almost pathological conservatism, he was second to none in his support for the bakufu, and enthusiastically endorsed the current court-bakufu setup. Japan's very identity as a nation, he believed, required the presence of a shogun. As he saw it, Choshu was a rebel domain—and with rebels digging in and fomenting civil war at home, and foreign powers keeping a close eye on Japan from without, ready to invade at the first opportunity, how could the office of "barbarian-quelling generalissimo" be left vacant?

But Keiki, for whatever reason, would not give in.

The bakufu had no other suitable candidates. A handful of people did have some traditional claim on the office, but none was suitable. Little Tayasu Kamenosuke, whom the ladies of the Ooku in Edo were backing for shogun, was a mere infant, and the head of the Tayasu family, Yoshiyori, was a fool. Tokugawa Yoshikatsu, daimyo of Owari, was past his prime. There was no one but Keiki—a fact that Keiki himself, with his sharp powers of discernment regarding personnel matters, knew full well. And yet, to one and all he replied that he would not stand for the office of shogun, reminding them firmly that once he had given his word, he never altered it. That much was certainly true. Among the daimyo, he was sometimes referred to as "Stubborn One."

Perhaps because Keiki was a man of such strong individuality, he had a number of nicknames, of which Stubborn One was about the friendliest. Edo hatamoto hostile to Kyoto called him Two-faced One behind his back, a reference to his close ties with the imperial court—ties they believed might lead him to betray Tokugawa at any time. In private conversations they never referred to him as Minister of the Center Hitotsubashi, his official title, but always as Two-faced. One reason for the nickname, surely, was his origin in the Mito loyalist camp, but the impression he gave of being a clever manipulator lent the name even greater plausibility.

Then there was that other nickname, "Swine-eater," made popular either by hangers-on in the shogun's camp or by Edo commoners. Unlike his father, Mito Nariaki, or Mito scholars who touted Japan as the land of the gods, Keiki was a man of westernized tastes, extending even to his dining habits. Beef and pork were sent daily from Yokohama for his pleasure. This nickname was a contemptuous slur, carrying the implication that he was defiling himself by eating the flesh of four-legged beasts. From the days of Ieyasu on down, never before had anyone associated with the house of Tokugawa been saddled with derogatory nicknames from below.

It was Matsudaira Shungaku, trying hard to persuade Keiki to become Iemochi's successor, who gave Keiki a new sobriquet. "He is what's known as an 'arm-twist drinker,'" he said. The expression commonly referred to the kind of man who twists logic and lashes out at people when drunk. But it had another meaning as well: At banquets, a certain type of man declares he's had enough to drink, and yet when pressed hard enough, goes on to consume a surprising amount of liquor. And unless someone does press him to drink, he is out of sorts. Apparently it was this latter type of "arm-twist drinker" that Shungaku had in mind.

The description came at an important juncture. It was now a full week after Iemochi's passing, and Shungaku had called on Keiki at his residence near Nijo Castle. It was ten in the morning.

Keiki's quarters were small. When Shungaku entered, in the room just inside he found chief senior councillor Itakura Katsukiyo, who had set up camp there to continue reasoning with Keiki. That morning the temperature was already high. Exhausted after his marathon attempts to persuade Keiki, Itakura sat with his neckline slightly loosened—a shocking lapse for a daimyo—as his personal retainer fanned him.

Surprised by Shungaku's entrance, Itakura hastily started to tug his kimono to rights, but Shungaku stopped him. "No, don't bother," he said, and quickly loosened the neck of his own kimono, commenting as he did so that it certainly was a devilishly hot day. The man had a disarming ability to adapt himself to others.

"What's the latest word?" he asked. Itakura, whose rank as chief councillor was equivalent to that of a European prime minister, shook his head despondently. "It's not going well at all," he said. "It's as if Lord Hitotsubashi has forgotten the word 'yes.'"

But after hearing the details of Itakura's exchanges with Keiki, Shungaku smiled. "From what you say, I would say that we have every reason to be hopeful," he said.

"Really?"

"Certainly. I am quite serious. He is what they call an arm-twist drinker. Someone who gives in and has a drink only after a bit of arm-twisting. Give him enough time, and he'll come round."

But arm-twist drinkers generally are unaware of that habit of theirs, and so it was with Keiki now. His rejection of the proposal was by no means a ploy. Rather, he was passionately convinced that it was his duty to refuse. Keiki's intellect gave him an all-too-clear grasp of the existing situation. What good would it do for him to become shogun now?

In the first place, he knew better than anyone that those in Edo whom as shogun he would have to lead held him in slight regard. Indeed, they seemed capable of outright treason. Once he became shogun, bakufu officials would start a slowdown. What was worse for Keiki, not only shogunal vassals felt that way. Even in the Mito family, an anti-Nariaki faction let it be known that in case of Keiki's accession, his life would be in danger—that they were prepared to stop him with force of arms if need be.

A still more awful situation was unfolding in Kyoto. Lords Abe of Bungo and Matsumae of Izu had previously been dismissed from the senior council, and samurai in both their domains laid the blame at Keiki's door. Keiki had heard that at a meeting of domain officials in Kyoto, and a public declaration was made to this effect: "If Lord Hitotsubashi becomes shogun, so that we are required to declare fealty to him, we would not be able to continue living as samurai for a single day. If such a thing comes to pass, we vow to storm his residence, swords drawn." Never before had any man nominated for shogun faced such intense hostility.

"My heart is not set on being shogun," Keiki confided to his closest retainer, Hara Ichinoshin. Yet even Hara doubted whether Keiki was speaking straight from the heart.

That morning, before seeing Shungaku, Keiki had told

Hara, "It is not meant to be. The Tokugawa bakufu is doomed, and the end is not far off, either. It could come in as little as a year; not more than two years, I think. To become shogun now would be like running headlong into a burning building that is already a sea of flames."

It was Keiki's misfortune that he saw the future all too clearly.

"What can I possibly accomplish by becoming shogun now?" he asked. Hara understood. That Japan could no longer be run under the old system was clear to anyone with eyes to see. Up until 1853, the imperial court in Kyoto had served a purely decorative function, but as a result of pressure brought to bear by certain domains and individuals, the court had acquired power of veto over government affairs until now the worst possible situation existed: a system of dual sovereignty. The bakufu was hamstrung, unable to make a single foreign policy decision.

English diplomats, seeing this anomaly, offered an explanation of the national polity and form of government of Japan based on a European-style analysis. Japanese sovereignty resided with the imperial court, they claimed, not with the shogun, who was merely entrusted with power by the court. Hence the French, who understood the shogun to be the crowned head of Japan, were wrong. This opinion was published in the newspaper of the Yokohama settlement, and shared with loyalists of Satsuma and Choshu. Furthermore, they said, the shogun was not even the liege lord of daimyo across Japan.

Unfortunately, the man best equipped to understand this European-style legal analysis was Keiki, who thought it largely accurate. Both Toyotomi Hideyoshi and Tokugawa Ieyasu had been leaders of non-Tokugawa daimyo, not ruling monarchs. They both had been nominated by the other barons to positions at the apex of the feudal system, the one as *kanpaku*, or imperial regent, the other as shogun (an abbreviation of the ancient title *seii tai shogun*, or "barbarian-quelling generalissimo"). When their influence was at its greatest, the shoguns had been able to rule like virtual monarchs over the rest of the daimyo, but with bakufu authority on the wane, and its control over the daimyo weakening, the truth—that the shogun was only a leader, not a ruler—was bound to emerge. The trend was evident in the second punitive expedition against Choshu, now under way. Satsuma had resisted the bakufu's call to mobilize, refusing to dispatch any soldiers. This was because, strictly speaking, an order from the shogun was not the same as an order from one's liege lord. The Satsuma domain did not regard disobedience in this case as an act of disloyalty. Clearly, the shogun lacked the ultimate power of a sovereign.

Success as a leader required strong military power, reflected Keiki. Military might was what had enabled the house of Tokugawa to hold three hundred barons in subjugation for the better part of three centuries. The barons had lived in fear of Tokugawa arms. Now, however, that power was sadly enervated. In the ongoing Choshu campaign, the bakufu troops were losing badly to a tozama domain worth barely 370,000 *koku*. News of defeat had arrived from Choshu battlefields. The shogunate was losing its last vestiges of power. Keiki knew full well what it would mean to step into the office of shogun now.

"It would mean going down in history as a traitor," he told

Hara. The Tokugawa bakufu was destined to fall, but the end would not come naturally, like that of a dead tree felled by the wind. If it only would! Then to be shogun even for a day, and gain the glory of a place among the great Tokugawa rulers, would be fine. But history taught that the collapse of power did not come as peacefully for men as for plants. Keiki was a great believer in history. His roots in the Mito family, cradle of scholars, only intensified that belief—although the Mito view of history was not congenial to his rational mind. His way of thinking, his way of understanding events, were based on history. And history, he noted, contained no examples of an enfeebled power coming to a natural, peaceful end. Someone new would inevitably appear on the horizon, embrace the emperor and brand those in the old order as rebels, then join forces with supporters from all over the country in attack. Keiki, were he to become shogun, would be the target of that attack.

"I'll be damned if I do," he ended defiantly.

After listening to all this, Hara Ichinoshin bowed low with a gasp of amazement at Keiki's sagacity. Even as he did so, it struck him that Keiki was not wholly averse to becoming shogun. Should some other candidate become shogun (limited though the field admittedly was), Keiki would certainly be displeased. In fact, Hara was conducting a discreet campaign to promote Keiki's candidacy, having spoken to both Prince Nakagawa and Matsudaira Shungaku.

Hara was a peculiar man. In Mito, he had been a radical exponent of *sonno joi*, yet on becoming Keiki's aide he had switched sides, convinced of the necessity of opening the country. He had urged Keiki to take the decisive step of sentencing his old comrades, Takeda Kounsai and the rest, to be beheaded; and in the end, his arguments had prevailed. He had eventually gone on to cast aside the doctrine of *sonno*, respect for the emperor, as well.

"Respect for the emperor is a spirit, not a political principle," he was fond of saying. "No matter how arrogant the gentlemen of the court may become, while I'm alive they won't lay a finger on the bakufu."

Hara Ichinoshin was a man of exceptional intelligence and ability. Men of such gifts derive the greatest stimulation from continual testing of their own limits rather than from devotion to a particular cause or belief. Hara's ambition knew no bounds. He had to make Keiki shogun. Once that was accomplished, power over the whole country would be within his, Hara's, reach.

And yet Keiki was wavering, tormented, like a man who wanted to eat blowfish yet feared it might be toxic. It was up to Hara to find some way to remove the "toxins" from the office of shogun—a daunting task, one that would require all his ingenuity.

It appeared to Hara that Keiki was mulling the same problem, no less preoccupied than he. That morning after breakfast he had summoned Hara and said, "Why not just give the game up?" He meant, why not relinquish any claim on political power? This was not a conclusion he had come to after careful thought; rather, he was giving voice to his thoughts even as he worked them out, a habit he frequently indulged with this trusted retainer and no one else. Although still in the process of working out his thoughts, he added, "There is no other way," as if he had come to a firm conclusion.

He was proposing to cast aside the political power of the Tokugawa bakufu. If that power could be likened to a tiger, it was a genuine tiger, to be sure, but a dead one—or if not exactly dead, all but dead, its internal organs nine-tenths failed, its pulse feeble. To inject life into that dying tiger was a task of Herculean proportions. Better to make up their minds to abandon it on the road, for the court to find, or for Satsuma—either way was fine. When pressed to the wall, the only thing to do was change your way of thinking—perform a feat of mental gymnastics. In this case, to accept that the house of Tokugawa would be reduced to a single daimyo. What did Ichinoshin think of that idea? Keiki wanted to know.

"Well—" said Hara, and then stopped. For a few seconds he froze, forgetting to breathe, his eyes fixed on Keiki, before beads of sweat began to break out on his forehead. "If I may say so, sire," he said carefully, "it appears that from time to time you are rather too farseeing." He went overboard in taking the long view, in other words. As Hara saw it, politics required a more direct confrontation with immediate realities. Keiki was himself a Tokugawa nobleman, and yet he spoke of the future of Tokugawa rule with dispassion, dissecting it coldly on the chopping board of history exactly as an ordinary samurai or scholar might, without any sense of personal involvement or responsibility. This would not do. It was most inappropriate for Keiki himself, in a position to become the next shogun at any time, to dismiss the matter as if it were none of his affair.

Then, because he was a provincial man of Mito, he pushed his point home bluntly. "Calamity begins behind the lord's screen, they say." In other words, a lord must never, not even to his own retainer, let slip any imprudent words, for if he did, they could lead only to disaster. "Never say to anyone else what you just said to me," he further admonished Keiki.

"I see." Keiki stroked his chin, keeping his face a mask. He was beginning to be aware of this flaw in himself. For a politician, his mind was if anything too incisive. All would be well if he kept his thoughts to himself, but whenever he came into contact with fools, he couldn't help speaking his mind. His words were then spread far and wide, probably sowing needless misunderstanding and creating needless enemies.

Keiki then got up and crossed over, his silk *hakama* rustling with every step, to the drawing room where Shungaku sat waiting. He knew very well why Shungaku was there. He had come to push his case yet again, to force the office of shogun on him, Keiki.

As Keiki seated himself in the place of honor in the room, an elevated alcove, Shungaku knelt formally before him. Inching closer to Keiki, he said in his voice that sounded like the singing of a bird, "I'll lose no time in asking. Have you reached a decision?"

"It is of no use."

It was all hopeless, no one could be shogun anymore, the bakufu, as it was, was unmanageable. Forgetting both Hara Ichinoshin's counsel and his own reflections of a moment before, Keiki proceeded to launch into a cogent analysis of the situation.

"No use? I beg your pardon?" repeated Shungaku, bewildered.

"Think about it. The political structure is antiquated. No one could possibly make it work." The system set up by Tokugawa Ieyasu to end the chaos of the Warring States period was still in place—a two-hundred-sixty-year-old relic. Any effort to use it to deal with the foreign powers, and the novelties they brought with them, was doomed. New realities required a new order. This was the gist of his discourse.

Shungaku was a good listener. He said little, nodding deeply from time to time as Keiki scored a point. Encouraged, Keiki waxed loquacious.

"And what are we to make of the hatamoto system?" he demanded. This was a highly sensitive issue. For the past two and a half centuries, Keiki pointed out, hatamoto had lived idle lives. Supposedly military men whose duty it was to protect the bakufu, in fact hatamoto no longer served any purpose whatever. Today's military required the ability to shoulder a gun and fire a cannon. But hatamoto insisted that this was the duty of lowly *ashigaru*, "foot soldiers," and refused to hold a gun or undergo any training. In the end, it had been necessary to recruit a new infantry from the common people. As Shungaku was of course aware, the bakufu's French-style infantry battalion, and its artillery as well, were drawn from those recruits. They had also participated in the expedition against Choshu—but what about the hatamoto? They lived in a fool's paradise in Edo, collecting salaries they did nothing to earn. No government in the world could afford to support tens of thousands of idlers, and tens of thousands of new recruits besides; financial ruin was inevitable. That alone was enough to bring down the bakufu. The hatamoto were eating them out of house and home.

"Aha." Shungaku was hard-pressed for a response. Certainly his keen mind had no trouble grasping Keiki's point. The only route to salvation for the Tokugawa, he was saying, was for the bakufu to carry out its own revaluation, abolish the feudal system, and set up a European-style centralized authority something like that of France's present ruler, Napoleon III. Naturally, this would put all three hundred daimyo out of work. "A fine thing for him to say," Shungaku thought. He himself was lord of Echizen, with a stipend of 320,000 *koku*.

The opinion Keiki had just voiced was spreading throughout Satsuma and other western domains, as Shungaku well knew. It was said to have originated with Finance Minister Oguri Tadamasa, who had absorbed that way of thinking during his tour of the United States. Some said that he had been influenced by Kurimoto Joun, the commissioner of foreign affairs, others that he had gotten it directly from Leon Roches, the French minister to Japan. Rumor had it that Keiki was another supporter of that line of thought, but Shungaku, knowing that Keiki had little use for Roches, had never given the idea much credence. And yet here he was, sounding suspiciously like a convert.

"It only makes sense for him to buy into it," thought Shungaku. Keiki was known for his fondness for France, and had at one time even briefly taken up the study of the language. He was also partial to French weaponry and military drills, and liked to hear about French government and history. Moreover, the French minister, Roches, had so ingratiated himself that he was unofficially special adviser to the bakufu. While the English minister, Parkes, and others referred to the shogun as "Your Highness," Roches alone called him "Your Majesty," convinced that Ieyasu's descendants were the crowned heads of Japan. Doubtless Roches had shared his plan for rebuilding the nation with Keiki.

In retrospect (although Shungaku's knowledge did not extend this far), Roches was psychologically well equipped to devote himself to such a cause, being the servant of Napoleon III. The situation of his master, Charles Louis Napoleon Bonaparte III, was reminiscent of Keiki's own situation. Nephew of the illustrious Napoleon I, he became his successor because his own elder brother died young and so did Napoleon's son, the Duke of Reichstadt. The age of Napoleon was over in France, consigned to history, but Napoleon III gathered troops and declared himself emperor. For that he was arrested and exiled to the United States, but after the revolution of 1848 he became a congressman, then French president, and finally, in 1852, he was elected emperor by popular ballot. Napoleon III took great interest in Japan, beyond the requirements of diplomacy, and he was sympathetic to the bakufu's position. He never came right out and advised the shogun to follow his example, but through Ambassador Roches he came close.

That was all well and good.

What troubled Shungaku was that this approach of Oguri and others would be certain to pique the strong western domains. Oguri's plan (as popular rumor had it) called for a second Battle of Sekigahara—the battle of 1600 that had established Ieyasu in power—in order to establish a central governmental authority based on the Tokugawa family. The bakufu's French-style army would be greatly expanded, and used to stamp out all antibakufu movements, whether in Choshu, Satsuma, Tosa, Shungaku's Echizen, or wherever. Then at one stroke the system of feudal lords could be abolished, and a new Tokugawa regime brought into being. On hearing this, even Yamanouchi Yodo of Tosa, staunchly probakufu, slapped the tatami flooring in indignation. Shungaku was present when it happened. From the time such rumors began to surface, the attitude of Satsuma toward the bakufu underwent a sudden shift. This was only natural for a non-Tokugawa, tozama domain, thought Shungaku. Yet here was Keiki, unabashedly saying such dangerous things to him.

"Since I am a collateral Tokugawa, it's all right, but what if some other daimyo heard this?" he thought, and sought to put a damper on the topic. In so doing he tried to remonstrate with Keiki. But Keiki, quick to catch what was going through Shungaku's mind, stopped him with a look. Then, with a gesture, he indicated to Shungaku that he was not to interrupt. Shungaku, a fainthearted nobleman after all, dropped his gaze in silence. Over his head, Keiki went on.

"If the Tokugawa bakufu is doomed to perish, we should not be the ones to select the next shogun." By "we" he meant the Tokugawas themselves. Until the end of his days, Shungaku could not recall those words without marveling. Keiki's analysis was as logical and incisive as if he had had a thorough grounding in modern jurisprudence. Logically speaking, the emergence of a shogun was predicated on military prowess, and his position as lord among lords was based in both name and substance on the backing of all the daimyo, who met and pledged him their fealty. So it had been with

Ieyasu. If the military might of the shogun should fade over time, the daimyo were under no obligation to continue to look on him as their leader. The precedent had been established by warlord Oda Nobunaga (1534–82), who threw over the Ashikaga shogun. It was up to the daimyo to choose a new leader for themselves.

"What? The daimyo choose the shogun?" Shungaku could not conceal his surprise.

"Yes. We will leave it to them," affirmed Keiki the theoretician.

Shungaku said nothing, clearly thrown off balance. He could think of no response. Something in Keiki's words, uttered in such commanding tones, struck him as off, containing a central and fatal flaw; the theoretical framework of what he said, however, was a masterpiece of irrefutable logic. Shungaku was unable to remonstrate. Helplessly, he said only, "You would assemble all the daimyo?"

Keiki nodded. Of course, all three hundred daimyo would have to come together to hold discussions and elect a leader. The franchise would be theirs.

Hearing that, Shungaku thought he saw a way out. The daimyo included a number of fools, he pointed out, men who were virtual imbeciles. Would they not simply become confused to no purpose?

"The daimyo could decide among themselves whom to exclude as not being up to the task," said Keiki.

Enfranchised men would decide on electors by mutual agreement. A shogun chosen by this means would no longer be shogun, but something closer to a president. Napoleon III had carried out a coup d'état in 1852, after which he won

7,500,000 votes in a popular election and was elected to a ten-year term as president. Possibly that thought was running through Keiki's mind even now.

He continued: "It is just as you say, Shungaku; the daimyo are not all men of wisdom. But the foolish would be sent home, and only the wise would remain. Together they would choose a shogun, and after that hold deliberations on government, dividing up the various offices among themselves and using their strength to rectify the shogunate government as needed. They could dismiss most of the bakufu officials, reducing personnel, and give guns to the hatamoto, making soldiers of everyone down to the last hangers-on in the castle."

Shungaku gave a cry of intense relief. This was not the Oguri plan after all. The daimyo would be retained. Affairs of government would be conducted jointly by an elected shogun and a council of able daimyo. "Yes," thought Shungaku, nodding to himself, "this might well be the only way to save the Tokugawa house and the country."

Then he raised his head and said, leaning forward, "Tell me this. The man chosen to lead the rest—what if it turns out to be you, sire? Surely you do not mean to say that you would refuse power even then!"

"Of course not." Keiki smiled suddenly. "I always follow the course of reason. If that should happen, I would gladly accept."

"I am relieved to hear it." Shungaku heaved a sigh, and then brought up a different subject: the succession to the headship of the Tokugawa family. He had heard that Keiki had announced to chief senior councillor Itakura Katsukiyo the peculiar policy that while he would not accept the office of shogun, he would consent to become head of the Tokugawa family. Keiki reasoned that the Tokugawa line was a private entity. Even if the Tokugawa bakufu should perish, the family would not be affected, and someone would still have to become head in order to perform the ancestral rites. That would be a private affair, unlike the office of shogun, which was public. Keiki, in his highly analytical way, insisted on keeping the two separate.

To Shungaku—to anyone with a commonsense view—it was strange logic. The shogun and the head of the Tokugawa family were one in nature, and from the time of Ieyasu, no one had ever thought of them separately. Still, Shungaku had no desire to enter into a debate with this master logician. He did, however, want to make sure of what he had said.

"You say you will succeed to the headship of the Tokugawa family. Are you sure that you will not change your mind?"

"I am not eager to take it on, but to do otherwise would be disloyal to my ancestors. I cannot find it in my heart to refuse. Reluctantly, therefore, I agree to serve as head of the Tokugawa family."

"Really?"

"Yes, really," Keiki said decisively.

The words were barely out of his mouth before Shungaku began nodding vehemently. "I cannot tell you what a relief this is to me, sire," he said. Declaring himself eager to share the good news, he withdrew to another room, where not only Itakura sat anxiously waiting, but also Protector of Kyoto Matsudaira Katamori, who had dragged himself there from his sickbed in his concern, along with his younger brother Matsudaira Sadaaki. As soon as Shungaku entered the room, he told them everything.

They all exchanged glances.

Soon thereafter, the meeting broke up. Keiki's reasoning seemed to them convoluted and not always easy to follow, but one thing was clear: He was not entirely averse to becoming the next shogun. This was the impression they had all received.

"Well, well," mused Matsudaira Katamori, a model of probity. "Maybe Shungaku was right about him. Maybe he is an 'arm-twist drinker' at that."

The Choshu Fiasco

As promised, Keiki did become head of the Tokugawa
family.

Seven days had passed since Iemochi's death. Since Keiki
was not shogun, there was no precedent for the ceremony.
And since he was still in Kyoto, the rites of succession could
not be held in Edo Castle, as custom dictated. Of necessity,
the ceremony would be summary in form.

Perplexed at the situation, Itakura Katsukiyo, who as chief
senior councillor was also master of shogunate ceremonies,
finally went to Keiki and asked him what was to be done. In a
tone as confident and relaxed as if he had been a bakufu
functionary for a hundred years, Keiki proceeded to tell him.

Itakura followed the advice. First, in the name of "Shogun

Iemochi," who was supposedly ailing, he presented a memorial to the throne. In essence, it said that he, Iemochi, had been ill since late spring, that his illness had progressed to the point where he could no longer carry out his duties, and that should his condition worsen, he wished Keiki to succeed him as Tokugawa family head. The memorial was no sooner presented to the throne than it received imperial sanction. Nothing could have been simpler.

Keiki's rank remained the same, and the office of shogun remained occupied by a dead man, Tokugawa Iemochi.

Imperial sanction was granted on September 7, 1866. Itakura went to give Keiki the news at his residence in Kyoto. Keiki received it in silence, seated bolt upright on the raised portion of the floor. When the report was finished, he continued to say nothing.

Itakura looked up at Keiki, wondering what was wrong. The silence was bizarre. It was as if the very air around the man were of a different density, forming a blue membrane that cut him off from all else.

Finally, unable to bear the suspense, Itakura prostrated himself, paying his first respects to the new head of the Tokugawa family. Then he lifted his head slightly and asked humbly if Keiki had anything to say.

But Keiki said nothing.

His eyes were fixed on a point over Itakura's head, on the painting of bamboo on the room's sliding doors. Keiki was equally unprepared for his reaction at that moment. Try to speak as he might, his throat constricted and his vocal cords shut down. Why was he so moved? Even though he might not be shogun, he had indeed become the fifteenth head of the powerful house of Tokugawa. The weight of hundreds of years of history, tradition, and family honor, from the time of Ieyasu onward, now settled on top of him. That this weight would descend on him with such overwhelming pressure, Keiki had never anticipated. Nor was it necessarily the heavy, gloomy burden that his logic had suggested it would be. On the contrary, to his surprise, it was tinctured with bright color, evoking joy in the deepest part of his being. Keiki was bewildered. If he opened his mouth, he feared he might give in to his emotions and let out a wild cry of exultation. He struggled to control this strange fancy. His silence stretched on.

At last his brain began to function again, and resumed its normal lively workings. This joy—hateful joy to him, no doubt—would have to be converted into something else. He must transmute it, give it some other form so that he could cry out, and safely expel it from his body; otherwise he feared he would truly emit a yell of sheer ecstasy. Keiki's brain searched for a substitute. In a flash of intuition, he had it: Choshu. War.

The punitive expedition against Choshu that had begun in mid-July of that year had run into unexpected difficulties, the bakufu having suffered a string of humiliating defeats at the hands of the small tozama domain. *This* was what he should speak out about. Now that he was in command, the battle would have to resume on a completely new basis; they would send in a large new army, launch a major offensive, and annihilate Choshu in a burst of cannon fire and smoke, thereby recovering lost prestige and instantly restoring faith in the bakufu, now at an all-time low, both home and abroad. In order to accomplish this, he, Keiki, would have to march to the front lines to raise morale by exhorting the troops with his own voice, just as Tokugawa Ieyasu had done at the Battle of Sekigahara, when he laid the foundation of the bakufu. Otherwise, what was the use in his having become the head of the Tokugawa family?

"Iga! Iga!" In a thundering voice, Keiki called out for Itakura Katsukiyo, lord of Iga, though he was right there in front of him. "Launch a major strike on Choshu!"

Itakura was dumbfounded. Three times Keiki repeated the command, drumming it into Itakura's ears. He had invented the term *ouchikomi*, "major strike," on the spot. In a short while it enjoyed great popularity among the members of the bakufu and the court alike, as a vivid term for an offensive operation.

Keiki then made a further announcement: "I myself will go." He proceeded to elaborate on the structure of the offensive, his brain in high gear. No longer would the bakufu rely on the feudal domains for help, but would focus on their own troops. Except for the sword and lance outfits, all units would be accompanied by Western-style corps. In Edo and Osaka there were now thirteen infantry battalions. In addition, the artillery had eighty cannon. Keiki himself would lead them west to Choshu in a few days, he said. Itakura was to see to it that another twenty battalions' worth of new recruits were readied as an auxiliary force. All of this Keiki announced in one breath, as if reciting from memory.

He went on to discuss his own travel arrangements. There would be no more of those ridiculously long daimyo processions in which everything was taken along, including the bathtub. Like the army generals of Europe—like Napoleon himself—he would content himself with three knapsacks and no more. One would contain a warm blanket, one a change of clothes and underclothing, and one his watch and other personal articles. Food? Like every other soldier, he would eat rations.

Words poured out of him, as if spun by some whirling internal machine. Everything he said was resplendent with new ways of thinking, and full of concrete applications. Itakura was in a daze. What sort of super-brain did he have, this new master of the Tokugawas?

Next, Keiki summoned Hara Ichinoshin and his other aides, and held a war council. They would take the field within ten days, but first it would be necessary to purchase two battleships. There were reports that foreign traders had already come to sell one each in Nagasaki and Yokohama. "Buy them," Keiki ordered. And finally, he commanded everyone, "Spread the word about the major strike. Raise your voices loud and clear!" Publicity and advertising would demoralize the Choshu troops, and raise bakufu prestige in the rest of the country. Let them shout the news from the housetops!

Matsudaira Shungaku heard people shouting the news, and was astonished. Immediately he hurried to Keiki's residence and asked for an audience. Keiki had many visitors that day, and Shungaku was made to wait awhile in a side room, where he was served tea.

"The man is totally unpredictable." Shungaku had no idea what to make of Keiki. He himself had always been opposed to an expedition against Choshu. Not only he, but his friends—the so-called "wise daimyo," including Yamanouchi

Yodo, Date Munenari, and others—were equally opposed. Their main reason was that to start civil unrest under the watchful eyes of the foreign powers would only further imperil the nation and ultimately shorten the bakufu's precarious hold on life. In addition, the cost to the domains furnishing troops was a burden heavier than they could bear. Furthermore, if war sent prices soaring (when as it was, ever since the coming of the foreigners, prices had gone through the roof), the people would be restive, and riots and insurrections might break out across the land.

But beyond all that, the greater question now bothering Shungaku had, rather, to do with the tenor of Keiki's words and actions. Just the other day, had Keiki not told him that he wished to make a council of lords the highest authority in the land? How could he turn around and arbitrarily decide something so momentous without consulting anyone? It made no sense.

Finally, Shungaku was admitted to Keiki's presence, and offered these criticisms in his soft-spoken way.

Keiki was unmoved. "What I said then was that if someday I were elected shogun, that is what I would do," he said. "In fact, I have only succeeded to the headship of the Tokugawa family, and this is no time to call a council meeting."

His defense was plausible, but Shungaku was asking something deeper: He wanted to know where Keiki's true spirit lay. If what he said varied so much from one day to the next, the bakufu retainers and the general public would be bound to misjudge him, and question his motives. But Shungaku lacked the boldness to criticize Keiki to his face so openly.

Keiki looked at him as if to say, "Shungaku, don't you understand my real purpose?" What he actually said was "I want to strike a blow." He would land a knockout punch to defeat Choshu, thereby recovering bakufu face and bringing the war to a favorable close. To make the offensive work, he said, he himself would attack from the south, another Tokugawa commander from the north, each driving their way to the domain capital of Yamaguchi, where they would compel Choshu to enter into a pact. The goal of the operation was not military in nature, but strictly political. He had assumed that Shungaku of all people would understand this. Flattered, Shungaku relented somewhat.

Keiki intended to use the imperial court to maneuver. Choshu activists were still branded "enemies of the throne," and Keiki sought to have the coming expedition designated an "operation by imperial command." The psychological impact on the people of Choshu was bound to be huge.

At court, all Keiki's requests were approved. The noblemen and princes were nearly all supportive of the bakufu, and Emperor Komei despised Choshu, so this bold plan of Keiki's met with general approbation.

Finally, the preparations were done. Several days later, Keiki donned his official robes as Minister of the Center and paid a palace visit as shogunal proxy, commander-in-chief, and supreme power-holder in the country.

The emperor was waiting for him in a small palace within the larger palace grounds. The two men greeted each other wordlessly, and then the emperor retired to his library, with Keiki following in attendance on him. There, the emperor gave orders for Tokugawa Keiki to attack and subjugate Choshu. In addition, he bestowed on Keiki his sword.

In both China and Japan it was traditional for the commander of imperial expeditionary forces to receive a special sword from the emperor with which to strike down insurgents. During the Nara and Heian eras, the practice had been followed frequently, but after Minamoto no Yoritomo established the Kamakura bakufu—Japan's first warrior government—in the 1180s, military affairs became the exclusive province of the samurai class. Military expeditions carried out in obedience to an imperial command were things of the past, along with the custom of bestowing the imperial sword. The sword that Keiki received thus represented the revival of an ancient tradition after a lapse of six hundred and eighty years.

Naturally, the ceremony was carried out not at the behest of the emperor but at Keiki's instigation. The court followed his plan exactly. More than a nostalgic revival, the ceremony was rife with political significance. Keiki's acceptance of the imperial sword marked the theoretical end of warrior rule for the first time since the days of Yoritomo. Like military functionaries in pre-Heian times, Keiki received the sword as a vassal of the emperor.

In any case, Keiki's drive against Choshu was off to a grand start, with even the emperor involved. At the court, orders were given that in accordance with ancient practice, prayers should be said at seven shrines and seven temples for the defeat of Choshu.

Yet barely six days later, Keiki stunned Kyoto political circles by announcing that he was giving up the attack.

The reason was unknown. In any case, the offensive was scrubbed, and because Keiki liked things to be done properly, he went so far as to request the throne to send him a letter canceling the expedition. The attack was announced September 13 and called off barely ten days later. Even Emperor Komei was infuriated.

The reason for the abrupt turnabout soon became clear. During the ongoing fighting with Choshu, the bakufu had had the advantage in the castle town of Oguri, but on September 10 the tide had turned. The Kiheitai, Choshu's crack volunteer militia, had stormed in under the command of Takasugi Shinsaku and overpowered the han forces. Castle lord Ogasawara Toyochiyomaru himself had set fire to the castle and beat a retreat. Senior councillor Ogasawara Nagamichi had fled to the bakufu battleship, leaving the battlefield, and gone up to Hyogo by way of Nagasaki. By the time he had returned to Kyoto and reported the defeat to Keiki, it was August 20. Partly in justification of his own flight, Ogasawara's every word painted a gloomy picture. The bakufu forces were in disarray; they could never defeat Choshu now.

"Victory is impossible?" Again and again Keiki pressed the point. "Impossible." Again and again, Ogasawara gave the same reply. The wheels in Keiki's head were turning fast. He knew better than to send troops into a war that was unwinnable. Nor did he have the boldness or battle experience of a Tokugawa Ieyasu, such that he might yet turn such a war around. Not long after Ogasawara Nagamichi left, he decided not to launch the offensive after all. Hara Ichinoshin and the rest of his retainers understood. Even to endure the shame of being branded a renegade, a man who could not be true to his own principles, was better than to lead an army into sure defeat. They explained the situation to the emperor's chief adviser at Nijo Castle.

"Then he's a damn coward." That was the opinion of the samurai from other provinces gathered in Kyoto. Even the court nobles on the side of the bakufu inwardly wrote off its chances of recovery from this fiasco. Matsudaira Katamori, Protector of Kyoto and longtime advocate of a hard-line policy against Choshu, was indignant; Matsudaira Shungaku, who had initially opposed the offensive, was filled with apprehension: How would this unpleasant twist affect public opinion of the bakufu? As far as he could tell, no one in the long history of Tokugawa military rule had ever committed such an act of folly as Keiki. And yet Keiki was no fool. His political instincts were at least a match for those of Ieyasu and Yoshimune, his education far better than theirs. Still, time after time he committed acts of folly more egregious than anything done by even the most idiotic of past shoguns.

"What it all comes down to is this," said Shungaku. "The man has wits and ability in spades, but not one iota of pluck. Without pluck, all the ingenuity and brilliance in the world is an empty charade."

Despite this rain of ridicule, Keiki felt neither inward regret nor outward shame. In this respect, he demonstrated tremendous pluck. He supported all his own actions, and was quite content to have himself as his sole supporter. More than mettle, or mere stubbornness, his quiet confidence and self-sufficiency were the mark of the true aristocrat.

His quickness to deal with the altered situation was beyond words. No sooner had he reported the cancellation to the emperor than he dispatched his naval minister to Choshu to begin peace negotiations.

The Fifteenth Tokugawa Shogun

AFTER A NUMBER OF FURTHER TURNS AND TWISTS, KEIKI was proclaimed shogun at last, formally taking the name Tokugawa Yoshinobu. However he might stress his peculiar notion that he would succeed to the headship of the Tokugawa family but not become shogun, thus attempting to create a private niche for himself alone, neither the court nor the bakufu could tolerate the awkwardness and unnaturalness of the situation. In the end they prevailed, practically browbeating him into acquiescence. Keiki pointedly ignored their pleas, but his aide Hara Ichinoshin worked hard behind the scenes to bring the two sides together. And in the end Keiki—or Yoshinobu, as we shall now refer to him—did become shogun.

"I have no taste for the office of shogun." Over and over, through words and actions, he had made his distaste plain. A cautious man, Yoshinobu never undertook anything new without first preparing a way of escape for himself. In this case, having created an impression in the popular mind that he had been forced reluctantly into accepting the office, now whatever might befall him, he was protected. In the case of any difficulty, he would be able to extricate himself easily and flee to some other, safer place. His sharp eyes had already made out that something would happen, and he had begun preparing for the performance that would be required of him then, carefully polishing his acting skills, studying his lines, and thinking about the theme of the script. But if that "something" were never to happen? Then he'd be shogun for a hundred years, he told himself brazenly. Cowardice and courage were strangely intertwined within him.

Yoshinobu was appointed the fifteenth Tokugawa shogun on January 10, 1867, more than one hundred and fifty days after the death of the previous shogun, Iemochi. During that long, leaderless interval, the bakufu future had looked bleak indeed.

What augured still worse for Yoshinobu and the Tokugawa line was this: Barely three weeks later, Emperor Komei fell sick and died.

"The bakufu is finished," thought Yoshinobu at once. At a time when it was fashionable to believe in restoring direct rule to the emperor, Komei himself had always been staunchly probakufu. He had supported the continued existence of the shogunate. For the activities of Aizu domain, which was coming more and more to embody bakufu prestige in Kyoto, he had had high praise. And he had trusted and loved Matsudaira Katamori, the Protector of Kyoto and lord of Aizu, more than any of his court attendants.

"With this emperor on the throne we can carry on," the probakufu activists had thought. The theoretical foundations of *kobu-gattai*, a movement to unify the imperial court and the shogunate in the belief that without the bakufu there could be no respect for the emperor, also came from Komei. And now he was dead.

The new emperor-to-be was a mere youth of fourteen. His maternal grandfather was former Great Minister Nakayama Tadayasu, and his mother was named Yoshiko. His grandfather was his official guardian and custodian of the privy seal required for all imperial proclamations. Simply by making an ally of this old courtier, any schemer at court might easily have an imperial proclamation issued to the effect that the true enemy of the emperor system was the bakufu, and that it should be brought down.

There were in fact two such schemers. One was Iwakura Tomomi, who had been banished by the former emperor, and the other was his alter ego and behind-the-scenes manipulator, Satsuma's Okubo Ichizo. Furthermore, just as Yoshinobu had feared, ten months after Komei's death, Iwakura's secretary, Tamamatsu Misao, penned a "Secret Imperial Decree to the Domains of Satsuma and Choshu." The elder Nakayama put the privy seal in the hands of the boy emperor and had him stamp it on the decree, while Okubo had brocade banners fashioned from women's obis made by the finest Nishijin weavers in Kyoto. Together they completed the final touches on their ultrasecret plans to over-throw the bakufu. Nothing requires the talents of great conspirators like a revolution.

Yoshinobu was forced on the defensive. He had to watch the conspirators like a hawk, never relaxing his guard for a moment, anticipating their every move, and taking swift preventive measures. This constant parry and thrust, blow by blow by blow, comprised the whole of his term as shogun, which lasted just over a year. During that time he was ensconced within Nijo Castle, yet forced to stay constantly on the alert, scarcely able to take a deep breath. Both for Yoshinobu and for Japanese history, the few months of his tenure were extremely critical. Even if he had been a superman, his mental and physical powers could hardly have lasted any longer.

Yoshinobu gained a reputation as a shogun not to be trifled with. No matter what daimyo or court noble came before him, no one ever got the better of him in an argument. When he presided over a council of daimyo, he was no mere ornament like shoguns of the past, but served as moderator, sponsor, and expositor of proposals, and skilled debater able to demolish the arguments of the opposition. He even served as a one-man reception committee, welcoming people to the chamber and being attentive to their needs.

This was just at the time of the debate in Kyoto political circles over whether or not to open Hyogo (present-day Kobe) as a treaty port. No other political issue of the day was so controversial.

"We will destroy the bakufu over our opposition to opening this harbor," declared Satsuma's Okubo Ichizo, and his friend Sir Ernest Satow, the British envoy's interpreter, observed that "the chance of a revolution was not to be lost. If Hiogo was once opened, then good-bye to chances of the daimios." Even a foreign diplomat could plainly tell that the bakufu faced a crisis.

A little over a year before, the bakufu had been reprimanded by the Western powers for failing to honor its agreement to open the harbor. Pressed for a response, the bakufu had ended up pledging that the harbor would open "very soon." They were now being held to that pledge, and had run out of excuses.

The bakufu's sole defense was this: "Imperial sanction has not yet been granted." The Western powers greeted this statement with derision. "We thought the Tokugawa bakufu was the only officially sanctioned government in Japan. Are you telling us that there is another, higher government after all?" This was the bakufu's Achilles' heel in its relations with foreign powers, and to have it thus pointed out was painful in the extreme.

The various foreign ministers had more to say: "There is no point in our talking with a government that has no authority. We would rather go to Kyoto ourselves and have an audience directly with your sovereign, the mikado. Is that all right?" Clearly, they expected the bakufu to respond with dismay. And indeed, a furor ensued. If foreign envoys were allowed to negotiate directly with the imperial court, the bakufu would be throwing away its primary qualification as the government of Japan in the eyes of the world. Domestically, too, such a development would mean instant disintegration. One way or another, the bakufu managed to placate the envoys. Meanwhile, the court was not about to issue the desired sanction. Okubo inflamed the ignorant, antiforeign sentiments of members of the court: "Nagasaki and Yokohama are one thing, but to admit foreigners to Hyogo, which is so near Kyoto, would be a gross defilement of Japan and an unpardonable insult to His Majesty. Besides, it was the previous emperor's wish to keep the harbor closed." With these arguments he got the court nobles lined up on his side. As long as the court issued no imperial sanction, the bakufu's grip on power could only weaken. If the bakufu should enter into a treaty without imperial permission, as Tairo Ii Naosuke had done, it would be playing into the hands of its enemies, who would then be swift to cry foul, rally the daimyo, and launch an antibakufu campaign.

No sooner had Yoshinobu become shogun than he had to solve this knotty problem. In April 1867 he met with representatives of England, France, Holland, and the United States, assuring them with confidence, "Hyogo will be opened." The Western powers were amazed at this unprecedented show of vigor from the bakufu. Considering Japan's precarious internal situation, Yoshinobu's words were extremely explicit. Ernest Satow, well versed in the complexities of Japanese politics, was skeptical. Through the senior councillors he inquired whether it would be permissible to publish what the shogun Yoshinobu had said in Yokohama and British newspapers. Yoshinobu's reply was still more blunt: "That would not be a problem."

Despite his friendly ties with Satsuma, Satow was favorably disposed toward Yoshinobu. In his memoirs he wrote that the shogun was "one of the most aristocratic-looking Japa-

nese I have ever seen, of fair complexion, with a high forehead and well-cut nose—such a gentleman."

Yoshinobu's mind was made up. First, he called for a council of the great reform-minded daimyo. The identities of
these lords changed from time to time, but on this occasion
they were Yamanouchi Yodo of Tosa, Matsudaira Shungaku
of Echizen, Date Munenari of Uwajima, and Shimazu
Hisamitsu of Satsuma. The four did not necessarily think
alike on the issue.

Satsuma's Shimazu, primed by his adviser Okubo, urged
that the Hyogo issue take a backseat to the question of
Choshu. "First withdraw bakufu forces from Choshu. After
that is time enough," he insisted, and by introducing this extraneous topic succeeded in throwing a monkey wrench into
the discussion.

Yoshinobu was eloquent in dissent, but his political
enemy—for that is what he was—Shimazu, being a poor
talker and naturally taciturn, only shook his head stubbornly
from side to side like a doll with a bobbing head, sometimes
even retiring to another room to receive advice from Okubo.
The discussion went around in circles, and no conclusion
was reached. Five days later, Yoshinobu invited the same four
men back to Nijo Castle. Yamanouchi Yodo was ill and unable to attend, but the other three all did.

This meeting, which lasted from noon till six o'clock in
the evening, was dominated by Yoshinobu. On and on he
talked. Even though he was shogun, he addressed his listeners frankly, as equals. This he did on the advice of the absent
Yodo, to avoid antagonizing Shimazu Hisamitsu. Even
though the council members were being granted the distinct

privilege of special audience with the shogun, he announced that they were welcome to smoke, and had ashtrays brought in. To lighten the atmosphere further, he even served sweets, which he personally encouraged everyone to sample. Had any of the preceding fourteen shoguns looked down from heaven and seen this, they would have been horrified, and doubted their eyes. Not only that; the sheer number of words uttered by Yoshinobu on this occasion doubtless surpassed that of all the words ever spoken during public audience by his fourteen predecessors combined.

When his audience wearied, Yoshinobu called for a short break, and led them out into the garden to pose for souvenir photographs. The art of photography was by no means new, but it was only five years since the first professional photographer had set up office in Nagasaki. With his delight in all things Western, Yoshinobu loved to have his picture taken, and had various portraits done of himself, including one with him seated on horseback while dressed in an imperial-style military uniform presented to him by France.

On this day, to relax the three lords he had hung a white curtain in the garden to create a small outdoor studio, and there he invited them to sit. After getting a group picture of the quartet, he had each man sit alone in a chair for an individual portrait. Shungaku's photograph shows him in what was evidently a familiar pose, looking down with a suggestion of weakness, his hands laid formally on his knees. Shimazu Hisamitsu is shown with legs spread wide and back erect, looking away from the camera, his boyish yet stubborn-looking face tilted to one side. The camera perfectly captures his air of triumph as the leader of the powerful Satsuma domain. Uwajima's long-visaged Date Munenari also appears.

Again this day, however, the deliberations were to end inconclusively, with Keiki defeated by the silent opposition of Shimazu Hisamitsu.

Keiki was tired. With all his efforts, it appeared that he was dancing alone, without a partner. The bakufu retainers in Edo saw him as a one-man show and nothing more, while his longtime allies, Yodo and Shungaku, were unable to join in his dance due to the complicated political situation in their home domains. Even Matsudaira Katamori, lord of Aizu, ever loyal to the head of the Tokugawa house, saw Keiki as a man of wiles whose word was not to be taken at face value. Never had there been a shogun so able, so gifted, or so alone.

Meanwhile, underneath it all, the times were drastically changing. The more furiously Keiki danced his lonely dance, the more he felt the sand giving way beneath the tips of his toes.

At night Keiki invariably sought the company of a woman. He had a number of bed companions in Kyoto, and only when he was with them was this lifelong philanderer able to revert completely to himself, master of his own body and nothing more. Only in that limited sense was he able to escape his isolation. Of all the women he had with him, his favorite was the one he had summoned from Edo, O-Yoshi, daughter of the head firefighter Shinmon Tatsugoro. She was tawny-skinned and, though slight of build, had a thickset neck and a no-nonsense, lively way about her, with a style of speech to match—all of which made her seem every inch the daughter of an Edo firefighter. With her whole body she helped Keiki fight off the intermittent pangs of homesickness. To O-Yoshi alone Keiki would suddenly let slip what was going on in his mind—to her everlasting discomfiture.

"One hundred plans and one hundred arguments cannot prevail against the spirit of the times," he told her. He was recalling the round, nut-brown face of Shimazu Hisamitsu, who met everything Yoshinobu said with stubborn silence and opened his mouth only to say no. Against him, the shogun felt that all his best plans and arguments were of no avail. Why? It could only be that the times were on Shimazu's side. That incompetent man—as Yoshinobu could not help judging him to be—was seated squarely before a massive screen representing the spirit of the times. Yoshinobu might dance in front of him all he liked, but the irascible Shimazu, like a fretful baby, never once smiled.

As Yoshinobu himself possessed an uncommon ability to catch the drift of the times, his conviction regarding the invincibility of a man in tune with the times came no doubt from his inmost depths. By rights, the narrow-minded and ultraconservative Shimazu should have been sitting in his place, and vice versa. And yet, to Yoshinobu's intense grief—for so he sometimes felt—he himself was shogun.

He had another idea about how to settle the Hyogo issue. He would hold a council meeting on the grounds of the imperial court, that den of opposition to opening the ports, invite the most powerful nobles and daimyo, and argue down their opposition all at once. He set about executing his plan immediately.

But Satsuma resisted, Hisamitsu absenting himself at Okubo's instigation. As a result, Uwajima's Date Munenari took a wait-and-see attitude and also absented himself, fearing he might be forced to cast in his lot with Yoshinobu once and for all. Not even Shungaku came. He had all but given up hope on the future of the bakufu, so that even after all his past support, he now feared to go along with Yoshinobu lest he be tarred with the same brush. Shungaku, too, had belatedly adopted the position of the other domains, that of quietly slipping the bonds of the Tokugawa and creating a system of independent domains with which to respond to the coming national emergency. If he did not separate from Yoshinobu soon, his domain of Fukui would share in his same fate of destruction.

And yet, he was weak-willed. Yielding to the shogun's insistent persuasion, he alone visited the palace. The courtiers consisted of Nijo, the ministers of the left and right, two former imperial regents, five great ministers, and two others. The location of the meeting was the Tiger Room in the imperial palace.

The meeting was held on June 25, a scorching hot day. In accordance with palace custom, it began after sundown, not getting under way until eight in the evening. The meeting turned into a marathon that lasted all night long and on into the next day, not ending until eleven P.M. at night. There were several breaks, and time for a brief nap, but as moderator, Yoshinobu permitted no more time off than that. "At a time of such crisis for the empire, you must sacrifice your rest," he said, admonishing those who attempted to leave early. From his point of view, the only way to manage the courtiers and the daimyo was to coop them all up in one room and force them to fight it out. That was his aim. Moreover, throughout the entire twenty-odd hours of the meeting, he declaimed with such spirit that no one could nod off, completely wearing out his voice in the process. Everyone in attendance was stunned. No one had the ability or the strength to argue with him. Finally, toward eleven o'clock on the second night, they yielded to his persuasion, and it was official: The port of Hyogo would open.

In this way, the bakufu narrowly averted a disaster and succeeded in extending its life a little longer. Those plotting against the bakufu were naturally left gnashing their teeth. Rather than wallow in disappointment, they learned to fear Yoshinobu. Saigo Takamori of Satsuma took such an apprehensive view of the shogun that in his opinion, unless Yoshinobu were killed, the young emperor's future would be in jeopardy. He never altered his opinion of the shogun Yoshinobu until the end, when he planned an attack on Edo Castle.

Kido Jun'ichiro, leader of the Choshu domain, took an even sterner view than Saigo, warning his comrades: "His courage and resourcefulness are truly like a reincarnation of Ieyasu. As long as he is our direct enemy, both Satsuma and Choshu must show great resolution, or we will be cast into the abyss." He added, overestimating his enemy, "Yoshinobu has renewed the government ordinance of Kanto, and the military administration is amazingly reformed. Instead of falling, the bakufu may well rise again!"

This was crediting Yoshinobu with too much. And yet such overestimation generated fear, and just after Yoshinobu's successful opening of Hyogo, secret plans to bring about the military downfall of the bakufu proceeded apace in Satsuma and Choshu. At the same time, plans to draft the "Imperial Rescript to Overthrow the Shogunate" got under way in Kyoto among Iwakura Tomomi and other members of the court. Only swift action could keep Yoshinobu's influence from growing day by day.

The Decision to Surrender

YOSHINOBU SENSED THAT PLANS WERE AFOOT IN KYOTO among the men of Satsuma and Choshu to overthrow the shogunate. He had information amounting to proof. One outstanding feature of Tokugawa politics was the sophistication of intelligence-gathering capabilities. The Aizu lord, Protector of Kyoto, relied on spies, and so did the Shinsengumi, bakufu ronin troops at his command. Yoshinobu's trusted retainer Hara Ichinoshin used all means at his disposal to obtain secret information. Everyone's sources made much of the singularity of Satsuma movements. What this elaborate intelligence network failed to pick up on, however, was the secret alliance between Satsuma and Choshu that had been mediated the previous year by Sakamoto Ryoma of

Tosa, binding the two once-warring domains in the cause of overthrowing the bakufu. Still, even for those kept in the dark, Satsuma's subsequent actions strongly suggested that something of that nature was brewing.

After the Hyogo issue was resolved, Tosa's Yamanouchi Yodo judged that the Satsuma and Choshu patriots must be in league. He foresaw that there would be an armed uprising in Kyoto before long, and predicted that the bakufu would then be doomed. Yodo was generous of heart, and felt greater loyalty to Yoshinobu and the bakufu than to the fudai daimyo; nevertheless, he was not sufficiently devoted to their cause to fight for Yoshinobu and share personally in the bakufu's fate. Tosa, his own domain, came first. Should the country revert to the age of rival warlords, it would be all he could do to cheer on the bakufu from the side while retaining an official neutrality. He knew, moreover, that highly placed men from his own domain, including his military commander, Itagaki Taisuke, were apparently in collusion with Saigo and the rest. Things had reached the stage where not even as firm a disciplinarian as Yodo could exert any restraining influence over the radical elements among his samurai.

There was no way to save the bakufu now. Yodo looked on the state of the country with despair.

Just at that time, early in August 1867, Goto Shojiro, the Tosa elder who had gone from Nagasaki to Kyoto, came rushing back in excitement with a startling claim: He had a wonder-working plan that would save the day, he said, bringing back the Tokugawa from the brink of disaster, and even placating Satsuma and Choshu. It was a plan to restore the reins of government to the emperor, devised by Sakamoto Ryoma and enthusiastically embraced by Goto. Goto never mentioned Sakamoto's name, however, presenting the plan to Yodo as if he had thought it all up himself. In order to unify the present political system, with its division between the imperial court and the shogunate, Yoshinobu would have to yield power. But the house of Tokugawa would survive—and emerge, indeed, as the most valued contributor to the revolution.

"Why, that's brilliant! Hurrah for you!" With a slap of his knee, Yodo roared approval. This was a way for Tosa, now outmaneuvered by Satsuma and Choshu, to put both those domains in its debt and leap to national prominence and hegemony. It was sheer political genius.

All that remained was to persuade Yoshinobu to go along with the plan. Yodo ordered Goto back to Kyoto. He sailed aboard the han steamship to Osaka, and went from there to Kyoto, where he and Sakamoto together won over the men of Satsuma and other friendly domains, as well as some of Yoshinobu's most trusted councillors in the bakufu.

Yoshinobu knew nothing of any of this. His source of information had been cut off. On September 11, his most trusted aide, Hara Ichinoshin, was cut down by antiforeign fanatics. Certain hatamoto in the shogunate had long despised Hara, blaming him for what they saw as Yoshinobu's bizarre and inscrutable behavior. Being a samurai of the loyalist house of Mito, he must be attempting to persuade Yoshinobu to sell out, they reasoned. Two men participated in the assassination, both of them shogunal vassals. They stopped by Hara's residence in the morning, announcing themselves as "men of Mito," then forced their way inside. Coming upon Hara as he was dressing his hair, they raised their swords, killed him, and fled with his head. A valiant youth in the Hara family chased after the assassins and felled one of them.

When he heard of the incident, Yoshinobu covered his face with his hands and wept silently, shoulders heaving. Assassins had taken the life of his first retainer, Nakane Chojuro, outside Kijibashi Gate of Edo Castle; then Hiraoka Enshiro had been slain in Kyoto, and now Hara Ichinoshin was cut down as well. Yoshinobu's critics refrained from killing him, lopping off the heads of his closest advisers instead. The death of those three was proof that Yoshinobu's political actions since leaving Edo impressed most people as devious and inscrutable.

In any case, deprived of his able retainer, Tokugawa Yoshinobu swiftly lost touch with what was going on. He did not learn of the plan to return power to the emperor until well after Goto and Sakamoto had succeeded in winning over key lords and members of the shogunate. It was Inspector General Nagai Naomune who mustered his courage and broke the news to Yoshinobu—though as it turned out, his trepidation proved groundless. To Nagai's astonishment, Yoshinobu displayed no sign of anger or agitation. Rather, his expression was unaccountably cheerful. Having delivered himself of the news, Nagai remained prostrate in the adjacent room, fearful of the shogun's wrath. Yoshinobu then spoke: "I see." That was all. Then silence.

Yoshinobu did not say so to Nagai, but undoubtedly this was one of the happiest moments of his life. Ever since becoming the fifteenth Tokugawa shogun, a position more dangerous than trying to balance on the blade of a sword, he had seen returning political power to the emperor as a possible way out of his predicament. Were he to find himself hopelessly trapped by events, he had only to take the burden of political power and toss it over the imperial fence into the lap of the emperor before heading back east. He had even thought of a parting line: "From now on the court can do as it pleases." But only to the slain Hara Ichinoshin had he spoken of this secret plan; to no one else had he breathed a word of it.

He was a clever one, that Yodo, thought Yoshinobu, secretly impressed by the man's ability to read his mind. Little did he guess that the insight came not from Yodo but from another Tosa man, Sakamoto Ryoma, whom Yodo was never to meet.

Yodo's agent, Goto, continued working tirelessly behind the scenes, finally succeeding in gaining the partial consent of Satsuma and in formally presenting a written memorial to the bakufu urging restoration of imperial rule. The date was October 29, 1867.

However, Satsuma, while giving the appearance of conceding reluctantly to the terms of the plan, was making final preparations for an armed uprising. By coincidence, on the very day of Goto's memorial, Shinagawa Yajiro, secret liaison officer of Choshu, entered Kyoto secretly and concealed himself in the Satsuma quarters.

Numerous reports of suspicious activities in the Satsuma men's residence reached the ears of Aizu and the Shinsengumi, and were made known to Yoshinobu by his new assistant, Nagai Naomune. By now Yoshinobu had ceased in effect to be shogun; he was merely a man waiting for something to happen. Even Shinmon Tatsujiro and his Edo fire-fighting brigade were sent out to keep their ears pricked, in the pleasure quarters and elsewhere, as Yoshinobu's secret agents. Still, no one came up with any proof.

Yet something was definitely brewing. Yoshinobu made up his mind. "This is the only way to cut off Satsuma and thwart their ambitions," he argued to the senior chief councillor, Itakura Katsukiyo, trying to get him to see how advantageous such a plan would be. According to Goto, nothing could be more to the Tokugawa advantage than this plan, which would allow them to maintain their lands and armies, casting off only the encumbrance of political power. Goto had taken out the sting of Sakamoto's plan, presenting it in this sweetened form to leading members of the shogunate cabinet, and this was how Yoshinobu, too, understood it.

Still, what would the court do then? It was a stupid idea, he thought. Given the incompetence of the court nobles and the pitifully low income of the imperial court, they could never hope to establish a national government. Who had ever heard of a government lacking a single soldier or a single warship to aid in its defense?

Moreover, under Sakamoto's plan the new administration would be backed by a bicameral legislature similar to that of the United States, which would conduct all the business of government. In his presentation of the plan, Goto tacitly suggested that Yoshinobu would head the legislature. In that case, Yoshinobu would suffer no actual loss of political power. What could the new government do without land, money, talent, or an army? They would be forced to rely on the Tokugawa, which had easily four million *koku*, a dozen warships, and tens of thousands of infantry.

Why, if anyone stood to lose from a transfer of power, it was the imperial house itself, said Yoshinobu. After years of suffering at their hands, he found the prospect rather enticing. On the other hand, he doubted that the Tosa plan would be adopted without change. Whatever alterations were made, they would have to go along with them, and adapt to situations as they arose. In any case, in order to dodge Satsuma's tricks now, they should agree to the plan. This was how Yoshinobu argued his case to Itakura—who, unable to offer any rebuttal, gave in reluctantly.

That left only the bakufu officials to persuade. Yoshinobu would explain things to them directly himself, he said, and win their consent. Itakura, knowing himself to be unequal to the task, humbly prostrated himself. "I beg your lord to do so." If he himself broached the topic, he would almost certainly be killed. Nor did he have the necessary powers of persuasion. There was nothing he could do but ask the most eloquent speaker in the realm, the shogun Yoshinobu, to handle it.

"I'll persuade them," Yoshinobu said, arching his eyebrows in anticipation. His was a strange personality. About to announce the self-destruction of the venerable Tokugawa shogunate, Yoshinobu forgot to register emotion at the enormity of the bitter event. It was not sentimentality that moved him now, but a rush of excitement of a different kind. He would explain his plan to his retainers himself, using his own talent for oratory, and make them submit to its logic. Yoshinobu, of course, knew nothing of the observation that Matsudaira Shungaku had made about his personality: "He is not free of the fault of relying overly on his own efforts, without taking others into consideration."

On November 7 of that year Yoshinobu invited all of the bakufu officials in Kyoto into the central audience hall of Nijo Castle. They waited breathlessly to find out what it was all about.

Finally, Yoshinobu came in and was seated. Instantly, they prostrated themselves before him as one man. Yoshinobu had someone read aloud his document on the return of political power to the emperor, and shortly thereafter he began to speak. His words were eloquent and forceful.

"We have no other hope but this.... This alone is the way to ensure the survival of Ieyasu's great legacy....

"Rumor has it that a gang of rebels lies in ambush, ready to rise against the shogunate; we do not undertake this plan in fear of them. However many they may be, we could conquer them with ease—but no such disturbance can be allowed in the streets of the imperial capital....

"Go on as you are, some may say, but that is scarcely possible. To maintain the status quo would require a reform more drastic than the mere relinquishing of power. Yet what can be done is limited. To accomplish anything, I would have to do away with the hatamoto and the daimyo alike—but these are extensions of my own self, whom I could no more cast aside than I could pluck out my bones and bowels and hack them to pieces....

"The present situation is full of anomaly toward the Western powers as well. Vassals of the shogun travel on missions abroad. From the court's perspective, these are vassals of vassals, mere secondary retainers. For Japan to send such second-tier representatives to call upon the crowned heads of the world, while other countries send us their first-tier ambassadors, is a breach of etiquette. Once the government ordinances are issued from a single source, then even if a Tokugawa vassal should be sent abroad, he would go at the emperor's command, and as a direct representative of the Japanese government. There would be no anomaly, no breach of etiquette....

"The lords of the various domains are now each fighting for themselves, as in the age of warring states. The authority of the bakufu is weak, the lords do not come when called. At this rate Japan can only splinter into three hundred separate, tiny estates. If the house of Tokugawa returns the reins of government to the emperor, unity will be restored. This plan will preserve peace and order in the land. More than three hundred years ago, Ieyasu founded the shogunate in order to do that very thing. Now, to the same purpose, I renounce power. My purpose is the same as that of our hallowed ancestor. In surrendering what he established, I carry out his wishes."

For hours he went on, talking backward and forward, until finally he said, "Are there any objections? If there are, speak up."

No one moved.

Added to their initial astonishment, a kind of hypnotic stupor had befallen them. "We were drunk with his eloquence," wrote one man in his journal to describe the peculiar air of the gathering.

"Very well, then. I will return rule to the emperor," said Yoshinobu, nodding in satisfaction as his gaze swept the room. Not for a full ten minutes after he had stood and left the room did people rouse from his spell. A wild clamor broke out, and people swarmed around the senior councillor and the inspector general, but it was over. He had deliberately invited dissent, but no one had broken out of the collective trance. Then, when he said "Very well, then" and rose to leave, no one had seized the moment to awaken and grab his sleeve to detain him.

"Tomorrow, gather together all the samurai of all the domains," ordered Yoshinobu. This was a surprise. Samurai were not entitled to an audience with the shogun. It would be more appropriate, argued the members of his cabinet, to summon all the daimyo from around the country, since only they were entitled to meet with the shogun in person. But Yoshinobu shook his head. "What can the daimyo do?" he asked.

He knew that power had shifted away from the daimyo toward their capable retainers. The thing to do now was appeal to them, to shore up public opinion on his side. The next day, the cabinet made the necessary arrangements.

On the afternoon of November 8, over forty men crowded into Nijo Castle, representing over thirty different fiefs. Keiki repeated his announcement and explanation. When he finished, he said, "If any of you have any doubts over this plan, I will meet with you later to discuss it."

People were astounded less by the unheard-of break with precedent than by the shogun's tremendous confidence. He was willing to grant special audiences in order to debate the issue. Six men took him up on it, from five provinces: Satsuma, Aki, Tosa, Bizen, and Uwajima. Among them were Satsuma's Komatsu Tatewaki and Tosa's Goto Shojiro. At that meeting, as fearless a man as Goto was so overcome at his first-ever personal audience with the shogun that he sweated copiously about the forehead and neck. They were utterly incapable of raising any objection. Unable to utter a syllable, it was all they could do to prostrate themselves before Yoshinobu and praise his decisiveness to the hilt. Yoshinobu took advantage of the occasion to deliver another peroration.

"Oh, I said something, I forget what." Years later, toward the end of the Meiji era, Yoshinobu answered his biographer's query with those offhand words.

The six men did nothing but prostrate themselves and repeat words of praise, lauding Yoshinobu's courage.

They did not leave the castle grounds till nightfall. Because Goto, the proposer of the plan, proceeded after that to pay a call on the regent, the hour grew late as Sakamoto Ryoma, drafter of the plan, waited anxiously in his lodgings for word of his brainchild's fate. At one point Sakamoto despaired, and told his men that a bloody transition was unavoidable. Finally, however, a hasty message from Goto arrived. As he took in the news, Sakamoto was overcome with emotion and crumpled over sideways in a heap. After years of struggle to overthrow the shogunate, he exclaimed passionately, "What must the shogun's feelings be on this day! How courageous of him to do this thing! I swear that I would gladly give my life for so great a man."

Yet it would not be long before Sakamoto himself was brought down by a band of bakufu assassins in Kyoto. Years later, Yoshinobu became fond of reading materials having to do with the Restoration; that was how he learned for the first time of events that had transpired outside the castle.

Two days later, on November 10, the plan for a transfer of powers was formally approved by the imperial court. The thing was finished.

Or, rather, from then on things began to happen.

Satsuma's plans for a bloody coup had been successfully thwarted, but the conspirators had not yet given up. Instead, they accepted that delay was inevitable and bided their time. Nor did they wait passively, but took every opportunity to provoke the bakufu, seeking to create an occasion for armed uprising. They sent ronin to Edo to commit acts of arson, breaking and entering, and other outrages in the shogun's city. Worse, they prompted the court to deal the severest possible blow to Yoshinobu: They demanded not only his resignation but also the abolition of his offices and the surrender of the vast Tokugawa lands.

16

Retreat to Osaka

Iᴛ ᴡᴀs Oᴋᴜʙᴏ Iᴄʜɪᴢᴏ's ɪᴅᴇᴀ ᴛʜᴀᴛ ᴛʜᴇ sʜᴏɢᴜɴ sʜᴏᴜʟᴅ be stripped of all that remained him and reduced to a mere commoner. Forcing Yoshinobu to return the rich Tokugawa landholdings to the throne would cause him to wind up not even a daimyo, but a penniless ronin.

"You never know what he'll do; he may just go along without a fuss," said Okubo to his crony the Kyoto noble Iwakura Tomomi. The two men took as their base of operations a teahouse in the city. When he went there, Iwakura had to disguise himself by dressing as a samurai and wearing a hood.

"Could be," said Iwakura, nodding. Even this pair of clever schemers was in awe of Yoshinobu's ingenious stratagems, his remarkable ability to scent out their most secret plans and dance his way around them. Clearly, Yoshinobu had grasped the farthest implications of the current political situation, and rather than resist the tide, he had chosen to gain sympathy, thus minimizing the damage that he and the Tokugawa would suffer. It was always his principle not to swim against the current, but to move with it. Otherwise, how could he have carried off that daring feat the month before, summarily handing over his powers without any outside pressure whatever?

"The man is as crafty as a fox," Saigo Takamori had declared in astonishment.

"Still, surely he will balk at this," said Iwakura, inclining his head thoughtfully. To give up title and lands alike would leave the shogun a ronin, a nobody. "Even if he's faced with an imperial order, I can't believe he would be willing to give it all up without a fight."

Yoshinobu had after all performed a service to the state without parallel in history, by voluntarily handing over his administrative powers to the throne. His awareness of the magnitude of what he had done would make him all the less likely to swallow these demands.

"Ah, but the beauty of Yoshinobu," said Okubo (or his weakness, he might better have said), "is his fear of the court."

In fact, no man feared becoming an enemy of the court as much as Yoshinobu did. Above all, he dreaded being branded with the name of traitor. How otherwise could a man so calmly rational have been so susceptible? His great ancestor, Tokugawa Ieyasu, had harbored no such weakness. His total lack of such fears had given him freedom. Unlike

Ieyasu, Yoshinobu was born in an age of too many readers, and Yoshinobu himself was far better read than Ieyasu ever was. For that reason, he could not help worrying about how he himself might go down in print. The verdict of future historians worried him most of all. In part, that was his legacy as a Mito. He was descended from the founders of Mitogaku, that school of thought whose unique perspective on history was based on the vilification of medieval shogun Ashikaga Takauji as an enemy of the rightful emperor; and, as a Mito, he had been thoroughly indoctrinated in that view. Terrified of becoming another Ashikaga Takauji, he became obsessed with the notion that he must not be seen as a turncoat.

All of this was well understood by Okubo Ichizo, a man of similar constitution. Only put the demand for the abolishment of the bakufu's court offices and the forfeiture of its lands in the form of an imperial command, and he was quite sure that Yoshinobu would rush to fall down, strip off the last trappings of power, and make himself a commoner.

But, added Okubo, while Yoshinobu himself would do so without hesitation, his force of eighty thousand troops would not go down without a fight. The shogunate's lands were estimated to be worth four million *koku*—some said eight million. If all of that were handed over to the imperial court, the shogunal vassals would be left high and dry, thrown out on the street with nothing but the clothes on their backs. Would they agree to such treatment? asked Okubo rhetorically. Of course not. Without a doubt, they would rebel. "Then," he added, "all we would have to do is declare them enemies of the throne and call in the daimyo to mop them up. That's our best plan."

"I see," said Iwakura, adding, "First we've got to reform the court." But how? He himself was only a low-ranking courtier, not powerful enough to see that such an "imperial command" was issued. Moreover, he had on his side no more than three other members of the court nobility. Fortunately, Nakayama Tadayasu, maternal grandfather of the young emperor Meiji and former chief councillor of state, would do Iwakura's bidding, and through him they could freely issue an imperial edict. If it were passed off as the emperor's will, a reform of the court could be carried out to Iwakura's design.

For the next few days Iwakura was immersed in plans. Before long he had the necessary men and system in place to make the extra demands of Yoshinobu. He put the bumbling, good-hearted Prince Arisugawa in charge of political affairs, and beneath him, as someone likely to do exactly as he was told, he put the imperial prince who had taken holy orders at the Ninna-ji temple, returning him to secular life as Prince Ninnaji. He also found positions for the former chief councillor of state Nakayama Tadayasu, as well as for his childhood friends Nakamikado Tsuneyuki and Sanjo Sanenaru. In addition, there were Tosa's Yamanouchi Yodo, Echizen's Matsudaira Shungaku, and Satsuma's Shimazu Mochihisa. These men were all assigned their parts in the temporary government by Iwakura, virtually single-handedly.

To Okubo he explained, "Of them all, Shungaku is most likely to weaken when the time comes. Yamanouchi Yodo will raise a storm, but he is the only one. If the rest rally 'round, there will be nothing to worry about."

On January 3, 1868, the system was put through, and at

the same time, the restoration of imperial rule was formally inaugurated.

"Sire, have you heard?" said Itakura Katsukiyo to Yoshinobu surreptitiously the day before the announcement was to be made. Yoshinobu's name was not on the list. Before resigning his administrative powers, Yoshinobu had reassured Itakura and his other vassals in Kyoto by declaring, "Even after the restoration I will attend to affairs of state in the new government and work with all the daimyo to aid His Majesty. It will hardly be any different from the way things are now." And yet, unaccountably, his name was missing.

"It's all right," said Yoshinobu laconically, aware that behind this turn of events lay the machinations of the Satsuma conspirators. Time and again they had outmaneuvered him. His mind worked fast. Rather than waste time lamenting how he had been tricked, better to reassess his position on the board and plan his next move. Failing to understand the way Yoshinobu's mind worked, Itakura misjudged his nature and lamented that he was incapable of feeling either sadness or rage.

"Tosa's strategists lost to Satsuma's strategists," said Yoshinobu, analyzing what had happened. For Tosa, the deaths of Sakamoto Ryoma and Nakaoka Shintaro, activists killed in December by a shogunate patrol squad in Kyoto, were a bitter blow. Since the assassinations, all communication with Satsuma and Choshu had ceased. But of course Yoshinobu was not referring to those two men, both of whom were figures of national stature rather than narrow proponents of Tosa thinking. The master strategist of Tosa, so far as he was concerned, was Goto Shojiro. For the last few weeks Goto had traveled hither and yon at Yamanouchi Yodo's behest, working for the salvation of the Tokugawa; but unlike Satsuma and Choshu, he lacked contacts in the court, and so lost out in the end to Okubo. It was apparent to Yoshinobu that the imperial court was now rife with Satsuma and Choshu sympathizers.

Yamanouchi Yodo, who was to be appointed to high office in the new government, had arrived in Kyoto the day before the grand announcement, taking lodging in an inn called the Daibutsu. Goto filled him in on the state of the city and rumors of what lay in store for Yoshinobu, but before he could finish speaking, Yodo burst into a paroxysm of rage.

"What the devil is Shimazu up to! He's got the mind of a fox. He's using the cause of imperial restoration as a cover to take over the realm by military force. If I attend the meeting tomorrow, I'll be vastly outnumbered. I won't be a party to it. I don't care if it is an imperial command, I'm not sending a single soldier, and that's that!" Loudly vociferating, he called for sake and spent the remainder of the evening getting stone drunk. The next morning he started off drinking again, even though he was expected at the palace. Finally, prevailed upon by his retainers, he climbed into his palanquin and headed off.

In accordance with custom, the meeting began late in the day, continuing through the night until dawn began to break. During that time Yodo spoke on Yoshinobu's behalf with increasing passion, finally declaring, "The doings of two or three nobles are sly and insidious. I suspect their plan is to take the young emperor under their wing and usurp his authority." One of the court nobles in attendance later wrote:

"Yodo was excited in spirit and arrogant in expression. His behavior was outrageous."

As the night wore on, however, Yodo gradually lost ground to Iwakura. In the end, he sensed that further resistance would be futile, and fell silent. He had done all he could. His silence signified tacit acceptance of the harsh terms attached to Yoshinobu's surrender after three centuries of Tokugawa rule. For Matsudaira Shungaku it was the same. A resolution was even passed requiring Shungaku to go to Nijo Castle with the lord of Owari to urge Yoshinobu to accept those terms, a task he accepted. Once again, as so many times before, at a critical turning point in Yoshinobu's life, Shungaku acted as messenger.

Yoshinobu was in the castle.

Also inside the castle grounds were the troops of Aizu and Kuwana, ready to a man to lay down their lives in the bakufu's defense. Shungaku entered the castle in ordinary dress, and as he threaded his way through the assembled throng of soldiers, they yelled at him in anger: "Satsuma and Tosa brought down the house of Tokugawa!" Ignoring their cries, Shungaku pushed on and soon found himself face-to-face with the shogun.

Yoshinobu listened carefully to Shungaku's message, and when it was over he repeated, "An imperial command, you say? In that case, I must change into formal clothes." With that, he left the room, retiring to his inner chamber and remaining there until evening. For two hours he was deep in thought. He consulted with Itakura Katsukiyo. But Itakura was by then fog-brained, and of no use as an adviser.

Yoshinobu then reappeared. "I agree to resign as shogun,"

he said. "Next is the matter of the other demands put before me."

The previous night Shungaku had argued fervently on Yoshinobu's behalf, finally winning a pair of significant concessions. First, the official posts would not all be abolished, but only those of the first rank. Second, of the Tokugawa landholdings, instead of the full four million *koku*, only half that amount would be returned to the throne.

"I have no objection there either," said Yoshinobu. But he went on to take issue with the widespread impression that the Tokugawa lands were actually worth four million *koku*. Bakufu land income amounted to only two million *koku* a year. The imperial order that he present two million *koku* thus would force him to turn over all Tokugawa territory. In time he would accede to this command as well, but at this moment, the agitation of public opinion prevented him from making a timely reply. He would convey his intentions to the emperor later, when calm had been restored.

Public opinion was indeed agitated. In Edo, the fudai daimyo got together and agreed to renounce the titles they had been given by the court. "By so doing, we sever our ties with the imperial court. We wish to die together as vassals of the Tokugawa," they declared. The leaders of the bakufu's Western-style troops in Edo, too, were outraged at the turn events had taken, and without awaiting orders they quickly set about assembling their men and leading them out of Edo onto warships bound for Kyoto. The number of those troops has been estimated at five thousand, or as many as ten thousand.

Of the probakufu troops stationed in Kyoto, five thousand

were infantry and hatamoto under the direct control of the Tokugawa; three thousand were from Aizu, and another fifteen hundred or so were from Kuwana (now northern Mie Prefecture), for a grand total of just under ten thousand. Satsuma, in contrast, had barely two thousand troops. That month, for the first time since 1863, Choshu troops had come openly into the capital and were even now camped on the city outskirts, numbering over one thousand strong. Together the two domains could muster a good three thousand men. If the Tokugawa army had a mind to take them on, it had them well outnumbered and might claim an easy victory, perhaps even destroying the combined Satsuma-Choshu forces in a single night. That was also why the Tokugawa army surged madly inside the castle walls, clamoring for the battle to begin. Yoshinobu, fearing an eruption, ordered all the soldiers out of their barracks and inside the castle walls, with gates barred. Summoning the commanding officers, he gave strict orders.

"Listen to me," he told them, his voice hoarse. "When you hear that Tokugawa Yoshinobu has committed *harakiri* and died, do as you please. But as long as there is life in my body, obey my commands. There will be no troops running wild."

Emotions were running so high at this point that some men crouched in a room of the castle and committed harakiri. The bodies were whisked out of sight, but there was no one to mop up the blood, and because of the crowd, no one even knew the names of the dead. Every time he strode down the hall, Yoshinobu looked at the pooled blood of those nameless dead and thought to himself that now a cataclysm was unavoidable.

Turning to Matsudaira Katamori, the lord of Aizu and former Protector of Kyoto who had never left his side for the
past few days, Yoshinobu looked at him and asked, "Can you
understand how I feel?" If there was to be a cataclysm anyway, instead of relinquishing his powers to the throne, he
could have chosen to annihilate the Satsuma troops in
Kyoto, bring down his army en masse from Edo, and put the
entire city of Kyoto under military occupation. Then, of
course, he would be branded as a traitor—or at the very
least, civil war would break out. If it came to that, the Tokugawa would lose. Having made up his mind not to respond
to Satsuma's provocation, Yoshinobu was determined to stick
unwaveringly to his principles.

"That is the only way to counter them," he concluded.

Matsudaira Katamori also sensed the folly of rising to the
bait. As he was nodding in agreement, suddenly Yoshinobu
proposed, "Let's go to Osaka." As long as this enormous
army was kept stationed in Kyoto, there was the danger of
unwelcome contingencies. They would have to leave.

"Flee the capital, you mean?" Katamori blanched. Quickly
recomposing his features, he stated firmly that the shogun's
soldiers would never pay heed to such an order. Some of the
Tokugawa vassals were threatening to kill Yoshinobu, he
knew. He was the real ringleader behind all this trouble, they
were muttering, that Mito shogun who had sold out the
house of Tokugawa, and they would kill him in tribute to the
earlier Tokugawa shoguns. Their logic was peculiar, but
these were extraordinary times and apparently they had won
a surprising number of listeners. It was precisely because he
understood the danger so well that this faithful brother of

the Tokugawa never left Yoshinobu's side for an instant. Should the disaffected soldiers storm the castle, he was ready to fight them back with Aizu troops.

Of all this, Yoshinobu naturally knew nothing. He supposed that the men of Aizu would be most opposed to leaving for Osaka Castle, and in that much he was correct. No one hated Satsuma as much as they, no one was as ready and determined as they to lay down their lives in battle in Kyoto. If ordered to retreat to Osaka Castle, they would no doubt die in an apoplectic rage.

Yoshinobu proposed a plan to win them over. He believed only in his own plans; at heart he trusted in them and nothing else—not his own vassals, not the Aizu loyalists. Yoshinobu told Katamori that he would meet in person with his chief retainer. Summoning Tanaka Tosa, chief elder of Aizu and general commander of forces in Kyoto, he had him come close and said, "I will speak to you from my heart." With that, he told him of his plan to retire to Osaka, and Tanaka concurred.

Tanaka went back to the soldiers' camp and explained the plan, but Sagawa Kanbei and Hayashi Gonsuke, heads of the combat units, furiously refused to listen. They thirsted for blood. When Yoshinobu heard this, he summoned the two men and first extolled their indignation: "A brave soldier is to be cherished," he told them. "And yet," he went on, his voice dropping, "I have my reasons for withdrawing to Osaka. More than that I cannot tell you now. Unless I keep my plan secret, I will lose. Do not trouble yourselves needlessly over such matters, but leave them to me," he urged.

The two men's hearts beat high. Interpreting the shogun's

words to mean that he would dig in at the mammoth Osaka Castle, the largest fortification in western Japan, and fight to the end against Kyoto, they went straight back to their men and told this to them. In no time the Aizu troops were appeased, and indeed began to clamor to leave quickly, the sooner the better.

"Ah, they've quieted down, have they, good," said Yoshinobu when he heard the report, nodding in satisfaction. But then he set down the tea he was drinking and for several seconds considered in silence: Why was it that his genius for tactical strategy should be devoted always to the retreat of his own troops, never to advance and victory? He had been born in the wrong place, he told himself. But then he picked up his tea bowl again and drained it. By the time he had drunk the last drops, all such foolish laments were banished from his thoughts. He had much to do. They would leave Kyoto that very night, he resolved, and ordered that preparations begin.

Escape and Aftermath

LATER IN LIFE, AS HIS BODY GREW OLD AND FRAIL, YOSHINOBU was haunted in his dreams by the events of that night. Few people can have seen as much drama in their lives as Yoshinobu did in his, but nothing seared itself into his brain like the memory of what happened on the night of January 7, 1868.

That evening he gathered several thousand samurai in the castle yard and broke open a barrel of sake. Each man was given an unglazed earthenware cup to drink from, embossed with a paulownia crest in gold. The Higashi Hongan-ji temple, then probakufu, had once presented them to Yoshinobu. He himself was first to raise his cup to his lips and drain it. Everyone then followed suit, smashing their emptied cups on the ground in the time-honored custom of soldiers departing for the front.

The hour was six P.M. The sun had set, and the castle gates swung open into darkness. In no time the first platoon set out, but their orders were to march without lights; a single lantern at the head of each platoon lighted the way. For identification, they each had tied up one sleeve with a white cotton cord. Only Yoshinobu, traveling on horseback in their midst, wore double sleeve-cords with a black crested kimono, to identify him as shogun. The white cords moved forward through the darkness, all else invisible.

They went down Omiya Avenue, turned at Sanjo, and headed west. Then from Senbon Street they came to an intersection, where they took Toba Highway, and so left behind the streets of the capital.

He was fleeing the capital. As the lights of Shichijo receded in the distance behind him, a cold sense of reality flooded through Yoshinobu. Five years had gone by since the spring day when he first entered the capital as shogunal guardian and called at the palace. No one in the history of the Tokugawa line had ever been as busy as he was during the intervening years. He had served the imperial court and his country with every ounce of strength he possessed, but to no avail. Now he was forced to flee the city like a refugee. Usually Yoshinobu was able, by the force of his intellect and will, to keep himself from waxing sentimental over his own dramatic situations—but for once his efforts at objectivity failed. As he sat astride his horse, Yoshinobu's cheeks were wet with tears.

"I'll never come back here again." The thought made him

as sentimental as a girl, but he resisted the impulse to cry uncontrollably. Gathering the reins in his hands, his spine straight in the saddle, he moved forward with his face tilted slightly upward. Not even Matsudaira Katamori at his side was aware that Yoshinobu was weeping.

Yoshinobu's intuition that he would not return to Kyoto proved correct. Never again in his lifetime was he to tread on Kyoto soil.

Dawn broke at Hirakata.

When they reached Osaka Castle, it was four P.M. The decision to leave had been made so abruptly that the castle was not prepared to receive Yoshinobu and his men. When dinner arrived, there was food enough only for Yoshinobu. With his own hands he broke it in half and shared it with Matsudaira Katamori.

After that, the new civil government in Kyoto—actually, Iwakura Tomomi and the men of Satsuma—was imperious. In an attempt to provoke Yoshinobu and his men, insistent pressure was applied for the speedy fulfillment of the court's demands. Yodo and Shungaku did all they could to negotiate a relaxing of the harsh terms, but then in Edo a calamity occurred. When Satsuma ronin deliberately disturbed the peace to provoke the bakufu, the shogunal council lost patience and ordered troops from Yamagata to set fire to the Satsuma headquarters. When word of the incident reached Osaka, the shogun's troops were enraged, and without waiting for orders from Yoshinobu they took up their positions, spreading out between Kyoto and Osaka to be ready for battle on a moment's notice. The situation had escalated far beyond the ability of chief senior councillor Itakura Katsukiyo to control.

Going to Yoshinobu, who was laid up with a bad cold, unable to leave his room, he urged him over and over to lead his troops to Kyoto. Yoshinobu could not get out of bed. For the past few days he had thought of various plans, trying to guess the intentions of the men in Kyoto, but no brilliant move presented itself. If he went back to Kyoto for a showdown, he might enjoy a military victory only to lose on the political front. Okubo Ichizo and Saigo Takamori might well manipulate their own military failure into a political victory. The politicians most on Yoshinobu's mind were not Itakura and other bakufu council members, but the enemy—Okubo and Saigo. He felt as if he were engaged in a game of chess with them, stretching across thirteen miles of the Keihan highway between Osaka and Kyoto.

As a sign of how heavily those two weighed on his mind, he opened a chapter of Sun-tzu's classic treatise, *The Art of War*, which he was then rereading, and showed it to Itakura. Then he commented, "It says here, 'He who knows the enemy and knows himself is invincible in a hundred battles.' So I ask you: Among all our fudai daimyo and bakufu retainers, is there any the equal of Saigo Takamori?"

Itakura thought awhile before answering, "There is not."

Yoshinobu then asked, "Is there any man the equal of Okubo Ichizo?"

Itakura dropped his head and answered no. Inwardly, he was amazed that Yoshinobu knew the names of the Satsuma fighters. On and on Yoshinobu brought up the names of one Satsuma man after another, asking about each one, "Do we have any man his equal?" Again and again Itakura answered regretfully, no.

"That is why even if we wage war against them, we cannot win," said Yoshinobu. In his view, the only way to avoid falling victim to the enemy's stratagems was to adopt a submissive posture of nonresistance; give up that policy, and the game would be over.

But events began to sweep Yoshinobu along with them. The prowar faction of his retainers resolved to make an armed attack on Kyoto, and on January 26, with an anti-Satsuma banner waving in their van, the entire Tokugawa army of fifteen thousand men headed north with cannons in tow, on the march. Yoshinobu had no choice but to acquiesce. And, with his army on the move, he dreamed now of victory. The Satcho troops in Kyoto were few in number. They should be able to gain the ascendancy over them, at least for now. With the capital in control of the military, he could accede to headship of the court government and hold sway over the country, carrying out necessary reforms while attacking the Satsuma-Choshu forces as enemies of the state. It was an appealing scenario.

"But it's only a dream." Yoshinobu's reason was able to laugh at his fancies. Even if they were defeated in battle, Saigo and Okubo would never be so boneheaded as to leave the youthful emperor behind in Kyoto. No, they would take him with them, and then from a safe location issue an imperial mandate to the lords and samurai of the nation. Given the domination of *sonno* ("revere the emperor") sentiment, it would not be long before millions of men from all around the country flocked to Kyoto to destroy Yoshinobu and the last vestiges of the Tokugawa regime.

Events rumbled forward like the wagon wheels under the

cannons. At five P.M. on the afternoon of January 27, a battle commenced in the village of Toba, and subsequently the bakufu army opened fire on Sat-cho forces along the Fushimi highway. The booming of the gunfire reached all the way to Osaka Castle. After dark Yoshinobu looked out from the castle to the north and saw that the town of Fushimi was burning, for only that part of the night sky glowed a dull red.

The outcome of the battle was unknown.

There was no more news from the front. The roads were jammed, and no official messengers made it through to Yoshinobu. Over seventy hours from the outbreak of hostilities, at seven P.M. on the evening of January 30, the outcome was finally clear. The news was brought not by messenger, but by the defeated soldiers themselves, streaming back to Osaka Castle in retreat. The castle grounds were in an uproar such as had not been seen since the overthrow of Toyotomi Hideyori more than three hundred years before.

But the battle fever of the Aizu retainers was not in the least abated. With an intensity tinged with pathos, they called for the shogun to personally lead his forces into battle, a cry echoed by the bakufu troops. With damage limited to the annihilation of the spearhead troops, if Yoshinobu would lead the unharmed rear guard, morale would soar and victory would be theirs, they asserted. Military wisdom confirmed this.

Unable to quiet the clamor of voices urging him to take charge, Yoshinobu entered the great hall, where his troop commanders sat assembled. In the glow of candlelight he saw a room packed with men swathed in bloody bandages, some of them too severely wounded to prostrate themselves before the shogun as convention demanded. Before this appalling sight Yoshinobu was for once speechless. Itakura quickly stepped in, asking the assembled men, "What shall we do now?"

With a roar came the instant, unanimous reply: "Fight!"

"Handle them somehow ..." These were Yoshinobu's next words. There was nothing else for him to do but deal somehow with these people. Before long he left the room and summoned Itakura and the inspector general, Nagai Naomune. "I'm going back to Edo," he said.

Itakura was taken by surprise. If word of Yoshinobu's intention should leak out there in the castle where people were seething with lust for battle, there was no telling what might become of him. Not only that, but Itakura himself had been converted to the pro-war position. To go back to Edo without a fight seemed to him like running away. Nor was Nagai convinced either. Yoshinobu was now isolated from his closest advisers. He would have to deceive these two as well.

"I will go back—and I have an idea what to do then," he said, making it sound as if he intended to dig in and make a last stand in Edo. Itakura and Nagai rejoiced. In that case, better that he return to Edo Castle as soon as possible, but in the meantime how were they to handle this uproar in Osaka Castle? How could he even hope to escape from there?

"What will you do, sire?"

"Can't you guess?" Yoshinobu was impatient. In Osaka Harbor was the Dutch-built frigate of the bakufu, *Kaiyo-maru*; if he could make it that far, he would need only to weigh anchor.

229

Abandoning your officers and men. That was what Itakura's reproachful expression said. But Yoshinobu took issue with that silent protest: "Those are not my officers and men now," he said. "That is a mob."

He would take with him Matsudaira Katamori, lord of Aizu, and his brother Matsudaira Sadaaki, lord of Kuwana, he said, looking at the two men. To leave them there would be extremely dangerous, for it was their forces that were the most excited of all. Once Yoshinobu was gone, they would no doubt entrench themselves in Osaka Castle with their commanders and lead a fight against the forces of the new government in Kyoto. The only way to prevent that was to take them with him as virtual hostages.

Itakura looked at the two daimyo for their reactions. With their leaders gone, what would the men of their two domains do? They would have no choice but to flee, and a harrowing escape it would be.

But the Matsudaira brothers said that in these times of emergency, they wished above all to protect His Excellency, Yoshinobu. All too trusting, they believed to the end that Yoshinobu wanted them with him for his own self-protection.

"Leave the escape plans to me," said Yoshinobu. At times like this, he thought and acted with characteristic incisiveness. Quickly he got up and went back out to the hall packed tightly with the crowd of retainers. Men were spilling out into the hallways too, and they crowded around Yoshinobu as he made his way forward, all but pulling on his *hakama* as they implored him to lead the army into battle.

Finally, Yoshinobu stood and cried, "All right! If we are to go into battle, let there be no delay. Let us rise now and fight. Everyone, make your preparations."

The crowded hall shook as the men cheered and sprang outside to prepare for battle, each man dashing to his post, while Yoshinobu withdrew into the castle recesses. Immediately he slipped out, taking with him eight or nine men, including the Matsudaira brothers. All were dressed in plain clothes. They ran through the castle grounds, but in the crowd and the darkness, no one recognized them.

It was then about ten o'clock. They stole out through the back gate. The guard leveled his rifle and issued a challenge: "Who goes there?" Yoshinobu answered without missing a beat: "The pages are rotating shifts." He had an undeniable genius. Yoshinobu's gift for thinking quickly under pressure was probably what led people to call him a master of deception. In any case, he succeeded in pulling the wool over the eyes of his entire army.

They got into a riverboat and traveled downstream till they came to the sea, reaching the offing late at night. In the blackness it was impossible to tell where the *Kaiyo-maru* lay anchored. All they could make out was a huge American battleship before their eyes. Yoshinobu declared that they would rest aboard the American ship until dawn, and ordered one of his men to handle the negotiations. The American captain approved their request, and had food and drink brought out for his unexpected visitors. At dawn the whereabouts of their own frigate became plain, and the group piled into a small boat furnished them by the Americans and made their way to it. The *Kaiyo-maru* lost no time in steaming out of the harbor in the morning mist. Yoshinobu's disappearance was just then becoming known in the castle.

When the frigate reached the Kii Channel, Yoshinobu seemed to relax. He sent for Itakura and the rest, and for the first time spoke frankly about his thoughts and plans for the future. After returning to Edo he would not show any resistance, but would continue to pledge his unswerving allegiance.

"We were fooled," they thought. Surrounded on all sides by sea, without a single retainer of their own at their sides, Katamori and Sadaaki had no way to pressure Yoshinobu.

"You understand, do you not?" said Yoshinobu to Katamori, pressing the point. Katamori was staring at the table before him, head down, his face ashen. Yet having once sworn to cast his lot with Yoshinobu, come what may, he could only nod.

The *Kaiyo-maru* entered Shinagawa offing, and anchored there on the night of the eleventh. They spent the night there and ventured out on land before dawn on the twelfth, heading straight for the palace on the beach. The locals realized from the thunder of hooves that a band of men on horses had galloped by, but naturally they had no inkling that the shogun had returned. The hour was so early that Edo was not yet astir, and the hatamoto remained unaware of what had transpired.

When the sun had risen completely, the captain of the warship, Enomoto Takeaki, fired a cannon salute toward Edo. At home in Akasaka, Katsu Kaishu, the former commissioner of warships, silently counted the number of times the cannon went off and realized that it was in honor of a great minister or shogun. "It must be Yoshinobu returning in defeat," he thought. Soon a messenger appeared at the Katsu residence, bearing a summons.

Katsu Kaishu had already guessed the content of the message. He was not in favor with Yoshinobu, had never been given a position of any importance by him, and was in fact now under domiciliary confinement, relieved of office. For Yoshinobu to turn to him now was most extraordinary. It was because he had lost, Katsu thought. Of all the Tokugawa retainers, only he, Katsu, had earned the love and respect of the Satsuma and Choshu patriots. Probably Yoshinobu wanted him to take charge after the fighting was over.

Katsu rushed to the beach palace, entered the compound, and was shown to the lawn of a large courtyard, where two Western-style chairs were set out. That arrangement had been chosen for his audience with Yoshinobu despite the cold, no doubt to ensure that their conversation remained confidential. Soon Yoshinobu came into the courtyard and was seated. For a while he was silent, but then a change came over his face. Hurriedly, Katsu leaned forward. Yoshinobu's eyes were shining. The next moment, sparkling tears spilled from his eyes and coursed freely down his cheeks. They were the first tears Yoshinobu had shown to any retainer of his since leaving Kyoto.

"They carried the brocade banner," he said simply.

The battle had begun on January 27, 1868, and on January 29 the brocade banner that signified an imperial commission had appeared, transforming Satsuma and Choshu into imperial forces. That automatically made Yoshinobu a rebel, a traitor to the throne. The stigma would never vanish. He had finally been pushed into the position he had most dreaded. As soon as he had heard the news, Yoshinobu had abandoned the castle, abandoned his troops, and returned to Edo. He knew that Katsu, so like him in disposition and ability, would understand everything from that one statement, without need of explanation.

"Take the appropriate measures to deal with the situation," he ordered, and got up. Then, leaving the beach palace ahead of Katsu, he hurried to Edo Castle on horseback. It was the first time he entered the castle since his proclamation as shogun. He went straight to the women's quarters, intending to pay his respects to Seikaku-in, the former Princess Kazu, who was the royal-blooded widow of the previous shogun, Iemochi, and also his own relation. He announced himself to her lady-in-waiting, but his petition was summarily turned down. She could not meet with an enemy of the throne, said the former princess.

Next he requested to see Tensho-in, the Satsuma-born widow of the shogun Iesada, daughter of his old ally Shimazu Nariakira. She agreed, and met with him that afternoon at about four P.M. He told her all that had happened leading up to the calamitous Battle of Toba-Fushimi: how his troops had set out for Kyoto, hoping to dislodge the Satsuma-Choshu forces from the Kyoto palace, only to be intercepted at Toba and Fushimi, south of the city, and suffer a terrible defeat. He unburdened himself of his inmost feelings. So skillfully did he express himself that Tensho-in forgot the gravity of the situation, lost in the power and beauty of his words. Her lady-in-waiting, Minoura Hanako, who would live on many years into the Meiji era, said over and over that Yoshinobu's words on this occasion surpassed even the eloquence of the famous actor Danjuro, and that she wished she could have recorded them verbatim. Probably no defeated general has ever spoken of his defeat with such brilliance. He was furthermore a superb actor who never volunteered another syllable on the subject, maintaining silence about the past for the rest of his life.

Yoshinobu needed personally to talk to the castle ladies at this time, but it was a matter of pressing urgency in a political sense as well. He hoped that Tensho-in, with her Satsuma ties, would conduct diplomatic negotiations with the imperial army on his behalf, and he also wanted to gain the sympathy of Princess Seikaku-in with her ties to the imperial family. After first turning him away, she later consented to see him at Tensho-in's intervention, and when she heard the details of his situation, she took his side and even made an appeal to Kyoto for him. Such was the miraculous effectiveness of Yoshinobu's gift with words.

The next political policy he needed to adopt was one of absolute allegiance, at whatever cost. Allegiance not so much to the familiar, living powers of this world—the court nobles, daimyo, and politicians—as to the history of the next, in order to remove the nasty aura of rebel from himself, secure a favorable impression, and escape the stigma of "traitor." There was no other way for him to contend with the politicians.

He sought steadily to position himself as underdog. The nation's theater-loving public was particularly fond of tragedy, with a special weakness for tragic heroes. The real-life tragic figure of Minamoto no Yoshitsune, brilliant but ill-fated warrior of the Heian era, was a beloved national icon.

Yoshinobu tried to live out that theme in his own life. As long as he made a point of it, society would overwhelmingly view him as the underdog, and as long as he was the underdog hero, Satsuma and Choshu would be painted in the public's mind as black-hearted villains. This was the last trick in the bag of Yoshinobu the schemer.

In order to guard this allegiance of his, he sacrificed others remorselessly. To the bakufu retainers he announced, "Do not live in Edo. Those of you who have a fief should go live there and make new lives for yourselves." His words caused discomfiture and aroused antipathy. Most pitiful of all were the Matsudaira brothers, Katamori and Sadaaki, who had spared no effort in serving Yoshinobu. Because they were despised by the imperial court and by Satsuma and Choshu, they were also refused admittance to Edo Castle and forced to leave the city—kicked out, as it were. Katamori returned to Aizu, while his younger brother, Sadaaki, unable to return to Kuwana because it had fallen under the influence of the imperial army, led the remnants of his defeated army to Echigo (now Niigata). Already enemies of the imperial throne, abandoned now by the Tokugawa as well, there was nothing left for them to do but fight and die in the moors and hills. Bitter at Yoshinobu's treatment of them, Katamori found an outlet for his feelings in poetry, writing mournfully, "How could such a great tree abandon its own limbs?"

Day by day, Yoshinobu's submissiveness and allegiance grew more complete. On March 6 he left Edo Castle and retired to the Tokugawa-affiliated Kan'ei-ji temple in Ueno, confining himself there in seclusion. Finally, on May 3, he had Katsu Kaishu surrender Edo Castle to the imperial forces. On the morning of the castle's takeover, he left the temple and departed from Edo for Mito, his ancestral domain, condemned to live there in retirement.

The following year, in October 1869, Yoshinobu was given his freedom, and at the same time he was forgotten by the times. Around then he moved from Mito to Shizuoka, the new Tokugawa fief. From then on Yoshinobu vanished forever from history.

In Shizuoka, he lived in a mansion that had once belonged to a magistrate. He was young for retirement, only thirty-two.

The day he arrived in Shizuoka, Yoshinobu said, "Now I must live out the endless days of my life." It struck his chief page, Shinmura Takeo, that Yoshinobu sounded uncharacteristically nihilistic and mournful, and the thought that even his master was prone to such moods and regrets made his throat tighten—until he realized his error. Yoshinobu meant that because the days stretched out endlessly, he would have to work hard to keep himself entertained.

Yoshinobu absorbed himself from then on in pursuing his varied interests. His favorite pastimes were archery, polo, hunting, and falconry. He was a perfectionist in all he did. Every day he practiced releasing a falcon from his fist; after that, it was Noh chanting of the Hosho school, followed by oil painting. Yoshinobu was fond of painting, and in his Hito-tsubashi days he had studied traditional landscape painting under the master Kano Tan'en, but he took to oil painting with even more abandon.

"The one time I am glad I gave up being shogun is when I

am painting in oils," he said, a stranger to boredom. He learned the rudiments of oil painting from a former retainer named Nakajima Shotaro, who had some knowledge of the art, but he lacked materials. So he fashioned his own. For a canvas he substituted cheesecloth soaked in alum water, and since oil paints were also hard to come by, he improvised those as well.

Photography had always fascinated him, and after going into retirement he took up its study scientifically, often spending long nights in his darkroom working on developing his photographs. He was especially partial to photographs of scenery, and captured on film virtually every scenic spot in and around Shizuoka.

It was the same with embroidery. He made purses and the like, embroidering them with rather ordinary designs of peonies and Chinese lions, or rape flowers and butterflies, and presenting them to his attendants. Once, he began a large project, saying that when it was finished he would give it to the family of Prince Arisugawa, his mother's ancestral line, but when it was finished he took a dislike to it and spent days unraveling the threads.

"Why not leave it as it is?" his attendant remonstrated, but Yoshinobu shook his head. If he did that, then after his death it would be shown to the world as an example of his handiwork, and that he could not allow, he said. Who cares? "It's only a piece of embroidery," thought the attendant to himself, but Yoshinobu was as ever acutely aware of his position in history, and overly sensitive to how later generations might look on him.

He refused to see his old retainers.

If he did see them, he would be forced to make some sort of comment. He feared that anything he said might be repeated and bandied about. He would consent to see only his old retainer Shibusawa Eiichi, and Katsu Kaishu, who was something like his sponsor with the Meiji government. When Shibusawa came to see him around 1877, bringing with him Nagai Naomune (the former inspector general, whom Yoshinobu had made his private secretary in his Kyoto days), Yoshinobu saw only Shibusawa, refusing to meet with Nagai. Whereas Shibusawa was now a businessman lacking any government office, Nagai was serving in the new government as well, as general secretary of the senate. Apparently Yoshinobu took this way of avoiding giving any false impression to the new government.

"But doesn't he want to see me for old times' sake?" wondered Nagai. During their days in Kyoto, after the assassination of Hara Ichinoshin, Nagai had served as his strategist while at the same time becoming a central figure in the bakufu; and from the time of the imperial restoration all the way until the surrender of Osaka Castle after Yoshinobu's return to Edo, he had handled all sorts of important business for Yoshinobu. The two men whom Yoshinobu would have most enjoyed talking over old times with were doubtless Itakura Katsukiyo and Nagai Naomune. But Yoshinobu was afraid to talk.

If he opened his mouth, inevitably some of what he said would be charged with bitterness. People would hear of it, and take it as resentment on his part, he feared. For that reason he refused to see any but the two men mentioned above—Shibusawa and Katsu.

He did not even meet with Matsudaira Shungaku. After the Restoration, Shungaku became one of the most highly placed men in the Meiji government, and moved from Kyoto to Tokyo, the new name given to Edo. On the way he stopped in Shizuoka. Bowing to the times, however, he made no effort to see Yoshinobu. Other officials as well, old acquaintances of Yoshinobu's whose business took them frequently back and forth between Tokyo and Kyoto, stayed away from Shizuoka for fear of inviting misunderstanding. Yoshinobu was not hurt by these men's attitudes. On the contrary, he was glad. He wanted to go on having as little to do with the world as possible.

Nagai Naomune professed to be able to understand Yoshinobu's point of view, but not his apparent lack of nostalgia. With new understanding, he recalled hearing that Yoshinobu's reputation among former shogunate retainers in Shizuoka was not very good. Before this the new government had declared Kamenosuke, a Tayasu boy, the new head of the Tokugawa house, giving him a stipend of 700,000 *koku* in Shizuoka, and moving him there from Tokyo. Some five thousand former bakufu retainers had accompanied him, knowing they would have no stipends. When they arrived, there were no houses for them, and they made do by billeting in merchants' houses and farmhouses, leading lives of extraordinary poverty. In the midst of all those goings-on, Yoshinobu with his old fondness for whatever was new and different would sometimes ride around town on a bicycle, causing the old shogunate retainers to whisper among themselves in displeasure that highborn people lacked feelings.

It seemed to Nagai Naomune, too, after he came all the

way to Shizuoka to see Yoshinobu only to be sent away, that Yoshinobu's emotional life was somehow different from that of people brought up in an ordinary way. Yoshinobu was to remain thirty years in seclusion in Shizuoka. In 1888 a train station was built a short distance from his house, and the noise bothered him so much that he moved. It was as though he would do anything to avoid other people.

Yet during that time he sired a large number of children; indeed, he seems to have devoted himself to fathering children during his retirement. In 1881 his first and second sons were both born. The following year they both died, and a third son came along. The year after that his third son died, and a daughter appeared. It was a busy time. Naturally, there was more than one mother. The number of children who survived to maturity was twenty-one—ten boys and eleven girls.

In 1897, when Yoshinobu was sixty, his residence was broken into by an infamous pair of burglars who destroyed treasures in the house and stole part of the Tokugawa riches. They were soon caught, but the incident left Yoshinobu leery of living in the house, and in November of that year he moved back to Tokyo, settling in Sugamo and becoming for the first time since the Restoration a citizen of Tokyo. He sought to continue his reclusive, quiet life, but Prince Arisugawa took pity on him and attempted to force him to call at the castle, saying things like "Here you are, living in Tokyo now, and still you don't come to see us. Why not?" But Yoshinobu declined. He had once been branded with the name of enemy of the throne. Even though he had since been pardoned, he was still living a life of self-imposed discipline, and had no desire to call at the castle, he said.

Prince Arisugawa misunderstood. Or, rather, perhaps he did understand in essence. He thought that Yoshinobu was making too much of being labeled an enemy of the throne, and perhaps he was. Yoshinobu was deeply resentful that after having voluntarily relinquished his power, he should still have received such treatment. His bitterest resentment lay not with the court itself but with Okubo and Saigo, both men of Satsuma.

Resentment against Satsuma and Choshu smoldered within him. Once he said to his attendant, "The men of Choshu saw the bakufu as their enemy from the start, so I think nothing of them. But the men of Satsuma were different. At first they were close to the bakufu, and together they brought down Choshu. But when circumstances changed, they pretended to remain close to the bakufu on the surface, all the while plotting beneath the surface and finally engaging in a double cross."

Those words got around, and came to the attention of Arisugawa. Thinking that Yoshinobu's refusal to call at the palace must stem from some such resentment, he told him, "It's now been over twenty years since those people"—an allusion to Okubo and Saigo—"met with foul play. Many of those who knew the events of those days are dead, and it's all in the past. It's no use going on talking that way forever."

Yoshinobu protested courteously that he did not hate those men, that on the contrary they were the country's elder statesmen—but then he could not go on. He was running out of reasons to refuse.

"I don't have any Western-style formal clothes," he said finally, coming up with a childish excuse.

Prince Arisugawa shook his head firmly and said there was certainly no need for any such thing. A black crested kimono was surely good enough, and what in the world did he want with Western-style full dress?

The prince had a reason for inviting him. Yoshinobu had no rank or title. He was neither a titled peer nor a samurai, nor yet a common citizen either. He had close blood ties to the Arisugawa family, and was moreover a distant relation of the current empress. The old daimyo, including both Matsu-daira brothers, had been made members of the peerage, while their former commander, Yoshinobu, received no recognition whatever. It was an odd state of affairs.

Besides, thirty years after the Restoration, it was all history. Now that things had calmed down and they could look back with greater perspective, there was room to imagine what might have happened if Yoshinobu had not peacefully handed over the Tokugawa power. No one in the Meiji government said so openly, but many thought privately that the greatest contributor to the establishment of the Meiji government was none other than Tokugawa Yoshinobu. There was a movement afoot to see that he received some sort of title in reward, and for that, it was necessary that he pay his respects at court.

Yoshinobu continued to hang back. He promised only to talk it over with Katsu. When he did so, Katsu refrained from encouraging him outright, but did say he saw no particular harm in it.

In the end, Yoshinobu did appear at court. The year was 1898, and Yoshinobu was sixty-one. Purposely refraining from having a set of Western-style formal clothes tailored for the occasion, he wore his black kimono with the hollyhock crest as he mounted the steps of the former castle, where he used to live.

He was shown into a Japanese-style room. It was not Western-style, partly because of the way Yoshinobu was dressed, and partly because the emperor Meiji wished to receive him as much as possible like a member of the family. He was offered a cushion to sit on, but did not use it. His hosts were the emperor and empress. She waited on him herself, filling his sake cup a single time. Yoshinobu knew her from his Kyoto days, when he used to call at the Ichijo house, and he remembered her as a little girl. She must have remembered him, too, since he was then the supreme ruler of Japan.

Yoshinobu safely withdrew from the imperial presence.

The following day the emperor called in Prime Minster Ito Hirobumi and said jokingly, "Yesterday I was finally able to do something to show my gratitude to Yoshinobu. I ought to be grateful; after all, I took the country away from him!" This reminiscence, so typical of Emperor Meiji, created a favorable impression on all who heard it, and was widely repeated.

The day after that, Katsu Kaishu called at court as a former shogunate retainer, to express his appreciation to the emperor.

Four years later, in order for Yoshinobu to set up a new branch of the Tokugawa, as required by law he was raised to the peerage and given the rank of marquis.

Later, in 1903, Yoshinobu took his first long trip since the Restoration, traveling to Osaka. Entering the castle, now under the control of the fourth army division, he climbed all the way to the top of the donjon and looked out. He was accompanied by the commanding officer of the fourth division and the armory head. They deliberately stood at a respectful distance as Yoshinobu lingered, not wishing to intrude on the thoughts and emotions that surely swept over him. Afterward they took him on a tour of the ordnance factory east of the castle, with its many chimneys. They knew that he had always had a special interest in firearms from old times. To their surprise, however, Yoshinobu showed not a whit of interest in the cluster of new cannons. What caught his eye and fascinated him above all were the soldiers' canteens then being made.

"How do you use this?" he asked, picking one up in his hand and hanging on to it. They explained in detail how to put in the rice and water, and presented him with one as a gift. He was delighted, but then inquired, "Begging your pardon, but is aluminum harmful to the human body?" He intended to use the canteen for his daily meals. The officers were not certain of the answer to his question.

Silver would be no problem, thought Yoshinobu, always aroused by a challenge, and after he went back to Tokyo, he sent a bar of silver to the ordnance factory with a request that they use it to fashion him a canteen. They did, and sent him the result, which pleased Yoshinobu so much that from then until his death, three times a day without fail he cooked his own rice in his own canteen.

Yoshinobu was an eyewitness to the hoopla surrounding the Russo-Japanese War, which broke out the following year, and to Japan's victory, but he acted perfectly indifferent to the outcome. He was not indifferent to current events for all that, however, and in old age he loved to read a number of newspapers every day. In 1910, when the anarchist leader Kotoku Shusui was arrested with eleven of his followers on suspicion of plotting to assassinate the emperor, Yoshinobu thought that the emperor and the emperor system were fated to go the way he and the Tokugawa shogunate had gone. Gathering his children around him, he admonished them: "In this age, to get along in the world it is better for everyone, even women, to find employment." That was the first and last time he ever dispensed such fatherly advice.

By now he was seventy. He lived on, catching a light cold at the age of seventy-six, in November 1913. In no time he had a fever of 103. Over and over he told his physician, in the same words each time, "If this is pneumonia, I'm ready to die. Do you think it is pneumonia?" In fact, just as he suspected, it was acute pneumonia, and when the fever came on him, both lungs were already affected.

Just before he died, his physician leaned over the pillow and asked, "Are you in pain?" Yoshinobu answered faintly, in an extremely accurate description of his condition: "No, I am just weak. The pain is gone." Those were his last words. A few minutes later, at 4:10 P.M. on November 21, 1913, he was gone.

The funeral took place in the afternoon of the thirtieth, at the Kan'ei-ji in Ueno, the Tokugawa family temple. From Ieyasu on, funerals of shoguns had always been performed by Buddhist monks of the Tendai and Jodo sects, but Yoshinobu's funeral followed Shinto ritual, as he had wished. Shinto was the official religion of the Mito, and it seems that

Yoshinobu wished to be seen off in death as a man of Mito.

An imperial envoy attended the funeral, along with over three hundred of the former daimyo. There were many mourners from the defunct hatamoto families, but what struck everyone most of all was the large number of representatives of foreign countries in attendance. From their perspective, the funeral marked the passing of a former head of state, and they were paying the proper respect. United States President Woodrow Wilson sent a formal message of condolence through the Japanese foreign minister. There could have been no greater mark of respect on the death of a former Japanese ruler.

"The last shogun is dead," people said, and people in the great town houses of Tokyo lined the streets as his coffin went by. Of particular note was the appearance of every firefighting unit in the city, decked out in brand-new breeches and livery coats ordered specially for the occasion, standing smartly at attention to pay their respects to this last shogun, who had shown such affection to one of them—Shinmon Tatsugoro.

With the death of Tokugawa Yoshinobu, the age of old Edo belonged suddenly to the distant past. From that day on, Yoshinobu began to live in the emotions of those who looked back with nostalgia on that vanished age.

Author's Afterword

Afterwords are of no use, but I am going to write one anyway because I find that even after finishing this book, my heart is rocked by waves that will not be stilled. Perhaps in penning these lines, I can achieve a measure of peace.

It is a long time now since I first thought I would write about Tokugawa Yoshinobu. Since then, the man has been in my thoughts on many occasions, as he was on a trip I took to Kagoshima—present-day site of the former Satsuma domain—one New Year's a couple of years ago.

While taking in the sights of the city, I stopped at a bookstore and purchased a book called *Rohen Nankoku-ki*, written by one Shimazu Tadashige, born in 1886, the nineteenth year of Meiji. He was head of the old aristocratic house of Shimazu, and grandson to Shimazu Hisamitsu. Known as an expert on England in the old Imperial Navy, he retired as a rear admiral, serving thereafter as head of the House of Peers. His father, Tadayoshi, would have been the twenty-ninth lord of Satsuma, Tadashige himself the thirtieth.

The next day a chill rain fell, making the prospect of outdoor excursions rather unpleasant. I had little choice but to remain inside and read my book. It was an autobiographical essay, from which I learned to my surprise that Yoshinobu never met face-to-face with the head of the house of Shimazu until the waning years of Meiji.

"[The meeting took place on] a day at the very end of the Meiji era," wrote Shimazu Tadashige. It could have been around 1909 or 1910, or even as late as 1912. By then the author would have been a naval ensign or lieutenant junior grade; Yoshinobu, past seventy, would have been pursuing his many interests with no sign of senility. Every morning he read the newspaper avidly, always keeping up with the careers of people who had figured in the Restoration. In particular he read everything he could find on the life of the Satsuma leader and master strategist Okubo Toshimichi, his old nemesis—striving for knowledge of the era that not even he had been privy to at the time. Apparently, his mental vigor was undiminished.

According to Tadashige's account, it was Tokugawa Iesato, of the main Tokugawa line, who brought the two men together. The setting was the palace. The following is Tadashige's description of the meeting in his own words:

Yoshinobu struck me as a rather small man. Already advanced in years when I met him, he seemed enervated, an affable figure who said very little. When Iesato introduced me, saying, "This is Shimazu Tadashige, son of Shimazu Tadayoshi and present head of the house of Shimazu," Yoshinobu's only response was "Indeed." Yet it struck me that as he scrutinized me, the eyes of this fifteenth and final Tokugawa shogun filled with tears. His taciturnity only reinforced my impression that he was extremely moved. Much affected by the mood of the moment, I hesitated to say much in turn. Yoshinobu died thereafter in 1913, at the age of seventy-six. Had I known that that was to be our first and last encounter, I would have spoken of many things.

This is all he has to say of the encounter.

Revolution or no, it was doubtless impossible for Yoshinobu to remain calm in the presence of the youthful head of the Shimazu of Satsuma, whose stratagems were what had tripped him up and toppled him from power. For the men of Choshu, Yoshinobu bore no ill will. But for the men of Satsuma, he bore a deep-seated grudge, one he alluded to long after the Meiji Restoration was history. What must have gone through his mind that day as he stared at Tadashige? Wondering, I could hardly sleep that night.

As it happened, I was staying in what was formerly the Shimazu villa, now a seaside inn called the Shigetomi-so. The sliding doors in my room were painted with the Shimazu crest, and outside my window was a large garden with an arbutus so venerable that old Shimazu Hisamitsu himself must have laid eyes on it in his time. Spending the night where history's aggressors once lived, as I contemplated the viewpoint and mental state of one of history's victims, I began to feel that the shadow cast by Yoshinobu on history was clearcut and intense. It was then that I decided to write about him.

Carrying out that decision was not easy, for Yoshinobu's is not a story that lends itself easily to retelling. He was a politician, and, except for Stefan Zweig's *Joseph Fouche*, few books with politicians as their subject have met with any success. Politicians can exist only in the midst of political events and can therefore be understood only amid the whirl of politics. Page after page of detailed political information must precede a few lines portraying the man at the center of events. Worse, if the events in question are long past, they are apt to arouse even less enthusiasm in today's readers than the political section of an out-of-date newspaper.

And yet, in that I was fortunate. The political turmoil of Yoshinobu's time is not a set of moribund facts in musty newspapers but a vital part of an era just beginning to gel into history. Knowing this gave me courage.

Saigo no shogun (The Last Shogun) was first published in a special edition of the monthly magazine *Bungei Shunju*. I had intended to publish it whole rather than in installments, but after finishing the first one hundred and twenty pages of manuscript I found I could not stop there, and ended up writing over one hundred more for the next issue as well. Even that was not enough; not until I had added on another two hundred pages in the next issue was I finished.

Tokugawa Yoshinobu was shogun for less than two years.

That so many words might be necessary to do him justice never suggested itself to me in the beginning. Why, then, do I still feel a nagging regret at not having written more? Leaving aside the question of my poor ability, I can only assume that my subject, Tokugawa Yoshinobu, is so high in alcohol content that he induces inebriation in the unwary. Nothing else could explain it.

Glossary

bakufu ("tent government") Same as SHOGUNATE.

daimyo Domainal lords; the largest of the landholding military lords in premodern Japan. All were sworn vassals of the SHOGUN, expected to provide absolute loyalty and obedience.

fudai Hereditary vassal.

han Domain.

hatamoto ("bannermen") Direct samurai retainers of the Tokugawa SHOGUNATE. Analogous to bureaucrats of a central government; the most responsible positions in the shogunate were often reserved for them.

joi See SONNO JOI.

koku A measure of volume for rice. In the Tokugawa period, one *koku* was equivalent to 5.12 U.S. bushels, supposedly enough to feed one person for one year. Samurai stipends and DAIMYO wealth were calculated in *koku.*

Ooku ("great interior") Large separate living quarters in Edo Castle for the women who served the Tokugawa SHOGUN then in power, employing some three thousand women. Generally closed to all men but the SHOGUN, the Ooku hierarchy often exerted considerable political influence.

ronin Masterless samurai.

sankin-kotai ("alternate attendance") A rule of the Tokugawa SHOGUNATE whereby DAIMYO were required to reside in alternate years at Edo (now Tokyo) in attendance upon the SHOGUN, thus dividing their time equally between the capital and their domains. Their wives and children were kept permanently in Edo.

shishi ("men of high purpose") Lower-ranking samurai on the fringes of the ruling class. Frustrated and volatile, with no stake in the existing structure of inherited rank and privilege, they played a major role in the movement to overthrow the SHOGUNATE, alone or under the protection of dissident daimyo or nobles.

shogun An abbreviation of the ancient title *seii tai shogun,* which is usually rendered as "barbarian-subduing generalissimo." As chief of Japan's warriors, a shogun was expected to keep the peace, controlling foreign trade and diplomacy while preserving law and order at home.

shogunate Synonymous with BAKUFU. Any of the three military governments ruling Japan during most of the period from 1192 to 1867; distinct from the civil government under the emperor at Kyoto.

sonno joi   ("Revere the emperor, expel the barbarians.") A political doctrine that developed during the late Tokugawa period, combining the idea that Japan should be unified under imperial rule with extreme resistance to foreign incursions. It became a militant rallying cry for the movement to overthrow the SHOGUNATE and restore imperial rule.

tozama   ("outside" vassals or allies) Hereditary vassal DAIMYO whose allegiance to the Tokugawa family dated from or after the Battle of Sekigahara (1600), which ended years of civil war and established Tokugawa Ieyasu as SHOGUN. Generally, tozama domains were larger and geographically farther from Edo than those of the FUDAI.

ABOUT THE AUTHOR

Ryotaro Shiba, one of Japan's best-loved writers of all time, was born in Osaka in 1923. He graduated from Osaka University of Foreign Studies, where he studied Mongolian, and served in the Imperial Japanese Army during World War II. Toward the end of the war his shock at the direction Japan had taken was put into sharp focus by a commander's chance remark showing complete disregard for the lives of Japanese civilians. After the war he embarked on a lifelong exploration of people and events in Japanese history, trying to understand how a nation's course is set. Working as a newspaper reporter, he began to write historical novels, and in 1959 received the Naoki Prize for *Fukuro no shiro* (*The Owl Castle*). His many works, which often provide new interpretations of turbulent times such as the Meiji Restoration, have had enduring success with Japanese readers. He was named a member of the Japan Art Academy in 1981, cited as a person of cultural merit in 1991, and was conferred with the Order of Culture in 1993. Shiba died in February 1996. He is survived by his wife, Midori.

ABOUT THE TRANSLATOR

U.S.-born translator, writer, and teacher Juliet Winters Carpenter has won two awards for her work. Her translations include essays, poetry, and fiction by modern authors such as Abe Kobo, Enchi Fumiko, Machi Tawara, and Shugoro Yamamoto, as well as numerous books on Japanese life, art, and culture. A native of Michigan, Carpenter has lived in Japan for more than twenty-five years, and is professor of English at Doshisha Women's College in Kyoto.